# DAISY AND THE EXISTENTIAL GOAT

## (AND OTHER STORIES)

### BY

### John McCotter

<u>The usual disclaimer:</u> The people in these stories are all figments of my warped imagination. They are not based on any person living or dead. I started with the idea of constructing each story around a holiday or a special occasion. As the stories progressed however, the special occasions seemed to become less and less important. They are still present in each story, however.

<u>Order of the stories:</u>

*Showdown at Santa's Village*

*Overlays*

*Conduit*

*Happy Birthday, Mary Anne*

*Foster Celebrates the New Year*

*Maria's Journey*

*Blockhouse*

*Daisy and the Existential Goat*

*Resurrecting Clayton Fenerly*

## SHOWDOWN AT SANTA'S VILLAGE

Larry liked to get to the mall at least an hour before it opened. He would arrive in street clothes and Sonia, the Hispanic lady who acted as his elf helper, would meet him at a freight entrance and let him in. Sonia was short and stocky and buxom and each year after Thanksgiving she would get her hair cut in a pixie style. To Larry, his Puerto Rican elf was so adorable it nearly took his breath away. He kept his attraction to himself, however. He was realistic. He knew what he looked like and he was very conscious of the difference in their ages. He imagined she had a young, handsome boyfriend somewhere. He loved working with her, however. Sonia seemed to bring light and laughter with her wherever she was. The parents and the kids gravitated to her, seeing nothing incongruous about an elf with a tropical accent.

Unlike Larry, Sonia would show up at the mall already in her elf's costume. She always had the electric cart at the door to whisk him away to the mall office just off the food court. There, she would help him into his Santa Claus suit. The hardest part of course, was the boots. His large stomach—so necessary for his role—made it difficult for him to reach his feet. Sonia would patiently work with him. She would kneel in front of him, working the shiny black imitation leather over his ankles and calves. On this particular morning, Sonia slapped him lightly on his knees and grinned up at him.

"Okay, Santa, you done," she said. Larry got a sudden flash image of Sonia kissing him. He had to shake his head to clear it. Sonia looked concerned.

"You okay, *Popi?*" She asked.

"Yeah, Sonia, I'm fine," Larry reassured her, taking secret pleasure in her use of the familiar and affectionate nickname. He thanked her and struggled to his feet. As he followed her to the electric cart, he tried to fathom what he had just seen. He had long been attracted to Sonia but this was the first time he realized there was a tiny chance that the fondness might be mutual.

In fact, it was the first time his flash images had involved Sonia. They had been part of his life as far back as he could remember. They only happened every now and then and each one lasted for no more than one second, but they appeared to be brief glimpses into the thoughts and imaginings of a person he was in proximity to. It's how he discovered that his wife had been sleeping with her boss several years ago. He remembered the color draining from her face when he confronted her about it. She couldn't believe that he knew. She had been so careful, she had thought.

The divorce had been amicable enough. He was grateful that there were no kids. Her lover was rich, and so she refused alimony. Larry got the house the car and the loneliness. He had stopped drinking and smoking years before the divorce and saw no reason to begin those habits again. But food was another matter. It became his drug of choice. A freshly delivered pizza or a large steak could temporarily fill the void inside of him. And so the pounds began to accumulate.

When he retired from the accounting firm, he let his facial hair grow out and it had turned a magnificent silver color. Friends began to remark on how much he resembled St. Nick. He had applied for the job as the Santa at the Sydney, Florida Mall on an impulse and was accepted. Surprisingly, he found he really loved the job. It was the one time of the year that his ponderous bulk was useful and appreciated. And he was a natural. He immediately discovered that all most kids really want is for an adult to look them in the eyes, listen to them, and take them seriously.

Occasionally, his flash images came into play while being Santa. Last year, when listening to one little girl, he got a flash image of her drunken father (who stood swaying glassy-eyed nearby) beating her with what looked like an electrical cord. When she got off his lap to return hesitantly to her dad, he could see strips of blood peeking through back of her light pink slacks. He had nodded to Sonia, to lean in. He whispered to her to go find Gordon, the mall security officer and ask him to follow the man and the girl. Fifteen minutes later, sheriff's deputies appeared. The man had started an argument with a merchant at one of the shoe stores and was threatening violence. Gordon had called the sheriff's department and had intervened enough to prevent the man from striking the clerk behind the counter.

As they led the man away, he was ranting some gibberish about how America was ruined by too much government. Larry had flagged down one of the deputies and told him about the bloodstains on the little girl. The officer's face turned grim. He thanked Larry and hurried back to his colleague who was escorting the man. The little girl seemed totally frightened and in a daze. She had followed behind the officer and her father at a distance, clearly not knowing what else to do. The deputy Larry had spoken to caught up with her and knelt down next to her.

Larry was glad to see him do that. Children are more comfortable dealing with adults at their eye level. After a brief conversation, the girl took the deputy's hand and the four of them left the mall. A few months later, Gordon had informed Larry that the man was serving time in the county jail. As Sonia drove him through the food court, Larry silently prayed that there would be no disturbing flash images this year.

"Santa's Village" in the mall consisted of a tiny fake cottage with Styrofoam snow glued onto the roof. It was surrounded by plastic fir trees and enclosed by a two-foot high green metal fence. Larry would sit in a large, comfortable armchair on what was supposed to be the front porch of the cottage. Parents and kids would line up at the opening in the little fence and Sonia would keep track of who was next, making jokes and chiding everyone with her adorable accent. When Larry had finished his session with each child, he would ring a silver bell on the arm of his chair and Sonia would escort the child back to his/her parent and then lead the next child to Santa.

As he got off the electric cart, Sonia touched his arm.

"Have a good day, Santa," she said. Once again the flash image of her kissing him surged in his mind.

"You too, Sonia," he managed. Sonia zoomed off in the cart to return it to the mall office. He moved his bulk slowly to the chair and sat down. The mall had not officially opened yet, and he liked this quiet time before the crowds came in. Even though no stores were open, there was still plenty of activity. Clerks were coming to work and the "mall walkers" were about. He admired these elderly folks who took advantage of the safe, air-conditioned area to get their exercise protected from the Florida heat outside. There were some regulars that he saw every day. Of particular interest was a large black man who walked with military bearing. Larry was to find out later that the man's name was Dodge.

Dodge was constantly correcting his posture as he walked. It was a battle he had been fighting for a couple of years. When he had played football, he tended to move leaning forward so that his helmet and shoulder pads would be the first things to greet an opponent. In the Marines, he habitually leaned forward to compensate for the weight of a heavy pack on his back. Now that he was retired and elderly, he found his 76-year-old lower back was complaining at the strain caused by the leaning. He would realize he was leaning about thirty times each day and try to stand straighter. The result was a tall, chunky, elderly man whose body was bent at a slight angle at the waist. The back was straight from the waist to the shoulders, however. As he passed the display window of the Book Nook, he could see the failure of his attempts to achieve a totally ramrod-straight posture. It seemed to him that he resembled an overfed praying mantis.

A few yards ahead of him, he could see he was about to pass his friend Arnie for the fifth time. Arnie was one of the reasons Dodge had become conscious about his posture. Arnie was a rotund little man who was permanently hunched over. He had to use a four-point cane to balance himself as he lurched painfully around the shopping mall each morning. Besides the curvature of Arnie's spine, there also seemed to be something wrong with his hips. So his gait was very jerky and painful to watch.

Dodge had met Arnie for the first time a couple of years earlier. He had just started walking at the mall for exercise and he admired Arnie's determination. The little man was at it every morning, forcing himself to lurch as rapidly as possible around the half-mile indoor expanse of the shopping center. As Dodge strode by, Arnie cocked an eyebrow at him.

"Going for three miles today, Dodge?" he asked.

"That's the plan Arnie," Dodge replied.

"Show off!" Arnie pretended to scold. Dodge shrugged in reply. He knew that Arnie's routine was to do a mile, then rest at the food court and get coffee and something to eat. Arnie's mile and Dodge's three seemed to always end at the same time. They would sit together in the food court after getting coffee and a donut at the only shop open—the Coffee Kitchen. There they would chat comfortably and watch the other "regulars" doing their laps. Years of repeating their routine had taught Dodge that if Arnie was feeling especially good, he would walk some more after about a half-hour of coffee and conversation with Dodge.

Both men were widowers and they had bonded self-consciously (as men will do) in their shared pain. Both looked forward to seeing each other on these mall walks. The encounter had become a major part of their routine, although they would never admit as much to each other. To some men in their situation, routine becomes a kind of refuge. Having lost the loves of their lives, they sought the predictable, the safe, as they tried to figure out what their existence would be like in this strange, unsettling situation. The air-conditioned mall with its familiar stores and layout was the perfect metaphor for how they were living now.

"Mutt and Jeff," Wanda thought to herself as she watched the two men stride by the bookshop in which she worked. The disparity in their heights brought to mind the old comic strip from her childhood. Weekday mornings were always pleasantly slow at the store, giving her time to read and to stare out the display window at the passersby. She appreciated the solitude and the quiet.

It had not always been this way. When her marriage came crashing to an end years before, the divorce had left her terrified of being alone. The generous alimony settlement enabled her to find an affordable condo in Sydney, Florida near the mall. She had forced herself to apply for the part-time job at the bookshop because she reasoned that it would impel her to leave the condo and relate to the rest of the world. It wasn't that she needed the money. It was an exercise in self-discipline. She was glad she had done it. Gradually, over the months, she had gotten used to being by herself, and occasionally actually enjoyed it. Besides, working at the store gave her the opportunity to turn her attention outward, away from herself and her many fears.

She had observed the two men for months and took some comfort in the predictability of their routines. They were like solid signposts in the course of her day. She found the taller of the two kind of attractive. He carried himself with projected authority, but she was perceptive enough to see that this was a façade. It was a convincing protective barrier to most people because its performance had become an unconscious habit for the man. On the few occasions she was able to see his eyes, however, she saw confusion and loneliness there.

"We are all shell-shocked by life," she thought to herself.

She admired the determination of the smaller man. It was obviously very painful for him to move, but he refused to surrender to the pain. Just as she had refused to give in to her fear of being alone, he was determined to combat the limits of his condition. Her thoughts were interrupted by the sound of a buzzer. Someone was at the back door. As she expected, it was her boss.

Pearl Warner was British and seemed permanently angry. It became clear to Wanda that part of her job as an employee involved being a sounding board at which Pearl could furiously rant about the latest tribulations life had visited upon her. It took a few weeks for Wanda to realize the fury was not directed at her, but at *them*—the people, institutions and forces of nature that constantly conspired to ruin Pearl's life. This morning it was weather and traffic.

"I never thought I would miss the cold and damp of the UK, but this heat and humidity is *insufferable*!" She muttered when Wanda let her in. Wanda decided to try to interject a cheerful note.

"It *has* been an unusually warm December so far. But the weatherman says a cold front is coming next week. I think that's when the gorgeous days will begin."

"It can't happen soon enough as far as I'm concerned," Pearl groused. "And the people around here drive so *slowly!* Wanda tried to sound sympathetic.

"Well this *is* a retirement community," Wanda supplied helpfully. Pearl snapped her head back and forth in rejection.

" I know they are retired, but they drive as if they are *dead*!" The fact that these same slow moving elderlies had provided Pearl with a comfortable income for a number of years seemed to have escaped the storeowner's memory. Her initial tirade spent, Pearl sat down at her desk in the tiny back office and began to shuffle papers about. Wanda took this as a sign of dismissal and returned to the front of the store.

She had already cleaned thoroughly when she had opened the place up, so there wasn't a lot for her to do until customers showed up. So she pulled the feather duster from below the counter and began walking around the shop, making a show of dusting the shelves of books. She hated doing this kind of charade, but she felt it was important for customers to see busy, active people inside. She was relieved when the back door buzzer sounded again.

It was Jeremy, the handsome young deliveryman. Even though Wanda knew she was old enough to be his grandmother, he always made it a point to be flirtatious with her and Pearl. The tactic worked. To Wanda, he was a burst of positivity. It was a testament to his attractiveness that Pearl got up from her desk each time he delivered to personally greet him and sign for the boxes he was delivering.

"Ah, my two hot young mommas!" Jeremy grinned when Pearl opened the door.

"Oh shush!" Pearl pretended to scold, her tone betraying secret delight. "Let's have a look at what you've got here," she said, taking the clipboard from him. She checked the order form against the label on each carton and nodded when she was through. She scribbled a signature on the form and chirped "Come through!' Her voice had assumed a breathless, almost girlish quality. She led him past the office and into the store. Jeremy wheeled his dolly loaded with boxes adroitly around the counter and deposited them in a neat stack in the middle of the store.

"This okay?" he asked.

"There is fine," Pearl cooed. "Wanda will sort them out," Pearl added dismissively. Pearl turned to lead Jeremy back to the door. As he rounded the counter with his empty dolly, the young man winked at Wanda. It was the shared joke between underlings in the presence of a pretentious boss. Wanda liked this kid.

After this pleasant interlude, Wanda began checking the labels on the various boxes and then carrying each box to the area where its contents would be shelved. After a couple of such carries, she noticed she was panting very heavily and her arms were weary.

"I am really out of shape," she thought to herself. At that moment, she heard chimes playing "The White Cliffs of Dover," and knew that Pearl's cell phone had gone off. Pearl answered in a low voice and then came out into the store.

"Wanda, why don't you take a break Love? I'll watch the store."

"Thanks, Pearl, I will," Wanda replied, grateful for the opportunity to catch her breath. Whoever had phoned her, Pearl was determined to have privacy while talking to them. Wanda got her purse from behind the counter and walked out into the mall. She turned left and headed toward the food court.

At that moment Buford Cletus Hutto was pulling his rusted old pickup truck into a parking spot outside the mall. Buford had been drinking heavily for several weeks—ever since Mona had left him. After being convicted of child abuse and spending nearly a year in the county jail, he had come home to the little cinder block house expecting to resume life as it had been. Instead, he had found an empty home and Mona's note. She had saved up some money and was taking their daughter, Bonnie, away. She left no indication of where they were going.

To Buford, this was the ultimate betrayal. He had especially picked Mona to marry years ago. He believed that because she was fatter and worse looking than he was, she would never leave him. After all, he had provided a good living for her and the girl. Oh sure, he had been rough with them a few times, but only when they deserved it. After all, he had been raised to believe this was his right as the man of the house. He snorted angrily at the injustice of it all. Being a dragline operator for a company that dug and cleared irrigation ditches did not make him rich, but it enabled him to buy a home for them. He had provided food and shelter and could not understand Mona's rejection of him. It was obvious to Buford that *he* was the victim here.

He had tried to ease the pain and anger in his soul by heavy applications of booze, but this seemed to have the opposite effect. In one of his nightly drunken rages a couple of evenings earlier he had tried to dramatically punch through the sheetrock of the living room wall. Unfortunately, he hit a stud behind the sheetrock and had cracked two knuckles on his right hand. He bandaged the hand badly and quickly resumed drinking to assuage the pain in his hand as well as that in his heart. Except for supply runs to the liquor department of his local supermarket, and to a fried chicken outlet, he had remained isolated at home for nearly a month, drinking and raging aloud to the empty house, often pleading his case to a non-existent audience.

The conservative talk radio station that was constantly blaring in the house fed his rage. The combination of fundamentalist religious programming along with talking heads denouncing liberals, gays, minorities and Muslims began to meld together in his mind. Mona's leaving was somehow related to evil forces plotting against America in general and him in particular. The idea of revenge came to him on this particular morning. This time he had awoken from passing out on the living room floor, lying in a pool of vomit.

He had risen slowly and had gone into the bathroom and cleaned himself up as best he could. He donned a relatively clean set of camouflage-patterned tee shirt and pants He then went into his bedroom and retrieved the .38 pistol from his night stand. He spun the cylinder and made sure it was loaded. He then fished a box of bullets out of a drawer and put them into the pocket of his pants. Wearing the cammies, spinning the chamber, and being smart enough to bring extra bullets made Buford feel macho and in control. He decided to celebrate these good feelings, so he opened another fifth of rum and sat at the kitchen table, drinking and envisioning the crusade ahead. Meanwhile, the talk radio station was playing patriotic music.

The more he drank, the more what he was about to do made sense to him. He would strike a blow for freedom. He would rid the world of some of its evil. What if he ended up dead or in prison? Had not the forces of evil imprisoned him here in his own home? After draining the bottle of rum in an amazingly short time, Buford stood and swayed beside the kitchen table. His mind tried to focus.

"Truck keys," he had said aloud. "Where'd I put the goddamn truck keys?" When he found them, he left the house, not even bothering to clean the puddle of vomit from the living room floor.

And now he sat in a parking place in the sunbaked lot of the Sydney, Florida Mall. He reasoned that it was fitting the crusade should start here. After all, this is where his troubles seemed to begin last year.

He had brought Bonnie to the mall to meet Santa Claus after punishing her for spilling her cereal that morning. He figured meeting Santa would make up for the beating he had given her. He shook his head in wonderment at what an even-handed parent he had been. Then he snorted when he remembered losing his temper at the snotty, dark-skinned clerk in the shoe store. If that security guard hadn't stepped in, he would have flattened the little shit. Then the cops showed up. Somehow, one of them had noticed Bonnie's bleeding bottom and all hell had broken loose after that.

Buford opened the truck door, but when he stepped out, the fresh air seemed to amplify the effects of the rum. His head swam for a few seconds and he clambered back into the truck and sat still until the spinning stopped. He rolled down the windows on the truck and tried to collect himself.

Meanwhile, Dodge and Arnie were enjoying their post-workout get-together. At first, they simply watched the other "regulars" passing by the food court. There was a lady they had nicknamed "the Cruiser." She was clearly as old as they were and they suspected she suffered from some kind of obsession. She was always dressed nicely in clean slacks and blouse and her hair was carefully died and coiffed. But she walked about the mall for hours in no particular pattern. She seemed to critically study everything she passed. Although she seemed prosperous,

Dodge and Arnie had seen her deftly steal things from some of the food stalls.

Then there was the "Angry Admiral." He was an obese little fellow who sported a Navy cap with a splash of gold braid on the bill. He wore a permanent angry frown as he walked his laps. It was as if he was infuriated by the fact that no one saluted him or even seemed to notice him.

"Typical officer," Dodge said, nodding at the Angry Admiral. Arnie nodded.

"Yeah," the smaller man speculated. "Some of us seem to resent the way we become invisible when we get old."

"I don't," Dodge replied. "I like being invisible." Arnie nodded in agreement.

"Yep. There's a lot to be said for being left alone." At that point, a nicely dressed older woman approached them.

"Hi," she said. "Do you mind if a stranger joins you?" Both men looked up, surprised, but Arnie recovered first.

"You're welcome to join us, but it might ruin your reputation," he chided. The woman laughed as she sat with her cup of coffee.

"At this point in my life, I would welcome a reputation," she replied. She then stuck her hand across the table to Arnie.

"I'm Wanda," she offered, shaking Arnie's hand.

"Arnie," he replied. Wanda then offered her hand to Dodge who seized the initiative.

"I'm Dodge," he said, returning her handshake. Wanda cocked her head quizzically.

"Dodge," she repeated. "Now that's an unusual name." Dodge grinned.

"It's a nickname I got when I was young," Dodge said. "I used to have an addiction to buying used Dodge Challengers, fixing them up and reselling them. The name stuck," Dodge explained.

"You don't do that any more?" she asked.

"I kind of lost interest in it when my wife died." Wanda nodded sympathetically.

"Sorry," she said softly. Dodge studied her face and could see that she meant it.

"I'm not usually so forward," Wanda explained. "But I work in the book store and I have noticed you two getting your exercise each morning. I was wondering if you would mind if I walk with you some time? I really need to get back into shape." Dodge and Arnie looked at each other in surprise. Their earlier comments about being "invisible" seemed incongruous now.

"But we walk, while you are working," Arnie said.

"Yeah, about that," Wanda began. "I'm getting tired of my boss and wouldn't mind using my time for my health instead."

"What about your salary?" Dodge asked. Wanda smiled wryly.

"The one good thing that resulted from my husband trading me in for a younger model is that he gives me enough to live on." Dodge nodded in comprehension. It was his turn to empathize.

"Sorry," he said simply. Wanda studied his face and could tell he was sincere.

It was Dodge who noticed Buford first. His eyes were drawn to the camouflaged pattern of the clothing of the man shuffling and swaying toward the food court. He could instantly tell by the stooped posture and slovenly appearance that this man had never served his country. He was obviously one of those local idiots who donned camouflage-patterned apparel to make people think they were ex-military when they clearly were not.

The food court was flooded with daylight from a large glass skylight overhead. This seemed to disconcert the man somewhat. A few feet away from Santa's Village there was an information booth that was never staffed. It was a circular wooden counter that was a convenient place to leave stacks of brochures about upcoming events at the mall. The man in camouflage stopped and steadied himself against it.

Larry noticed Buford next and instantly recognized him as the abusive parent from the year before. He got a flash image of Buford spinning the cylinder of a pistol. Larry picked up the silver bell and began ringing it furiously. Sonia came running over to him.

"Get Gordon *quick!*" He whispered. As she started to leave, he grabbed her hand. Once again the flash image of her kissing him appeared. He fought to clear his mind and make sense. "He's probably going to need to call the sheriff's office. Once you tell him that, stay away from here for a few minutes, okay?" Sonia glanced nervously around and saw the man weaving next to the information booth. Understanding came into her face.

"I'll get Gordon, but I ain't leavin' you, Popi." She muttered and was gone. Larry continued ringing the bell as loudly as he could.

There were not very many people in the food court and all of them seemed puzzled by the sudden racket Santa Claus was making. There were clearly no kids or parents waiting. Dodge, however, seemed to understand instantly.

"Excuse me," he muttered to Wanda and Arnie. He instinctively began to circle to the outside of the formation of tables.

"What's he doing?" Wanda asked Arnie. The smaller man followed Dodge's gaze, which seemed to be locked onto the fat man in cammies.

"I think it has something to do with that guy," Arnie said, nodding at the man. The small man struggled to his feet and grabbed his cane.

"Maybe you better wait here," Arnie said, and began his lurching movement toward the man who was steadying himself at the information booth.

For his part, Buford found the constantly ringing bell an irritation. He glared at Santa Claus and debated whether his first shot should be at the man in red, just to make him quit ringing the damned bell. Then he noticed the bent-over Jewish-looking guy lurching toward him. "No," he thought to himself, "*That's* my first target!" He fumbled in his pocket for the pistol but the baggy pouchlike opening seemed to claw at the weapon making it difficult to extract. He was so involved in retrieving the gun he didn't notice the large black man descending on him from the side.

When Dodge was about five feet away, he saw the gun appear. At that point, reflexes he had not used in years took over. He dipped his shoulder lunged the last two steps and rammed into Buford as hard as he could. His shoulder sank into the fat man's ribs just below the armpit. As both men sailed over the small green fence, Dodge felt his back seize up. The two men landed at the feet of Santa's chair. The large black man was writhing in pain and the fat white man was gasping for breath, the gun had fallen from his hand and had gone sliding across the tile floor.

The man in camouflage seemed to recover first. Flopping clumsily on his stomach he began to crawl toward the gun, reaching for it with a bandaged hand. Suddenly a four-pointed cane seemed to come out of nowhere and pin the hand to the floor. Arnie was leaning on the cane with all his weight. The fat man on the floor let out a yelp of pain and began flailing at the cane. He had succeeded in knocking it away when a huge red mass settled on top of him, squeezing the breath out of him once again and pinning him helplessly to the floor. A nicely dressed woman picked up the gun and pointed it at the man on the floor with a shaking hand. Even in his pain, Dodge noticed Wanda wisely kept her finger outside the trigger guard. An accidental shot could ricochet off the tile floor and hurt the wrong people.

Gordon appeared next to Wanda a few seconds later and she gingerly handed the weapon over to him. Sirens could be heard in the distance. Relieved of the weapon, Wanda knelt next to Dodge.

"How badly are you hurt?" she asked anxiously.

"I threw my back out again," Dodge grunted through clenched teeth. "It does that whenever I forget I'm not twenty-five any more." Wanda grinned.

When the sheriff's deputies arrived on the scene, they saw a small crowd gathered around a bizarre Christmas tableau. A fat man in cammies was on the floor, braying like a mule giving birth. Perched on top of him was the largest Santa Claus the deputies had ever seen. The mall security officer handed them the man's weapon and explained what had occurred. With some difficulty, the deputies helped Santa get back onto his feet. The crowd erupted into spontaneous applause at the sight of Santa's resurrection.

The deputies then turned their attention to the idiot on the floor. The smell of booze seemed to radiate from the man's skin. As they got him to his feet and cuffed him, he was slurring some nonsense about a crusade. As they led Buford out to the patrol car, he wondered through the fog in his brain about the curse that seemed to hang over him whenever he approached the Sydney, Florida Mall.

When he regained his feet, Larry was nearly knocked over again by Sonia who threw her arms around his neck, tears streaming down her face.

"Are you okay, *Popi*?" She asked between sobs.

"Yeah," Larry said smiling fondly into her upturned face. "I'm just fine, Sonia."

"Maybe you should take the rest of the day off," Gordon suggested. Larry shook his head and settled back into Santa's chair.

"No. Let's don't disappoint the kids." Larry glanced over at Sonia.

"What about it, Sonia? You willing to stay with me?" Sonia blew her nose with a tissue and smiled fondly through red-rimmed eyes.

"Always, *Popi*," she answered.

Three hours later, Wanda was driving Dodge back to the mall. She had taken him to the Sydney Medical Center where the emergency room staff checked him out and sent him down to X-Ray. There were no fractures and Dodge was given an injection of muscle relaxant. Dodge had asked her to drive him back to the mall so he could get his car. As she drove, however, Wanda was having doubts about doing that.

"So what's your real name?" Wanda asked. Lolling next to her in the passenger seat, Dodge was clearly feeling the effects of the shot. He snorted lazily.

"Archibald," He replied. Wanda laughed in spite of herself.

"Dodge it is!" She exclaimed.

"Thank God," Dodge mumbled.

Just before they got to the mall, Wanda seemed to reach a sudden decision and made an unexpected U-Turn at an intersection.

Dodge looked over at her with a dazed smile on his face.

"Are you kidnapping me lady?"

"Absolutely!" Wanda grinned. "The doctor said you are not supposed to drive in your condition, so I am going to take you to my place, feed you, and put you to bed.

"What about your job?" Dodge asked groggily.

"When I didn't come back from my break, I think my boss probably realized I was quitting," Wanda smiled.

"You don't know me," Dodge tried to object, but Wanda could tell his heart wasn't in it. "I could be an axe murderer or something," Wanda's smile broadened.

"I saw you take out an asshole with a gun," she said, smiling at him proudly. "I think I'll be perfectly safe with you around, mister."

"Yeah," Dodge slurred as he drifted off to sleep, his head resting against the passenger side window. "Sometimes I'm not too smart."

Wanda laughed to herself as she drove her new friend to her home.

THE END

# OVERLAYS

## CHAPTER ONE: WELCOME TO ST. IGNACIO

Margaret started seeing the overlays when she first came to St. Ignacio, Florida. In fact, it was seeing the outline of a building that was not actually there, that piqued her curiosity about the little town. It was a hot humid day in August when she first pulled into the village. She had stopped for gas at a station in the small downtown area that stretched along US Highway one. After filling her tank, she went into the convenience store to buy a cold drink. As
she came out of the store and looked across the street, she saw it.

The one-story cinder block building that stood on a corner was crowned for a moment by the transparent outline of a two-story wooden framed building with a porch running across the front of the lower story. She halted in her tracks at the sight. She was halfway across the sunbaked parking lot, and a man in a pickup truck had to stop suddenly to avoid hitting her.

The man rolled down his window and growled irritably, "You okay?" Margaret nodded and waved apologetically at him and returned to her car. When she looked across the street again the image was gone. She took a sip of her soda and tried to collect herself.

A tree-shaded community park was across the street from the gas station/convenience store, so she pulled into a parking space next to the lovely green area. She turned off the engine and tried to make sense of what she had just seen. She got out of the car and stared once again at the unremarkable one-story building on the corner. A sign in front of the building read ST. IGNACIO HAVEN. No ghostly image appeared, so she sauntered along the walkways in the welcome shade, sipping her drink as she walked. A nice breeze came off the Indian River, which flowed by one end of the park. She wondered if she was drifting into some kind of dementia. She grinned to herself.

"Well, old girl, you DID want your life to be different," she thought with a rueful smile.

Her intention had been to drive all the way to Key West. It's famous bohemian atmosphere would be a welcome change from the deeply conservative area of Washington State where she had spent a career teaching other people's children. She had planned this trip during her last year in the classroom and her aim was to completely change her life.

She had lived frugally, and had saved her money for years, plotting her escape from the expected and the ordinary. She had made the decision toward the end of her career that she would use whatever time she had left on earth to experience new things. First, however, she had to free herself from the stifling and conflicted expectations involved in being a teacher in the United States. Her one major purchase during that last teaching year was a new hybrid car. She would need dependable, gas-thrifty transportation for her excursion.

She had held several yard sales that spring. What she couldn't sell, she gave away to charity. When she left her little apartment on that last day, it was completely empty and thoroughly cleaned. She took great satisfaction in seeing it that way. "Out with the old; in with the new," She thought to herself.

Her drive across the country had taken a little over a week. She was content to not rush. Even though she had friends and acquaintances all over the nation, she had scrupulously avoided these. She badly wanted to be alone to forge her new life. She knew that well-meaning buddies would offer all kinds of suggestions as to what she should do now, but she didn't want that kind of interference.

That first night on the road, she was staying at a motel located in Grants Pass, Oregon. When she got out of the shower, she stood naked and looked at herself in the full-length mirror on the bathroom door. She saw a slightly overweight, woman in her early sixties with graying hair that hung below her shoulders. Her face was pleasant enough. When she put on her glasses, she could see the lines around her eyes and mouth more clearly. These apparent flaws did not bother her.

She had never married and had never borne a child, so her body had fewer stretch marks than most women her age, and the aureoles of her breasts were still small. She had long ago resigned herself to being a spinster and frankly, did not mind it. She enjoyed coming and going as she pleased, without answering to anybody. She had enough of children dealing with the ones in her classroom. She had showered on them, the energy she would have expended on offspring of her own. The last two years of her teaching career were the hardest. She was emotionally exhausted and she could feel her temper getting closer and closer to the surface.

As she stood looking at herself in the mirror, she had taken out her dryer and began to work on her hair. She had never understood women and men who fought against aging. She had refused to cover her gray hair when it started appearing in her forties. She saw no sense in frying her hair roots with chemical dyes. Nor did she see any reason to apply increasing amounts of make-up as the years progressed.

So the result of these decisions was a woman with healthy, shiny graying hair and clear skin. As she looked at the small tire around her middle, however, she realized she needed to do something about her physical conditioning. So for the rest of the trip across the country, she had made it a point to stop at hotels and motels that had grounds on which she could walk in safety in the early mornings before setting off again.

She never made it to Key West. It wasn't just the sighting of the ghostly building that drew her to St. Ignacio. There was something else—an indefinable familiarity about the little town—that seemed to pull at her strongly. Without really understanding why, she pulled into the town's one hotel belonging to a national chain and rented a room. This was the first step in what would be a rapid process of falling in love with St. Ignacio.

Her room had a microwave and a small refrigerator. Exercising her characteristic frugality, she got directions from the young lady at the front desk to a nearby supermarket. There she bought a baked chicken from the deli, some microwaveable vegetables, some milk, and a few other things that would enable her to eat well in her room. She was simply operating on instinct at this point. Something was telling her to prepare for an extended stay.

She then retrieved her laptop from her luggage and after signing onto the motel's Internet service, began researching St. Ignacio, Florida. According to articles she read, it had bean founded shortly after the Civil War by fishermen. The community was located where the freshwater of the St. Ignacio River intersected with the brackish water of the Indian River Lagoon. The Lagoon was a long waterway squeezed in between the mainland of Florida's east coast and a series of barrier islands that fronted the Atlantic Ocean. Inlets that brought seawater into the lagoon interrupted the chain of low, jungle-clad islands.

Because of the mix of fresh and saltwater species, the fishing in the area was good, and as land was drained further inland, vegetable farms and orange orchards sprang up. With the development of US Highway one and the north-south railroad begun by Henry Flagler, the little town began to grow...but not too much.

As Margaret read, it seemed to her that for most of the twentieth Century, St. Ignacio had existed in a kind of pleasant time warp. For decades, it was simply a place people passed through on their way to Miami or

Jacksonville. It did not seem to be a sought-after destination. When I-95 bypassed the town ten miles to the west, many of the roadside businesses on Highway one closed down, and the town's sleepy existence had continued.

That night in her hotel room, Margaret listened to trains passing by on the nearby track. It dawned on her that, given the town's linear layout along the highway and the parallel rail line, train traffic (mostly at night) would be a common element of living here. She found the rumble of the trains oddly comforting and she slept well.

## CHAPTER TWO: CANUCK'S REST

The next morning, she drove back to the community park and did her exercise walk among the oaks and then along the town's waterfront. The city fathers had apparently realized capitalizing on this area's natural beauty would bring more visitors and more money into the little town. In the lovely early morning, the well-preserved waterfront area was shown off to its best advantage.

She was impressed by the pedestrian walkway that paralleled the river. It was clean, bordered with neatly cut grass and free of litter and graffiti. As she walked, she watched pelicans and ospreys hunting in the shallows and occasionally would see the rolling fin of a dolphin break the glassy surface.

The town had also constructed a municipal pier that extended seventy-five yards out into the river. She sauntered out to the end and leaned on the wooden railing, looking down at the water. She realized that even this far from shore, it was probably no more that four feet deep. She could clearly see the bottom. Some large, striped fish were lurking around the pilings of the pier. The deepest sigh Margaret had ever experienced escaped her lips that morning as she leaned against the weathered wood of the pier. There was a slow moving peace about the place—an ease of existence—that she found irresistible.

She had breakfast at a local diner, and was amazed by how many northern and mid-western accents surrounded her. Many of the inhabitants of St. Ignacio seemed to be transplants. As she ate her scrambled eggs and bacon, it dawned on her that there must be a reason so many people had chosen this peculiar place to live.

After breakfast, she felt the urge to explore more of the area, so she drove south on highway one. Because only one chain hotel was located in the town, other smaller inns and cottages had filled in this vacuum. To Margaret, the absence of the usual large signs and multi-story buildings added to the small-town feel.

South of town, she encountered an odd sight: a huge Canadian flag. It stood at the entrance of an RV Resort aptly named CANUCK'S REST. Following the same instinct that led her to stay the night at the hotel, she turned into the large RV Park. The resort was situated between the railroad tracks and the highway and it stretched for nearly a mile. As she drove along its quiet streets, Margaret was surprised at the variety of dwellings here.

There were top of the line vehicles— practically palaces on wheels—as well as smaller, more modest models. Some of them were obviously occupied while others appeared to be vacant. There were a lot of empty RV spaces, and Margaret guessed that because it was summer, this was the off-season for visitors to the area.

Toward the southern end of the park, the RV's gave way to mobile homes and modular housing. All of them were neatly kept. As she headed back toward the entrance, Margaret noticed a large swimming pool and a green area in which there was a fitness course with an exercise apparatus stationed every few yards. When she drove by the office, she felt an irresistible impulse to pull in and ask about the Canadian flag.

The woman behind the counter was intimidating to look at. Her long dark hair was streaked with gray and her tanned arms were covered with tattoos. "Biker," Margaret thought to herself. At the sight of Margaret, the woman's face broke into an infectious smile. Margaret felt herself relax.

"Hi, darlin'," the woman drawled. "What can I do for you?" Margaret nodded at the greeting and smiled nervously.

"I was driving by, and I just had to know why there was a Canadian flag out front," she said. The woman threw back her head and laughed. Margaret liked her instinctively.

"You'd be surprised how often this happens," the woman said then offered Margaret a tanned, tattooed hand.

"I'm Sally, by the way." Margaret shook the hand. It was warm and smooth.

"Margaret," She responded. You're not Canadian are you?" Again, Sally's rich low laughter filled the little office.

"Naw, darlin'. St Ingnacio born and bred." Then Sally's eyes brightened with inspiration. "Hey! You wanna cup of coffee?"

"Sure," Margaret answered. Sally came from around the counter and headed for a coffee machine located against the far wall. She was a tall woman dressed in jeans and a black sleeveless pullover. Margaret could tell that this was a woman who dressed for comfort but had her own careless sense of style. They sat at a little table by the coffee machine.

"The place was started by a man who moved here from Vancouver, Canada," Sally said after taking a sip. "He was a big hockey fan, and Vancouver's team is called the Canucks."

"Do a lot of Canadians live here?" Margaret asked.

"In the winter, yes," Sally answered. "He rightly figured that he wasn't the only elderly

Canadian tired of freezing his ass off in the winter."

"So all these empty RV spaces..." Margaret began.

"Are filled up, starting in mid-October," Sally finished. "It's a good business," she continued. "We don't have to advertise, we have a steady clientele year after year, and the expenses are manageable." Then Sally cocked her head quizzically.

"So what brings you to the teeming streets of St. Ignacio, Florida?" She took another sip of coffee as she waited for Margaret's answer. Margaret chuckled nervously.

"You're going to think I'm crazy," she said. Sally's laughter once again flooded the room.

"Darlin', you pulled off the highway just to ask about a flag! That boat has already sailed!" Margaret nodded and laughed along with her. She really liked this woman. She hesitantly told Sally about what she had seen across the street from the gas station the day before, and how it had affected her. Sally listened intently. As Margaret talked, she studied Sally's dark eyes. There was no hint of derision, only fascination. When Margaret had finished, Sally's eyes grew excited.

"You know what?" She began, almost breathless. "If I'm remembering correctly, there used to be an old hotel on that corner!"

"Really?" Margaret asked, leaning forward.

"Yeah," Sally responded. "It seems to me it was kind of a famous place. A couple of well-known bird experts stayed there in the late 1800's."

"What happened to it?"

"I think it burned down in the early 1900's." Both women were silent for a while, each of them pondering the impact of Margaret's vision.

"What is there now on that corner?" Margaret asked.

St. Ignacio Haven," Sally replied. "It's an assisted living facility for the elderly." Both women were silent again for a few minutes.

"So what are you gonna do?" Sally asked. Margaret shrugged.

"I want to live here." Margaret was as surprised by her words as Sally was. It was the first time Margaret had admitted this to herself. Sally's eyes were excited again.

"All right!" Sally practically cheered. Then she looked serious for a moment. "Now do you mean live here in St. Ignacio or here in the RV Park?"

"St. Ignacio, but this is as good a place as any to start." Sally leapt to her feet.

"Say no more, girl!" She exclaimed. "Come with me!" The next thing Margaret knew she was sitting next to Sally in a golf cart as they whizzed down the streets of The Canuck's Rest.

"Are you interested in an RV or a mobile home or a modular home?" Sally asked.

"All I want is a safe place to live that is as cheap as possible," Margaret answered.

"I was hoping you would say that," Sally grinned and headed the cart towed the western edge of the property. Along the back row of RV's she pulled up to one standing alone. The motor home looked no more than a year or two old, and from the outside, looked to be in excellent condition.

Sally got off the vehicle and opened a metal box clamped to the back of the cart. She fished some glasses out of the pocket of her jeans and studied the mass of keys the box held. She picked a set of two out of the group and motioned for Margaret to follow her. Sally mounted the steps to the RV and unlocked the door.

Once inside, Margaret found herself in a cramped living space. A sink and kitchenette was to her left, and an armchair was to her right.  Beyond the armchair were the seats for the driver and passenger. A long sofa faced her and a dining table with padded bench seats abutted it. Sally went forward to the driver's seat and started the engine. The motor leaped to life.

"Battery's still good," the tall woman said. She left the motor idling and squeezed past Margaret to a set of buttons on the wall next to the dinette. She pushed one of them and amidst impressive rumbling and whining, the sofa and dinette began to move away from Margaret. Once the slide out was completely extended, Margaret found the cramped feeling was gone.

Sally then showed her the refrigerator and the microwave. The range had three gas burners on the top as well as a small oven. She then stepped back and let Margaret explore the back end of the unit. A round, clear sliding door enclosed a shower with a skylight at the top. Across the narrow hall from the shower was the commode and sink, complete with lighted mirror.

At the tail end of the unit was the bedroom. It consisted of a queen-sized bed flanked by a small closet and night stands. Sally walked around one side of the bed and opened the accordion shade. She pointed out a larger, newer RV parked a few feet away.

"That's me," she said proudly. "That's my home."

She straightened again and walked back into the living area. "So what do you think?'

From the moment the slide out was opened, Margaret had experienced a sensation of completeness, of safety, of warmth. "This is my home!" she thought to herself. But her cautious nature held her in check.

"How much?" she asked. Sally's throaty laughter once again filled the space they occupied.

"Girl, you get right down to it, don't you?" She regarded Margaret fondly. "If you want to just rent it, I can do that for $700 a month. That includes lot rent, but not electricity. Cable TV and Internet are free." Then she leaned in conspiratorially, one hand resting on the counter top by the sink. "If you want the rent to go toward buying it, I can do so for $900 a month."

How long would that take me to buy it?" Margaret asked.

"Five years," Sally answered. Margaret did some quick calculating in her head, but she already knew the answer before she had finished the juggling of figures in her mind.

"Let's do this!" She exclaimed. Sally laughed in delight and hugged her.

So it was that, on her second day in the town of St. Ignacio, Margaret had become a resident. Her decision was based on her gut feeling and the infectious smile of a woman named Sally. They rode in the golf cart back to the office where the necessary papers were signed and Margaret wrote a check for the deposit. Grinning in delight, Sally handed her the keys.

"Welcome home, girl," she said.

Margaret drove back to the hotel and packed the car with her belongings. She paid her bill then drove to the supermarket she had visited the day before. Keeping in mind the size of the refrigerator and pantry in the motor home, she bought groceries and cleaning supplies. The store had a housewares department and she bought some bed linens and pillows there. These she added to her luggage and other belongings in her car. Then, almost dizzy with excitement, she drove to her new home on wheels.

It didn't take her long to unload the car, but it was hot work in the Florida sun. When it was done, she found the air conditioning control and turned it on. The refrigerated air smelled a little of dust at first, but was welcome relief from the heat. She sat in the armchair next to the door and caught her breath.

Her suitcases, other belongings and bags of groceries faced her expectantly on the long couch. She surveyed her new domain and laughed out loud. It wasn't Key West. It wasn't the wildly bohemian existence she had visualized, but she knew in her bones that she had done well. Given her retirement income and her savings, this was a lifestyle she could easily afford.

As she looked at the belongings on the couch, she remembered reading *Robinson Crusoe* as a little girl. He had retrieved items from the wrecked ship that might help him to survive. The items stacked up on the beach of the island and he then had to decide where each item would go and how it would be used. Margaret loved that part of the story, and now found herself in a similar situation. Like Robinson Crusoe, she now had to figure where items from her old life would go, and how they would be used. Her heart was practically bursting with excitement. The smell of the dust in the air conditioning vent reminded her that this vehicle had sat closed up for months. First, she would need to clean.

By nightfall, she was thoroughly moved in to her new home. To her delight, she discovered that it does not take long to clean the interior of a motor home. Everything was in easy reach. She became fascinated by the ingenious use of space inside the vehicle. There seemed to be little storage compartments everywhere. Once the interior was cleaned, she had no trouble finding spaces to put her belongings and her food.

She ate supper, finishing off the last of the baked chicken. She then showered and crawled into bed among the new sheets tired but happy. She felt tremendous comfort knowing that her new friend was nearby. She fell asleep as the comforting sound of a train rumbled past, a few hundred yards away.

The next morning, Sally was just getting coffee when she glanced out of the window of her motor home to see Margaret returning from an early morning walk around the RV Park. Sally sipped her coffee and grinned at the look of stoic determination on Margaret's face. She had felt an instant kinship to this strong, self-contained little woman who had suddenly entered her life.

Her boyfriend, Phil, had been killed three years earlier, while riding his motorcycle down I-95. A drunk in a pickup truck had suddenly changed lanes without looking and sent Phil flying. After that, Sally had sold her motorcycle and got the job running the office at The Canuck's Rest RV Park.

The job had saved her life. Besides providing her with a place to live and a salary, it gave her somewhere to go and something to focus on as she passed through the stages of grieving the loss of Phil. Within a few minutes of meeting Margaret, Sally sensed that like her, this was a woman who was rebuilding her life.

Like Margaret, Sally was renting her RV and paying for ownership of it at the same time. Kinsey, the grandson of the original Canadian who opened the park, had wisely realized that if people were chosen carefully and he instituted this "rent-to-pay" plan, he would have a core population of permanent residents who would keep money coming in during the "off-season" of summer.

Like Margaret, Sally had slept especially soundly last night, knowing her new friend was close at hand. The loneliness that had plagued her since Phil's death eased a little when Margaret had entered the park's office and Sally was very grateful for that.

## CHAPTER THREE: ROLLY'S JOURNEY

Nineteen-year-old Rolly Collingsworth survived the Battle of Gettysburg, but just barely. A confederate minier ball had passed through his left leg just above the knee. He had fallen at the piled rock wall that led to the infamous "angle." Some of the Confederates in Picket's charge had managed to come over the wall. Before he blacked out, Rolly had shot the nearest rebel—a young boy with freckles and blonde hair. For the rest of his Life, Rolly was haunted by the memory of the shocked expression on that young face.

Rolly's wound wasn't that serious, but the gangrene that followed was. A butcher of an army doctor severed his rotting leg just below the hip joint. The man was nice enough to leave a sizable stump on which an artificial leg could be mounted.

As he lay recovering in the hospital back in Washington, DC, Rolly took morbid pleasure in designing his own artificial leg. His father, a New York cloth merchant, was wealthy enough to give his son the finest in prosthetics. Rolly, however, did not want any of the articulated wooden limbs that were just becoming available. Although the newer models made a valiant attempt to look real, Rolly found something incredibly sad about them. He wanted a good, solid, wooden peg.

He borrowed a few sheets of rag paper and a turkey quill pen from the hospital office along with a bottle of ink. It took him several tries, but he finally came up with a design he liked. He borrowed a tailor's cloth measuring tape and carefully measured his remaining leg to get the dimensions right.

Four months later, he arrived back in Albany wearing his varnished pine leg with its steel tip. He had selected pine because it was lighter than oak. Also, he liked the way its colorful grain showed up through the varnish. Rolly was determined to be as comfortable as possible so he had hunted leather shops all over the city until he found the softest strapping possible for the top of the limb. The strapping held a long extension of the peg that went up the outside of the leg to just below the hip. He also made sure the padding at the point of the stump was upholstered smoothly. Because he had measured accurately, the wooden leg was the same height as the remaining leg. As a result, he could walk without the side-to-side rocking motion that characterized many other amputees.

His life back in Albany had been a much more uncomfortable fit. His father had expected him to take up the family business and Rolly tried, but he found the factory floor a depressing place. Its seemingly endless rows of sewing machines and it's legion of underpaid immigrant women made him wonder what he had endured combat for. He felt tremendous guilt being part of a system that treated these women so shabbily.

Seeing Rolly's discomfort, his father tried moving him to the sales floor. After several weeks dealing with tailors, government purchasing agents, decorators and designers, it became clear to everyone that Rolly Collingsworth had come away from the war with a deep, abiding hatred of humanity in general. It was a major effort for him to be civil during even the most trivial encounters.

Eventually, he stopped coming in to work at all. His father was at a loss as to what to do with this moody, emotional hermit of a young man who had been so altered by the war.

Fall was coming to Albany and the thought of another freezing, gray winter seemed more than Rolly could bear. He begged his father for a portion of his inheritance so he could move to some place south. At this time, Florida was the wildest, most unsettled place in the eastern United States, and he was drawn to it.

So it was that he took a steamboat down the Hudson to New York City and caught a clipper ship heading south. He impatiently endured the many stops along the way at such ports as Baltimore and Charleston. A few weeks later the ship adroitly navigated an inlet between two low, jungle-clad islands and docked at the tiny community of St. Lucie on the Atlantic Coast of Florida.

It was a pretty fall day, unusually cool and dry for Central Florida. Rolly had the distinct impression that he was very close to his destination. He disembarked the clipper, carrying his backpack and blanket roll. He found lodging for a night or two at a fisherman's house. He felt no regret when the clipper ship set sail a day later, having replenished its supply of food and fresh water.

The fisherman he stayed with was an old fellow named Gus, who had lived in St. Lucie for about ten years. He had originally come from central Georgia. As the war clouds had gathered in the late 1850's Gus could see what was coming. He was too poor to own slaves and never did think the practice was justifiable. As he viewed the forthcoming conflict, he realized he was not willing to lay down his life defending rich planters.

So he had sold his small farm and had traveled south overland with his wife and two teenaged boys. After skirting the infamous Okefenokee Swamp, they had arrived in Jacksonville. Gus could tell that a thriving port like this would be a prize for either side in the conflict and so he booked passage aboard a southbound ship and, like Rolly, had been attracted to St. Lucie immediately.

He and his sons built the two-story frame house on the waterfront themselves. They had befriended a Christianized old Seminole named Karchee, who taught them how to fish the abundant waters of the Indian River. Karchee also taught them the complex craftsmanship of making dugout canoes from carefully selected cypress trees.

Between selling fish to boats putting into port, renting a room in their house to passengers, and building and selling canoes, Gus and his family had fashioned a comfortable life for themselves in only a couple of years. Gus's prediction about escaping the war bore fruit. During the war, the only reminder that a conflict was indeed raging somewhere was the occasional sighting of a Union blockade gunboat patrolling the waters out in the Atlantic.

"You lookin' like you uncomfortable around folks," Gus had observed over supper the first night Rolly stayed with them. Gus regarded the young man sympathetically.

"Can't say I care for people very much," The younger man answered, poking at the fried redfish on his plate.

"That why you came here?" Gus persisted.

"Yes," Rolly answered. "I want to find a place where I can keep to myself and not be bothered." Gus nodded and both men were quiet for a while.

"How you gonna live?" The older man asked. Rolly shrugged.

"Depends on what I find when I get where I'm going." Gus nodded again. He understood that instinctive draw to a place. Then an idea seemed to pop into the older man's mind.

There's a place about thirty miles north, where a good-sized freshwater river empties into the Indian River," Gus said, nodding his head in an upstream direction. I understand there is some high ground at that junction." Rolly's head came up and he felt goose bumps on his neck and arms.

"Can you show me the place?" He asked Gus. The old man shook his head.

"I got too much work to do around here son," Gus replied.

"I'll make it worth your while," Rolly offered. He then fished a $20 gold coin out of his pocket and slid it across the table. He could see Gus's eyes widen in surprise. Then the older man frowned in concern.

"Son," He warned. "I would be very careful where you showed that kind of money around here." Rolly patted the large Navy revolver at his side.

"I will," The younger man answered. "So can you show me where that place is?" Gus was silent for a while as he contemplated the young fellow in front of him. In the restless eyes he saw traces of himself years ago. He looked once again at the gold coin.

"I'll do better than that, son. Karchee and I will take you there and get you set up."

And so it was that three days later, three dugout canoes loaded with supplies headed north on the Indian River. The elderly Seminole led the way, stroking smoothly. When Rolly had first laid eyes on Karchee, he worried that the old fellow was too frail for a trip like this. In the water, however, Karchee's canoe seemed to glide effortlessly at an amazing speed. Rolly and Gus were not able to keep up with him and so trailed him by about a hundred yards.

They spent the first night on a bluff overlooking the water. It was a cold, crisp evening in late November.

"You were smart to do this during the cool weather," Gus remarked over their campfire. He was frying up a couple of fish he had caught.

"Smart had nothing to do with it," Rolly admitted. "I just couldn't stand to be where I was any more."

"Well, smart or not, you're here when the mosquitoes are not around because of the cold," the old man said. "And the snakes are all hiding out below ground." Rolly hadn't even thought about insects or snakes and as he dropped to sleep in his bedroll that night, he silently thanked whatever had led him to this place at this time.

Two days later, they arrived at the confluence of the St. Ignacio River and the Indian River. Just as Gus had heard, there was a high bluff standing about twenty feet above the water. It seemed to be composed of crushed seashells.

"This hill is an Indian garbage dump," Gus had said as they began hauling supplies from the canoes up to the top.

"Indians?" Rolly had asked, looking nervously about.

"Oh, they ain't around any more," Gus reassured. "They were a fierce bunch called the Ais." He set down a canvas-wrapped bundle. "They all died out from the white man's diseases before this century began."

"So they're not the ancestors of the Seminoles?" Rolly asked.

"Naw," Gus replied. "The Seminoles are actually runaways from tribes farther north, like the Creeks. Right Karchee?" The old man nodded in agreement.

Inland from the river, the area was covered with pine trees and palmetto bushes. Rolly and Gus began felling pine trees with a two-man crosscut saw. Karchee lopped off the branches with an axe. The men used peavey poles to move the logs into position.

After four days, a rough lean-to stood atop the bluff. The floor was raised off the ground on a supporting frame of pine logs. The logs that composed the floor had been smoothed somewhat with an adze. The walls and roof were overlapping palmetto fronds attached to a frame. It wasn't fancy, but Rolly was pleased with it. It allowed him to sleep off the ground and it kept the rain out. For the first time since Gettysburg, Rolly felt at home.

## CHAPTER FOUR: THE BRIDGE

Six months after she had moved into The Canuck's Rest RV Park, Margaret was riding with Sally to an antique store. The shop was located a few miles north of St. Ignacio on highway one. It was a balmy February day on the Florida coast. It was the kind of weather—sunny and warm without being hot—that made the rest of the country hate Floridians in the winter.

Sally was driving her old Jeep Cherokee that sounded and felt like one was riding in a truck. Margaret was content to simply gaze out the window at the now familiar downtown area of St. Ignacio. The instant fondness she had felt for the place upon arriving several months before had not abated. If anything, it had grown stronger. Old frame houses continued to border the highway in St. Ignacio as they had for years. What had once been the homes of prosperous families had been converted into some charming boutique businesses with parking in the back. It was a setting that invited sauntering from shop to shop.

As they headed north, the land rose slightly, culminating in a bluff where the St. Ignacio River met the Indian River. A concrete bridge spanned the St. Ignacio here, and afforded one an unobstructed view of either waterway. As Margaret looked out at the mile-wide expanse of the Indian River, she marveled at how this body of water seemed to change its personality each day. Today it seemed to laugh in the bright sunlight.

It was a Saturday morning. Sally had the day off and the two friends were laughing and chattering together. Sally had been telling Margaret about this wonderful jumble of an antique store they were about to visit.

"I usually don't buy much there," she had admitted. "I just love looking." Margaret could appreciate that. The six months of living in a motor home had taught her that the limited storage space forced her to be very judicious in deciding what she purchased. Rather than feeling restricted by this, she saw it as an interesting way to keep her life as simple as possible.

They were sitting at a stop light just before reaching the bridge when Margaret saw the second overlay. The modern concrete bridge was topped for several moments by the outline of a high, arching wooden span—and there was something else. On the part of the transparent bridge that slanted down toward them: there were the outlines of bodies. Then the image was gone. Sally had noticed Margaret's sudden intake of breath.

"You okay, Maggie?" Sally asked. Margaret smiled at the sound of her new nickname.

"Yeah," she answered. "Just saw something disturbing." Sally glanced up the highway just as the light changed and they started forward. She saw nothing unusual.

"What is it?" Sally asked.

"It was one of those things I saw when I first moved here," Margaret answered.

"You mean like the old hotel building?"

"Yes. Only this time it was an old wooden bridge over the river." Sally nodded when she heard this.

"There *was* a wooden bridge here until this one was built in the 1950's," Sally said. "It was long gone by the time I was born, but I've seen pictures of it."

"Where?" Margaret asked, surprised at the urgency in her own voice.

"The local historical society has a little museum in an old school building on Main Street."

"I want to go there sometime, Sally," Margaret said.

"Okay," Sally answered. "They are only open a few hours each week. I'll look into it."

Sally's description of the antique store was completely accurate: a wonderful jumble. It was housed in a low building made of weathered wood that fronted the highway. Inside, there was one large open room off of which a seemingly endless maze of smaller rooms branched. Just when Margaret thought she had reached one of the outer walls of the building, another little room would appear.

Each room seemed to have a theme of sorts. In one room there was a collection of old farm tools. Another room was dedicated to military regalia and old weapons. Margaret guessed that the owner had wisely put that room in to occupy bored husbands accompanying their wives.

"Smart marketing," she thought to herself.

She was not interested in buying anything she saw at first. She was enjoying fantasizing about who had owned some of the objects she scrutinized. She wondered what disruptions in their lives had resulted in their treasured belongings appearing here.

One room seemed to be dedicated to portraits of people. Some were paintings and some were fading old photographs. She looked at the weathered faces of generations past and marveled at how they had a different look in their eyes from modern folk. Some of them were clearly suspicious of the camera, and their expressions were unsmiling and sometimes downright hostile. Others seemed to assume a kind of bravado in front of the lens, and their faces seemed to say, "Look at me!" Then one picture stopped her in her tracks.

It was of a man her age; a yellowing oval portrait inside of a worn frame. Only his face and shoulders were visible. The tanned wrinkles formed an expression of cold anger. This man clearly did not want to be there all dressed up, sitting in front of that damned machine. There was something painfully familiar about his face that she couldn't quite identify.

As she looked at the scowling man, her left leg went numb. She wondered if she was having a stroke. She knew one of the signs of a stroke was paralysis to one side of the face, so she limped into the next room where a large, ornate mirror was hanging and looked at her own face. She made herself smile and frown and it was clear there was no paralysis. That's when it hit her: the man had *her* face!

She returned to the room with the picture and looked at it again. The numbness in her leg had passed. Yes. Underneath the beard and the gray, scraggily hair, the round, sunburned face was masculine but it was definitely hers. She carefully removed the picture from its hook on the wall and carried it into the main room. The proprietor sat inside of a little island of locked display cases loaded with jewelry.

"Do you have any idea who this person is?" Margaret asked the man. The man glanced up momentarily from his paperwork and studied the photograph for a moment.

"Some kind of local pioneer," He replied in what Margaret guessed was a New Jersey accent. "I think I've seen that picture and some others of him in a local history book."

"Do you remember his name?" She asked.

"Nah, sorry," the man replied. He glanced again at the picture then at Margaret.

"Wow!" He exclaimed. "He looks kinda like you! Is he a relative?"

"I don't think so," Margaret answered and paid the twenty dollars for the portrait. She had the man wrap it in newspaper and put it in a paper bag.


## CHAPTER FIVE: STARVIN' MARVIN

Starvin' Marvin was in an especially good mood. The Adored One had visited him before daylight that morning and they had made love as the sun came up. She had to leave when it got light, but she left him some donuts and some coffee and some money. He sat on the milk crate that served as a chair and stared out at the Indian River four stories below. He had finished the last donut and was sipping his coffee with satisfaction.

It seemed the ultimate coup to Marvin that he got to live for free in a place that other people would have paid hundreds of thousands to occupy years before. The abandoned luxury condo complex had been in the process of being built ten years earlier, when a hurricane came in off the Atlantic and gutted the unfinished structure. The tidal surge from the storm had swept in from the Atlantic and up the Indian River. It had inundated the first floor of the building, and the structure had been deemed uninhabitable ever since. The land had been turned over to the state, and the state seemed to be stuck in bureaucratic limbo as it tried to decide what to do with it. Starvin' Marvin was reaping the benefits of that indecision.

He had been living in the building for three years. Because the building was so far away from highway one and stood behind a curtain of jungle, it was completely invisible to passing motorists.  Boats plying the Indian River could see the building, but dared not try to land there. Besides the NO TRESPASSING signs warning boaters away, the building was still surrounded by wreckage from the storm. A dangerous-looking jetty of rusting construction equipment, twisted aluminum and broken, jagged boards fronted the Indian River.  It was an uninviting landscape to any watercraft.  Marvin liked to think of it as the outer works of his fortress.

Occasionally, a state officer of some kind would drive through the property in a jeep, but never ventured into the building. Marvin always kept his belongings in the center of the top floor of the building, out of sight from either the ground or the river.

In his thirty-two years on earth, the abandoned building was the closest Marvin had ever come to establishing a home of his own. He was nineteen when he fell from a scaffold on a construction site in Arkansas and suffered the traumatic brain injury that would characterize the rest of his life. His drunken father had left the family when Marvin was a toddler. While he was recuperating in a hospital charity ward, his beleaguered, exhausted mother had quietly taken the rest of her kids and had moved away with no forwarding address. Marvin was left to recover on his own. As it was, he recovered from the injury with only a vague memory of the family from which he had come.

He had never been a particularly stable person before the injury, but he emerged from the experience in a permanently heightened state of paranoia. He trusted no one and so he spent the next decade wandering throughout the southeastern United States.

He supported himself with a combination of thievery and odd jobs. During one of his jail terms for vagrancy, he got into a fight with a fellow prisoner and suffered a second concussion. It was during the recovery from this second traumatic brain injury that he became convinced that God was talking to him.

God's voice in his head closely resembled that of an elderly British man. The British accent seemed formal and exotic to Marvin and utterly believable. In Marvin's mind, God was guiding him as would stern but well-meaning uncle. The voice only seemed to speak to Marvin whenever he stood at some turning point in his life. Three years earlier, Marvin had been walking up highway one, heading toward the City of Sydney, Florida, when night began to fall. He ventured off the highway into the deserted flood plain and spied the abandoned building.

"HERE!" The voice had thundered. And here Marvin had stayed, fashioning a life for himself that he considered almost luxurious.

A further sign that he was in the right place was the discovery of the machete. He had discovered it in the overgrown hedge at the front of the building. Some gardener had apparently been working on the landscaping before the hurricane and had forgotten it there. "YOURS!" The British voice in his mind had proclaimed.

In the dim recesses of his fractured mind, there was the half memory of a story about a young king pulling a sword out of a stone. He carried the machete reverently into the building as if it were a holy relic. He found a large sandstone landscaping rock and used it as a whetstone. He had lovingly scraped the rust off the instrument and had honed it to razor sharpness. Wielding his machete, he felt immensely powerful, like the young king in the story.

Marvin prided himself on his ingenuity. He usually rose before daylight and rode his stolen bicycle out to the highway. There, he would wait until no one was in sight before breaking cover from behind some trees and becoming part of the rest of the world. Over the years he had lived in the building, he had developed several routes to turn up in public. Some mornings he would emerge from the woods on a residential street a half-mile to the north. At other times he would walk his bike to a ditch a quarter of a mile south of the building and emerge onto the highway after skirting the protective fence around the culvert. In the evening, he would return to the property using a route other than the one he had used that morning. Sometimes he would exit and enter the property by passing through the woods behind a nearby shopping center

Besides getting money occasionally from the Adored One, he survived by scrounging cardboard and bringing it to the recycling center. This would usually get him enough to buy a sandwich and a soft drink. He would pedal to a little picnic pavilion near the base of the bridge over the St. Ignacio River. He would eat his lunch there, looking out at the pelicans diving for fish. He had no idea that the picnic pavilion in which he sat was located on the former site of Rolly Collingsworth's cabin.

As often happens in small towns, he had become a kind of local character. "Starvin' Marvin" was a name the locals had dubbed him with, because of his permanently skinny, sunburned frame. He didn't mind the name. To him, it was all part of the camouflage of dealing with a world that he was never a part of and that he hated. In his mind, he was wearing a clever disguise and waiting for something that he sensed was coming. He took comfort in the fact that being obviously homeless and a little crazy kept most people away.

Occasionally other homeless people would discover the abandoned building, but Marvin quickly drove them away, brandishing his machete. Two years earlier, one of these threatened to tell the sheriff's office where he was. The old fellow's name was Stuffy, and he was a train-hopper. The more Marvin thought about Stuffy's threat, the more he became convinced that the man had to be stopped. His decision was finalized when the internal British voice shouted 'SILENCE HIM!".

So the next night, Marvin found Stuffy sleeping by the railroad tracks near The Canuck's Rest RV Park. He dispatched the old man with a single blow of the machete. It had cleaved neatly through the spine at the base of the skull while the old man slept in alcoholic peace. The kill had been quick and soundless. He had dragged the body into the patch of woods beside the tracks. Using a rusted shovel he had retrieved from the abandoned building, he had buried Stuffy there.

The woods along the tracks were a kind of no-man's-land, similar to the abandoned building in which he dwelled. People who had jobs and families never notice these vacant bits of land, so caught up are they in their lives. But the human discards of our society know these places very well. Marvin knew no one with any authority would ever venture into the strip of woods. But just to make sure, he occasionally visited Stuffy's grave to make sure it had not been discovered. A glance at the undisturbed pine needles would reassure him. Sometimes he would talk to the grave, explaining in a conversational tone why Stuffy's death was necessary.

In the meantime, Marvin had continued to live his role in St. Ignacio as a local harmless homeless character. He became a familiar sight prowling the garbage areas of businesses for cardboard, which he would load onto a wagon towed behind his bicycle. In the daylight, he wisely left the machete at the abandoned condo. No sense in alarming people. He enjoyed thinking of himself as a secret weapon.

## CHAPTER SIX: SANDRA

Sandra liked her job. As president of the St. Ignacio Historical Society, she got to run the tiny museum and talk to the folks that visited. She had always found it easy to deal with people. She seemed to be able to read them quickly and find the right tone of voice; the right facial expression to put them at their ease. In this way, she was vastly different from her husband, Clay. He was a blunt, simple man who had no patience with social interactions. He ran a profitable business installing fencing in the area and seemed to be happiest when he was away from home supervising an installation somewhere. When he would come home from work, he would eat supper and then fall asleep in front of the television. His snoring was so loud they had taken to sleeping in separate rooms.

As she drove through the streets of St. Ignacio, she was feeling especially good. She just had a long, luxurious bath and was sipping her coffee as she drove toward the little museum. As usual Clay had left before daylight to go to the storage yard of his company to do God-knows-what at this hour. He was obsessed with getting everything in order before his workers arrived.

She had met Clay when she was a college student in Georgia. He had been sent to Georgia by his boss to purchase some metal fencing stock that was being offered at a reduced price. He had encountered Sandra in a local bar where she was hanging out with a couple of her girlfriends He was ruggedly handsome and because he was obviously from blue-collar roots, he was "forbidden fruit" for a middle class college girl like herself. Their affair was sudden and passionate. They had eloped a few days later, to the consternation of her parents. To add to their distress, she had completed her rebellion by dropping out of college.

When Clay brought her to his hometown of St. Ignacio, she had felt an instant attraction to the place...at first. Just as Margaret was to feel years later, Sandra felt an overwhelming sense of familiarity with the village. When their son, Clay Junior was born, it seemed their happiness could not be greater. But when the second baby, Mindy, came two years later, Sandra had hemorrhaged badly and had slipped briefly into unconsciousness.

A few months after she was released from the hospital, Clay confided to a close friend, that the woman who emerged from the brief coma was not the same woman who had entered it. When asked what he meant, Clay as usual couldn't seem to find the right words. He said something about Sandra being a robot and left it at that.

For her part, Sandra had emerged from this near death experience more determined to make good use of whatever time she had left on earth. She still fulfilled her duties as wife and mother, but it soon became clear to all in the household that Sandra viewed them as just that—duties.

As children will sometimes do, her son and her daughter had moved away from home as soon as they were able. Clay Junior had joined the Air Force and at last report, was stationed somewhere in South Korea. Mindy went away to college in California and married a fellow she met there. Neither of them had children of their own yet. So given her husband's constant absence (both physical and emotional) and the empty nest that her home had become, she welcomed the diversion of the St. Ignacio Historical Society.

Sandra could not explain her growing passion for local history. Ever since she had emerged from the coma she was aware of a kind of restlessness—a hunger—and something told her that the antidote lay somewhere in St. Ignacio's past. She had joined the historical society shortly after Mindy was born, and she found the dithery old women in the group tiresome to deal with. She hid her impatience, however, and ingratiated herself to them. Using her formidable acting skill, she convinced them that she was a delightful, energetic partner in the society's efforts.

When Doris Hampton, the president of the society suffered a crippling stroke four years earlier, Sandra made it a point to visit her regularly at St. Ignacio Haven. She had been hoping to glean tidbits of local history from the older woman, but the poor dear's brains seemed to have been permanently scrambled. Doris simply stared vacantly at nothing when Sandra visited. But the younger woman continued to visit every couple of weeks out of a sense of duty. As time wore on, Sandra found it very comfortable to talk to Doris's vacant staring eyes while relating tidbits about her own life.

Given Doris's inability to function, it was decided to hold an election for a new president of the historical society. Because the other members were contemporaries of Doris, Sandra stood out as the youngest and most energetic candidate. So thoroughly had Sandra wormed her way into the affections of the members that she was chosen as the new leader by acclamation.

The first thing she had done in her new office was to move the museum. It had been housed in a drab little storefront on the highway. She was able to convince the city fathers that a more suitable location would be in the historic old elementary school building, which was no longer in use. Her insistence had paid off. Housed in its larger new quarters, the museum was attracting twice the attendance it had before. More and more locals seemed to be willing to donate articles of historical importance to the facility. Under her carefully researched scrutiny, the collection of historical memorabilia had grown to fill several rooms.

She pulled up in front of the building and parked in the space reserved for her. She took a moment to sip her coffee and look at the school building. It had been built in the 1920's when school buildings were edifices that complimented the cities in which they sat. It was a square, two-story brick structure, painted off-white. The bottom floor was the museum and the top floor had classrooms that were currently being used by the local community college. Sandra liked coming to work in the dignified, substantial structure. She took comfort in the solidity surrounding her and was a fastidious curator of the museum.

After opening the door, she put on a pot of coffee in the tiny back office and did a walk through of the exhibits. Satisfying herself that nothing seemed out of place, she settled in behind the reception desk. She was surprised when the door opened a minute or two later to reveal a short woman a few years older than her, with glasses and medium length salt and pepper hair. The woman was carrying a paper bag, with something inside. At Sandra's direction, the woman signed the guest register with her name and address. She then took a framed, oval-shaped yellowing photograph out of the bag.

"Do you recognize this man?" Margaret asked. Sandra smiled.

"Why, yes," Sandra answered excitedly. "That's Rolly Collingsworth, one of the founders of St. Ignacio." Sandra cocked her head quizzically.

"Where did you find that picture?" Sandra asked. "I didn't realize copies of it had been made."

"Copies?" Margaret looked confused. Sandra nodded at the wall across the room behind Margaret. There, in better condition and in a nicer frame was the same photograph Margaret held in her hand. She was distracted by the fact that there were two such pictures and had to force herself to deal with the question that had been asked.

"I—uh—bought this at that antique store north of here on highway one."

"You look a great deal like him, Sandra said. "Are you related to him in some way?" Margaret shook her head.

"I doubt it. I was born and raised in Washington State. How can I find out more information about him?"

"I have just the thing," Sandra answered and reached behind her. From a shelf she pulled up a large, soft-covered book entitled, *St. Ignacio Memories.*

"This was compiled by Doris Hampton who used to be the president of the historical society," Sandra explained. "She did a wonderful job and there is a lot about Mr. Collingsworth in here, as well as a copy of your picture," Sandra handed the book to Margaret. The price sticker on the front cover said $25. That seemed horribly overpriced to Margaret for a book that was about the size and thickness of an elementary student's workbook. But she was desperate to know more about the man who resembled her. So she asked Sandra to set the book aside and she began touring the various exhibits. As she did so, she was aware of a subtle uneasiness that seemed to creep over her.

There were pictures of many old homes and buildings that Margaret recognized as the sites of various stores and offices today. One of them was the Sunnyside Hotel—the two-story building she had seen in her first overlay. Posing in front of it were two older men and a woman of about the same age. The caption read, "Davis Buckley, famous ornithologist, poses with Mr. and Mrs. Stathis, proprietors of the Sunnyside Hotel." The men were bearded and stiff. The woman looked to Margaret as if she was wearing way too much clothing for Florida. Margaret gave a silent prayer of thanks for the more reasonable styles of today.

There was an extensive exhibit about men who had served in the world wars, Korea, and Vietnam. A long marble slab took up one end of the display case on which were engraved the names of local boys who had given their lives in warfare. Margaret counted almost a hundred names. For such a small town, St. Ignacio had paid dearly.

She then came to an exhibit dedicated to the history of the bridge over the St. Ignacio River. The earliest pictures were of the old wooden bridge she had seen in her second overlay. It was a level structure with a high hump in the middle to allow the passage of fishing boat masts. The hump rose higher than the current concrete span, and according to the caption beneath the picture, this had presented a problem during rainstorms. The wooden planks became quite slippery on both sides of the rise and skidding accidents were common. In none of these early pictures were there any dead people lying on the bridge.

Margaret stopped by the desk and retrieved the book she had just purchased. Before leaving she turned to Sandra.

"Was there some sort of violence on the old bridge?" She asked. For a split second, Margaret thought she noticed the younger woman stiffen.

"It's in the book," Sandra snapped.

## CHAPTER SEVEN: GOODBYE NOEL

Rolly sat on a palm log behind a clump of palmettos at the foot of the wooden bridge. In the east, across the Indian River, the sky was already light over the Atlantic. Dawn would be in a few minutes. He swatted another mosquito buzzing around his face and for the tenth time, checked the breech of his old Burnside carbine. The end of a brass cartridge peeked out at him and he closed it. He took out the old Navy colt and checked it again. It was fully loaded.

Across the way he could see Lucas, old Gus's grandson, who was sitting on a pine stump with his prized possession—a Winchester—cradled in his lap. He knew that to his right, hidden out of sight was Karchee's grandson Joe Gator. Joe's rifle was even older than Rolly's—an old Confederate Springfield muzzle loader. Joe would get one shot off and that would be it. So Lucas had given Joe his revolver for added firepower. And so they waited and watched the bridge 30 yards away.

Rolly found it hard to believe that just two hours earlier, he had been awakened from a sound sleep by knocking at his cabin door. He had opened it to find Deputy Johnny

Farley wounded and bleeding on his front step.

"Noel Taylor's bunch ambushed Sheriff Stinson, Charley and I," he had gasped. "We were at the Holcomb ranch!" He took in a ragged breath. "Stinson and Charley are dead." His speech was starting to slur. "I got away, but they're only a few minutes behind me. "They're comin' here next." Johnny's head lolled on his chest. Rolly had to lean in close to hear the deputy's last words. "They think the town is unprotected." Johnny went limp.

Rolly tore a blanket off his bed and wrapped the young man in it. He dragged Johnny inside his cabin and laid him on the floor. Hopping around the cabin on his good leg, he fumbled in the darkness to strap on his wooden leg and climb into some overalls. He got his rifle down from its hooks on the wall above his bed, strapped on his revolver and put a handful of ammunition in his pocket.

He had limped as rapidly as possible along the dirt road that would someday become highway one. At first it had disturbed him that in the thirty years he had lived at the confluence of the two rivers, more and more people began to move into the area. On this night, however, he was grateful to have two close neighbors that weren't afraid to fight. Both Lucas and Joe responded immediately when they heard Rolly's frantic knocking. Joe had sent his wife, Myra, to Rolly's cabin to tend to Johnny Farley. Within half an hour, the ambush was set. Now there was just the waiting.

Noel Taylor's gang had been terrorizing the local countryside for years. They were known as far south as Miami and as far west as Tampa. Their pattern was to find an isolated farm, Kill the males and do horrible things to the females before killing them. Then they would take whatever they could use and disappear. By the time law enforcement arrived, all they could do was bury the bodies and notify the next of kin.

Sheriff Stinson and his two deputies had been called out to Holcomb's ranch, about fifteen miles away, by a farmer who had heard gunshots and screams coming from the direction of the place. As they had entered the stacked wood fence that bordered the ranch, they could see bodies on the ground in front of the cabin.

Noel and his men had opened fire on them from several directions and Johnny was surprised to find himself unscathed. He had wheeled his horse around and started to ride hell-for-leather toward St. Ignacio. He had just cleared the gate when a bullet tore into his side just below the right shoulder blade. He could hear men trying to mount horses behind him. So he pressed on. His horse had won some local match races, and he knew he could outdistance the gang if he could just manage to stay in the saddle. It was logical for him to seek out old man Collingsworth for help. After all, everyone knew Rolly Collingsworth to be a tough, ill-tempered old bastard who was not afraid of a fight.

And now the Civil War veteran and aspiring hermit was waiting for another battle. The irony did not escape Rolly that a man who had moved heaven and earth to avoid people was now going to risk his life defending a scattered group of villagers that he hardly knew. Inspiration struck him, and he rolled up the leg of his overalls to expose his wooden peg.

His thoughts were interrupted by the clatter of horses' hooves on the bridge. Looking through the palmetto fronds, Rolly saw five men come over the hump in the middle. When they were halfway down the nearest side, Rolly stepped out into the road, keeping his rifle behind his good leg. He rightly guessed that in the half-light, the wooden leg would distract them. The five riders stopped at the sight of him. The lead rider, whom Rolly rightly assumed was Noel Taylor laughed and pointed at the one-legged old man.

"Hi, there, post-hole digger! What's your name?" Noel Taylor asked.

Rolly pivoted slightly on his peg. "My name's Rolly," the old man said. Swinging his rifle smoothly up to his shoulder, Rolly put a .54 caliber bullet into Noel Taylor's chest. The impact flung Noel off his horse and he lay gasping for breath on the planks of the bridge. The rest of the gang tried to return fire, but the sudden eruption of gunshots spooked their horses and ruined their aim. Their shots were going everywhere. Rolly stepped to one side to give Joe Gator a clean shot. Joe picked off the man closest to Noel. Lucas stepped into the road, firing and rapidly pumping the lever on his Winchester. Two more men fell to his volley. All three men then concentrated their fire on the remaining rider, who had managed to turn his horse around. By the time he mounted the hump in the middle of the bridge, they could see he had been hit several times. Swaying in the saddle he succeeded in crossing over the hump and out of sight, but they heard him clatter onto the wooden planks.

Rolly, Joe, and Lucas then approached the bridge. Rolly had his Navy colt in his hand and Joe carried the pistol Lucas had given him. Lucas carried the Winchester. Rolly came upon Noel Taylor who was trying to curse him through lips flecked with blood, but no sound came.

"Goodbye, Noel," Rolly said and put a bullet between the man's eyes. Two of the others were already dead and Joe finished off another one with Lucas's pistol. The three men walked up to the top of the hump in the bridge to find the last man lying in a pool of blood halfway down the other side. Joe walked over to him looked down and then looked up and Rolly and nodded. The entire battle had lasted less than three minutes.

Rolly looked toward the east. The sun was rising over the horizon in the Atlantic and it made silhouettes of the palm trees on the barrier island across the Indian River.

"Let's just leave 'em here," he said. As Rolly, Joe and Lucas walked off the bridge, Rolly turned around to look back at the scene. What he saw in that momentary glance is what Margaret had seen in her second overlay. Then all three men returned to their homes.

Late the following afternoon, the Sheriff of the little town that would some day grow into the city of Sydney, Florida came upon the scene He had been told of the bodies by a freight wagon driver who had crossed the bridge about an hour after the battle. It was clear to the officer that he was looking at the rapidly decomposing remains of the Taylor Gang. To taunt him Noel Taylor had sent the sheriff a photograph of himself. Looking down now at Noel's fly-covered face, the Sheriff smiled grimly as he remembered the cocky man in the photograph.

Locals had apparently helped themselves to the gang's horses and had picked over the corpses pretty thoroughly, taking anything of value—even clothing. As he thought about the mountain of paperwork that would be involved in the ensuing report, the Sheriff's stomach turned sour. He decided upon a simpler solution. He and his deputies simply tossed the bodies over the bridge railing. The alligators could take over disposal. That night a torrential rainstorm washed all traces of blood off the bridge. As far as the official record was concerned, the Noel Taylor Gang had mysteriously disappeared.

The detailed account of what eventually became known as "The Battle of St. Ignacio Bridge," was pieced together from three sources. Johnny Farley had miraculously survived his wound and had related his version of events to Joe's wife, Myra, who had tended to him. Myra had also heard the story from her husband Joe, and from Joe's friend, Lucas. She had outlived everybody involved in the episode and was able to tell the whole story to the mother of Doris Hampton, who then incorporated it into her book.

After reading the account of the battle, Margaret looked at the only two pictures of Rolly Collingsworth in existence. One was the portrait she owned and the other was apparently taken a few years earlier. In it, Rolly was standing in front of a substantially built pine log cabin, glaring into the camera, his peg leg clearly visible.

There was also the photograph of Noel Taylor that had been sent to the sheriff in Sydney. He was a tall man with a shock of brown hair that fell into his face. He was grinning slyly into the camera. Behind the smile the eyes were dead of emotion, which made the grin that much more grotesque. It occurred to Margaret that she had recently seen eyes with a similar expression in them, but she couldn't remember where.

## CHAPTER EIGHT: MEMORIES OF MEN

Margaret closed the book and leaned back in the armchair of her motor home. She suddenly felt exhausted and weak. The balmy weather that had brightened her trip to the antique store with Sally had disappeared. It was a cloudy, moody day outside and it matched her emotional state. There was an unusually chilly wind sweeping in from the north and grey clouds were scudding across the sky. On this day, Florida was more closely resembling her home state of Washington.

Earlier that morning, she had driven to the supermarket and the changeable waters of the Indian River looked unusually foreboding and cold in the grey light. She was reminded of Puget Sound on winter days in Washington. Over the years of living in the Pacific Northwest she had grown increasingly sensitive to Seasonal Affective Disorder. The seemingly unending gray winter days dragged at her emotionally with increasing strength each year. She had been relieved to be in the fairly constant sunshine of Florida.

But today was a throwback of sorts and she was feeling it. There is an old saying that "Winter in Florida lasts for a couple of days in February." It seemed to Margaret that these were those two days. When she got home with her groceries, she put them away, made herself a cup of coffee and sat down to read the book she had purchased at the museum.

Ever since she had found the portrait of Rolly Collingsworth, it was as if her metabolism had speeded up by a couple of gears. When she read the account of the

Battle of St. Ignacio Bridge, she got flash images that were not included in what she was reading. For a few seconds, she could actually *see* Joe Gator aiming his long rifle. She could *see* the hatred in Noel Taylor's eyes as Rolly finished him off.

When she finished reading the account, Margaret felt she had been through the battle herself, and leaned her head back against the cushion of the armchair. The speeded up metabolism had suddenly free-fallen into exhaustion and a mild depression. She jumped at the sound of a knock at her door. Sally was standing outside.

"I need company," Sally said, smiling entreatingly. "I bring pizza and ice cream. Can I come in?"

"Oh God yes!" Margaret exclaimed. "You are an angel of mercy!"

A few minutes later, they were sitting in Margaret's little dinette. They were eating slices of pizza and drinking coffee. On such an unseasonably chilly day, Margaret felt that something hot was called for.

"I've just been missing Phil a lot today," Sally confessed after sipping her coffee. "I go for long periods where I think I've made peace with the grief and then—wham! It sweeps over me once again."

"I've never been married," Margaret said. "I cannot imagine what you are going through."

"It's like one of my internal organs has been ripped out," Sally said. She told Margaret about how she and Phil would ride their Harleys together. Sally admitted she had been something of a hellion when she was young, but meeting Phil changed all that.

"He was big and strong, so he was respected by everybody," Sally said, her eyes staring fondly at nothing. "But there was a gentleness about him—an intelligence—that set him apart."

"He sounds wonderful," Margaret said softly.

"He was," Sally admitted. "I think one of the things I miss most about him was the laugher." She shook her head grinning. "He could always make me laugh." Both women were quiet for a few minutes. Margaret sensed that Sally needed time to enjoy her memories. Finally Sally shook her head and brushed away a tear.

"I'm sorry," she said. "I'm going on and on about Phil." Sally looked across the table at her friend.

"Wasn't there anybody in your life?" Margaret shifted in her seat.

"When I was a young teacher, I had an affair with a married fellow—a colleague." Margaret shook her head and smiled ruefully. "I was convinced I was madly in love."

"What happened?" Sally asked.

"The inevitable—he went back to his wife and ended it." Margaret took a sip of her coffee before continuing. "I was crushed, of course. I thought I had lost the love of my life."

"Was he?" Margaret shook her head.

"No. After years of hindsight and growing up I realized that if he and I had ever tried to live together, one of us would probably have murdered the other one." Both women laughed at this.

"And there's been no one since him?" Sally asked.

"Oh there have been occasional men, but no one I wanted to spend much time with." Margaret shook her head resignedly. "They all seem to be self-involved and boring. Besides, I've been on my own for so long, I don't think I could adjust to another person living with me. I'm pretty set in my ways." Sally nodded.

"The first impression I got of you when you walked into the office that day was that you were a very self-sufficient person." Margaret smiled.

"That's funny, because I had exactly the same impression of you." Sally laughed her wonderful laugh.

"It's all a brave front, as you now know. I spend a lot of my time lonely and scared."

"Of what?" Margaret asked. Sally thought carefully before answering.

"Nothing specific," she replied. "It's just that, ever since I was a teenager I've had a man of some kind in my life." She took another sip of coffee. "Ever since Phil's death, I haven't been able to even look at another man. I miss the friendship and the sense of belonging I had with Phil, but I just don't see anyone that could even come close to filling that void." Margaret nodded empathetically. Sally suddenly brightened.

"Enough about loss," she said. She nodded across the room where Rolly Collingsworth's portrait hung on the pantry door. "What have you learned about that guy?"

"According to the book I read on local history, he lost a leg in the Civil War, and moved down here from New York to make a new start."

"Sounds like an interesting man," Sally observed. "Did he start a family down here?"

"No. The books said nothing about him marrying. I get the impression that he was a loner like me." Sally nodded.

"He even looks like you," she said.

"That's what drew me to his picture in the first place," Margaret said. "And I think the images I sometimes see have something to do with him." Sally's dark eyes looked fascinated.

"Do you think it's reincarnation?" Sally asked. Margaret thought for a moment before replying. She shook her head.

"I have no idea," she answered. "But I get the impression that I am seeing things through his eyes."

"Why is that happening?" Sally wondered. Margaret frowned.

"I'm not sure, but I think Rolly Collingsworth is trying to warn me about something."

Margaret invited Sally to spend the night on her couch after the pizza dinner. Sally's eyes filled with tears at this unexpected generosity, and she had to run to her RV to get the extra bed linens that Margaret did not have. Both women slept soundly that night, knowing that the other was close by.


## CHAPTER NINE: A SHORT VISIT WITH DORIS

Doris Hampton didn't mind that her days were routine. The stroke had left her unable to speak coherently, but she could still write. She kept a journal by her bed at St. Ignacio Haven and wrote in it a few minutes every day. She could usually only manage about ten minutes of writing at a time, before becoming exhausted. She realized all too clearly that her life was winding down. She was not afraid of dying, but she felt a desperate need to get her last thoughts and feelings down on paper. So to her, those short bursts of writing each day constituted her most important work.

Alicia, the black teenager who was assigned to her wing of the facility greeted her cheerily each morning. Alicia would assist Doris into the bathroom and would help her wash up. Alicia would then brush Doris's thinning hair and pick out something for the older woman to wear. Doris liked and trusted Alicia, and felt comfortable resting in the young girl's care.

Alicia then would wheel Doris into the common room of the facility and place her at a north-facing window. This afforded Doris a view of the manicured grounds of the facility as well as some of the traffic on highway one. Because it faced north, she was never bothered by the glare of sunlight coming through the glass.

"You okay now, Doris?" Alicia would ask. Doris would nod and give the girl a crooked smile. Alicia would then leave to tend to other patients. Doris would have about a half hour to herself before being wheeled into the dining hall for breakfast.

Doris used that half hour to pray. Her prayers differed every morning. Sometimes she prayed for the soul of any resident of the facility who had recently passed away. Sometimes she prayed for Alicia, whose personal life seemed to be filled with teenaged drama. She always prayed for her grandchildren and great grandchildren, even though they rarely visited. She didn't blame them. They were busy living their lives as she had done. She understood.

She always ended her prayers by praying for the town of St. Ignacio itself. Her attachment to the place was as strong as what Margaret had felt that first day. Doris didn't see overlays around her, but her studies into the history of the town had given her a powerful sense of place. She was constantly aware, for example, that where she was now sitting had been the famous Sunnyside Hotel owned by Mr. and Mrs. Stathis. She had never been able to cross the bridge over the St. Ignacio River without remembering the bloody gunfight that had occurred there.

And now, it was starting to dawn on her that the town might be facing a new threat. What she sensed might be coming was quiet, even pleasant in appearance, but every bit as vicious as the Noel Taylor Gang. She had watched the threat emerge gradually, like a viper coming out of hibernation and stretching luxuriantly in the sunlight. The danger came from a most unlikely source and that made it all the more insidious. Doris had watched the threat emerge very gradually over several months, in a pair of brown eyes that seemed absolutely devoid of any emotion but anger.


## CHAPTER TEN: SANDRA AND THE ARCHANGEL

The seeds of Sandra's disintegration had been planted one day shortly after she had joined the historical society many years ago. She had been leafing through Doris Hampton's book when she came upon the photograph of Noel Taylor. She had read soppy romances as a teenager about women swooning when they first encountered the love of their lives, and had dismissed it as so much claptrap. But she *had* practically swooned when she gazed into the eyes of Noel Taylor. She felt suddenly lightheaded and almost dizzy with the recognition of a kindred soul.

Before Doris suffered her stroke, Sandra had used every opportunity to pump the older woman for details about Noel Taylor's life that were not included in the book. At first, Doris was happy to answer the younger woman's questions, sensing another person interested in local history. But the questions were so many and asked with such intensity that Doris had become increasingly uneasy in the younger woman's presence. Sensing the older woman's disapproval, Sandra began researching Noel Taylor on her own, haunting the county records offices in St. Ignacio and other areas of south and central Florida.

As she researched the bloody history of the Taylor Gang, Sandra found herself becoming increasingly fascinated by its leader. He seemed to hate everything and everybody and this hatred resonated with what felt like an undiscovered sea of rage inside of her. She marveled at Noel's complete disregard for the lives of other humans. She could imagine the incredible power it gave a person to be that far beyond the rules and expectations of others.

She identified thoroughly with his virulent hatred of "good folks," and their suffocating ways. Her husband and her kids were examples of "good folk," and they clearly wanted nothing to do with her. The ladies of the historical society were "good folk," and all they cared about was their social standing in this little backwater of a town. Charming little St. Ignacio gradually became in Sandra's eyes, the epitome of the kind of hypocrisy Noel Taylor so despised. He had been waging war against a society he wanted no part in, and Sandra was drawn to his beautiful fury.

As she drifted into her fantasy world with Noel Taylor, she made an effort to keep at least a semblance of sanity over the years. She had kept an immaculate house, had attended all functions involving her children, and had a hot meal waiting for her husband and offspring nearly every evening. She became less and less affectionate toward her son and daughter however, and she lost all interest in a physical relationship with Clay. When her husband and children were out of the house and she was sure she was alone, she would pleasure herself while visualizing Noel.

When each of her children had fled the nest to begin their own lives, she had pretended remorse and it was a convincing performance to all, save her son, daughter, and husband. Sandra secretly rejoiced in the empty nest. It took much less energy to maintain her façade with fewer people around. She immersed herself more deeply into the world of her idol.

As deeply as she had become enamored of Noel Taylor, Sandra had developed a cold hatred of the historical figure of Rolly Collingsworth. In her eyes, the one-legged old bastard had snuffed out the life of the only truly honest man that had ever existed. To her, Collingsworth had acted as the violent agent of the mass stupidity that passed for polite society. When Margaret had entered the museum wearing Rolly Collingsworth's face, it took all of Sandra's considerable acting skill to mask her desire to kill the smaller, older woman on the spot.

From her unrelenting research into Noel's life, Sandra had constructed in her mind the portrait of a person who had survived a horrendous childhood. Noel had been orphaned as a little boy and had been used as slave labor on the farms of various relatives. Her imagination was filled with righteous indignation at the images of physical and sexual abuse she was sure the boy must have endured. She ached to hold him, to console him, to heal his wounds. She also wished she could exact revenge on his torturers.

It made sense to her then that as a teenager Noel had run off to join a gang of Confederate raiders. This group had galloped about the South killing and pillaging at the ranches and farms of people reputed to be secret northern sympathizers. The fact that many of their victims were *not* actually "secret Yankees" did not seem to cause any pangs of conscience to the raiders. Sandra understood that, apart from his rebel sympathies, Noel was actually getting revenge on the culture that had abused him.

Noel had apparently honed his craft as a tactician riding with the raiders. Within a few months, his fanatical courage and utter brutality had made him worthy of a leadership position. When the war ended he, like other rebel sympathizers took the defeat bitterly. Noel and a few of the other members of the raiders had moved south into Florida to exact revenge on a region of the country that had proven too weak to win.

The more Sandra had fantasized about Noel, the more she had seen him as a kind of archangel of absolute truth. She could completely understand his contempt and hatred of folk that were labeled "law-abiding citizens." All other emotions seemed to have bled out of Sandra years ago, with the hemorrhage, leaving only rage, and she felt the righteous rage as Noel Taylor had felt it.

But it was cold rage. It was carefully managed rage. It was carefully hidden behind Sandra's expert social graces, as she manipulated her way into the affections of the historical society members. She had the luxury of feeling nothing, so she could easily imitate any emotion. She didn't understand completely what the outcome of this rage would be, but she sensed that it would reach fruition some day. She was convinced that she had become the disguised instrument of the archangel's final triumph over stultifying hypocrisy. She fancied herself a kind of "hidden apocalypse in plain sight." Meanwhile she had bided her time and waited for a sign.

A few days before Margaret had first entered St. Ignacio, Sandra got her first sign. She had brought a trashcan from the museum office to empty into the dumpster behind the building. There, she found a skinny, suntanned person digging through its contents. There was a kind of bestial urgency in his pawing at the detritus in the dumpster. His movements and furtive expressions were so raw and so primitive, they that had thrilled her.

"Are you hungry?" She had asked him. Marvin had looked up startled. Sandra was excited by the feral expression in the man's eyes. Behind those eyes, the god voice in Marvin's mind shouted "HER!" As Sandra waited for his reply, she saw him cock his head to one side for a moment as if listening to something before answering.

"Yes!" He replied. Sandra had led him into the building and into the back office of the museum she had found some cookies and made him a cup of coffee. Marvin had sat silently munching the cookies and drinking the coffee and studying her. Finally he spoke. It was a raspy voice. Sandra got the impression it was a voice that rarely spoke out loud.

"We belong together," He stated matter-of-factly.

"Yes," Sandra had replied, rising to make sure the doors to the museum and the office were locked. It was during that first encounter, over the desk in the back office, that Marvin began referring to Sandra as "the Adored One." Sandra liked it. It suited the person she had become since nearly hemorrhaging to death many years before. As she adjusted her clothing and prepared to open the museum, she looked at Marvin fondly.

"You will be my secret weapon," she crooned. "For now, we must meet in secret." Marvin nodded.

"Anything!" He rasped. She gave him some money and ushered him out the back door. After he had gone, she went into the museum's tiny bathroom and cleaned herself up, humming happily. It seemed to all be coming together in her mind. She sensed something important was coming and she was ready.

The second sign had been the appearance a few weeks after meeting Marvin, of the short, round older woman with Rolly Collingsworth's face. She knew this woman was important in the scenario that seemed to be constructing itself in her mind. But she still wasn't sure just how Margaret would fit into her destiny.

## CHAPTER ELEVEN: THE PEAVEY POLE

In early March Sally began to join Margaret on her early morning walks. Margaret was glad to have the company. Margaret usually exited her RV first and used the side of the vehicle to do her stretches. One morning as she had her hands pressed against the metal side of the motor home, she was extending one leg behind her, gently stretching her Achilles tendon. When she glanced to her right, she saw the third overlay.

The faint outline of a pole was resting against the wall of the motor home. It was about five feet long, with a spike at one end and a hook that arched out away from the pole and turned back inward. Even though she had never seen anything like it, Margaret was aware of feeling an instant familiarity with the tool before it vanished. On their walk, Margaret described what she had seen. Sally seemed to be at a loss to identify the tool Margaret had visualized.

After the walk, Margaret went immediately to her computer. She typed in "pole with hook at one end."
Nothing the search rendered resembled what she had seen. So she took out a sheet of

paper and drew the apparition as best she could.

Later that day, she went to a large home improvement store and wandered about the aisles looking for anything that resembled what she had seen. There was nothing. In desperation she stopped an employee who was putting boxes of nails on a shelf and showed him her drawing. He was an older man and he grinned when he saw it.

"Oh, that's called a peavey," he said. "It was used in the old days to move logs around."

"Do you have them here?" Margaret asked. The man shook his head.

"Naw. You need to go to one of those old fashioned hardware stores—you know the kind that's run by a family."

Margaret drove back to Canuck's Rest and found Sally in the office. She told Sally what she had discovered and asked if she knew of an older hardware store in the area.

"Not in St. Ignacio, but there's a wonderful old store in Oscar."

"Oscar?"

"It's a little farming town about ten miles inland." Sally's eyes lit up with inspiration.

"Look—I get off in a couple of hours. Let me drive you there."

And so it was that the two friends drove west into the countryside to Oscar. The county road passed by several ranches and a couple of churches before entering Oscar. Sally pulled onto the town's main street—a four block long stretch of paved road with a landscaped median ground. It occurred to Margaret that the leaders of the little community had decided to make the most out of its small-town atmosphere.

The old hardware store was as fascinating a place as the antique shop. It also was a "happy jumble" of things spread out on counters made of very old wood. Along with various types of fencing and galvanized tubs of various sizes, there were odd tools like the long-handled pincers used in changing horse shoes, or the triangular metal tool used in stretching barbed wire.

When Margaret asked the old man who greeted them about peavey poles, he looked at the two women quizzically.

"Hardly anybody uses those things any more," he said. "They've got these machines today called skidders that most folks use."

"I'm buying it for a friend," Margaret explained. The man shrugged and led them to the back of the store where an assortment of long-handled tools leaned against the back wall. Two of them were peavey poles like the one she had visualized. She picked up the closest one and discovered it was heavier than she had thought it would be. Two notions occurred to her simultaneously: she felt strangely comforted by the feel of the pole in her hands and she needed to work on her upper body strength.

She paid almost a hundred dollars for the tool, and the man helped her tie it on to the roof rack of Sally's Jeep. As she drove them home toward The Canuck's Rest, Sally grinned at Margaret.

"I've gotta say, girl," she teased. "You are full of surprises! What are you gonna do with that thing?" She nodded at the end of the peavey pole that projected above the windshield.

"I have no idea," Margaret shrugged. "I just know I'm supposed to have it." Sally thought for a moment.

"Did you see one of those poles when you were at the museum?" she asked. Margaret considered this, and shook her head.

"I might have seen it, but I don't remember it."

"Maybe we should go back to the museum tomorrow and look for pictures of that pole." At the mention of the museum, Margaret got a sudden, uneasy feeling she could not identify, but she nodded in agreement.

When they got to Margaret's motor home, they untied the pole and Margaret leaned it against the wall of the vehicle next to the door. That's where she had visualized it and so that's where it stayed.

For the next few weeks, it became part of her morning exercise routine to work out with the pole after her walk. She would repeatedly lift it as if she was doing curls with a weight bar. After every five lifts, she would turn the pole around in her hands so that the spike and hook were on the opposite side. Over the weeks she could feel her arms getting used to hefting the weight. She wondered with a smirk if the spirit of Rolly Collingsworth was acting as her personal trainer.


CHAPTER TWELVE: LINES IN THE SAND.

Sandra's final slide into action was promulgated by Margaret's second visit to the museum. It was a bright day in April when the Collingsworth lookalike returned to Sandra's realm. A tall woman with tattoos accompanied the short, older woman. After the two women had signed in, the taller one spoke to Sandra.

"Do you have any pictures of peavey poles?"

"I don't understand," Sandra replied. Margaret showed her the drawing of the peavey pole. Sandra studied it for a moment and shook her head.

"I don't remember seeing anything like that," she said. "Does it have something to do with the history of St. Ignacio?

"I'm not sure," Margaret replied hesitantly.

"Well, we're gonna look around anyway," Sally said. "I haven't been here since you moved into the school building." Sandra smiled her practiced smile.

"Enjoy!" She said brightly. Even Sally noticed, as Margaret did, how the expression in Sandra's eyes did not match the brightness of her voice.

Once the two of them were safely out of earshot, Sally whispered to Margaret.

"Is it just me, or is that lady a little creepy?" Margaret nodded.

"A lot creepy," she whispered in response. "I can't help thinking there's something going on with her."

As she and Sally went from exhibit to exhibit, Margaret once again got the uneasy feeling she had experienced on her last visit here. At one point, she and Sally were standing in front of a glass display case. In the reflection of the glass, Margaret could see the lady at the desk in the other room, studying them intently. Margaret couldn't stop thinking about the expression in the woman's eyes. It reminded her of someone— then the thought hit her—it reminded her of the photograph of Noel Taylor. The second that thought crossed her mind, he left leg went numb just as it had in the antique store when she first saw Rolly Collingsworth's portrait. She held onto Sally's arm for a moment to steady her self. Her friend looked concerned.

"You okay?" Sally whispered. After few seconds the paralysis went away. Margaret smiled at Sally.

"I'm okay," she smiled. "Just getting old." When they passed back into the main room of the museum, Sandra made another attempt at a bright smile.

"Did you read the book I gave you?" She asked. Margaret nodded.

"Yes." Sensing Margaret was hiding something, Sandra pressed on.

"And did you learn a lot about Rolly Collingsworth?" Sandra asked, repressing the anger that just saying his name out loud caused inside of her. Sandra was disturbed to notice that Margaret was now studying *her* very intently as she responded. The shorter woman looked as if she was realizing something for the first time.

"Yes," Margaret responded carefully and then said the unthinkable.

"I especially enjoyed the account of the battle at the bridge." Margaret was now studying Sandra's face intensely. Sandra felt rage building inside of her.

"You *enjoyed it?*" Sandra asked incredulously. Margaret smiled a cold smile, looking into Sandra's eyes.

"Yes," she answered in a quiet voice. "I think Noel Taylor got exactly what he deserved." The chair Sandra had been sitting in skidded back against the wall as she jumped to her feet.

"GET OUT!" Sandra shouted. Sally stepped in front of Margaret protectively, her fists clinched.

"What the hell is your problem, lady?" Sally asked. Margaret put her hand on Sally's arm.

"It's okay, Sally," Margaret said, still smiling into Sandra's eyes. "I think I just remind her of someone. Let's go." With that, Margaret turned toward the door. Sally leaned across the desk.

"My friend is too much of a lady to knock your goddamned teeth down your throat, but I'm not!" Sally then leaned back, glaring at Sandra and left.

Sandra sat back down in her chair, shaking. She was overwhelmed with mixed feelings of fear and rage. That dumpy little woman with Collingsworth's face *knew*!

Meanwhile, as Margaret and Sally walked toward Margaret's car, Sally shook her head.

I don't believe what I just saw!" she exclaimed. "What the hell is that bitch's problem?" Margaret shrugged.

"You know how I seem to be involved in things that happened a century ago?"

"Yeah, the visions," Sally answered.

"Well I think she is involved with that period too," Margaret explained.

"You mean she is seeing things like you are?"

"I don't know, but she is somehow really in tune with the battle that happened on the bridge." Sally pondered this for a few moments. Just as they reached the car, the taller woman's face lit up.

"So if you're in touch with Rolly Collingsworth..." Sally began.

"...She's in touch with the other side," Margaret interjected.

## CHAPTER THIRTEEN: THE SECRET SOLDIER

A few mornings later, Sandra parked her car in the shopping center parking lot as she had done many times before. She was disguised as a woman out for an early morning jog. She strapped a light runner's pack on her back, and began a slow, shuffling jog up the sidewalk that bordered highway one. When she was certain no cars were able to see her, she darted off to the right into the vacant land where the abandoned condo stood. Within a few seconds, she was out of sight of the highway.

She walked purposefully through the mixture of pines and palms and palmetto shrubs that masked the land from the highway. Within a couple of minutes, she had broken out of the trees into the open area that was intended to be the lush front lawn of the condo building. This vacant land, set aside to absorb tidal surges from hurricanes, had become very familiar to her over the past year. She felt safe and powerful whenever she came here.

When she arrived at the abandoned building, she said, "It's just me!" in a loud voice, and began climbing the bare concrete stairs. She had come to really enjoy having sex with Marvin in the early morning. Embracing his filthiness was so reckless, so divergent from the life she pretended to lead, that it excited her very much. She loved the savagery of fornicating on his bare mattress on the upper floor of the building. She could be as noisy and inventive as she wished, knowing that her acolyte would do anything for her.

On this particular morning, the sex had been unusually violent. When it was over,

Marvin had deep scratch marks on his bare buttocks. They sat naked together on the mattress, sipping the coffee she had brought in a thermos in the runner's pack. Marvin was hungrily eating the donuts she had bought for him.

"It's time for you to be my secret soldier," she told him. His eyes flitted up speculatively. He looked like a wild animal smelling scents on the wind.

"Anything," he rasped. She made her face look like love and tenderly caressed his cheek with her hand.

"You are my knight in shining armor," she crooned. Marvin's face lit up, as she knew it would.

A half hour later, after she had gone, Marvin struggled into his ragged denim shorts and put on his signature filthy tee shirt. He finished the rest of the coffee she had left for him and looked out at the river, deep in thought. She had left the methodology up to him. He unfurled the paper she had left with him. It was an address. He picked up the machete and hefted its comfortable weight. Yes. He could do this. Then the god voice in his mind shouted, "LOOK FIRST!" Marvin nodded, smiling. Of course! Look first! He thanked the god in his mind for this wisdom.

Two hours later, Margaret was planting vegetable sprouts into various plastic containers full of potting soil. She had wanted to start this project for some time, and late April seemed the perfect time of year to begin the container vegetable garden. So engrossed was she in her work that she did not notice the skinny man who pedaled quietly by on the street, studying her. Nor did she notice when he parked his bicycle and its little towed wagon behind some bushes at the end of the street.

Marvin melted into the patch of forest that separated the RV park from the railroad tracks and silently worked his way back toward Margaret's motor home. On his way, he checked Stuffy's grave and found it undisturbed. When he arrived at his destination, he remained hidden in the palmettos. Margaret had apparently gone inside. He barely noticed the long handled tool leaning against the side of the motor home.

With his eyes he measured the distance from his hiding place to her front steps. Yes, this would be easy. He was patient. He would wait here each night until he could get her outside in the dark. A quick dash, a slash with the machete and then he could melt back into the woods and escape. If he moved fast enough, she probably wouldn't even have time to scream.

He quietly made his way back to his bicycle and pedaled out of Canuck's Rest and down the highway to the shopping center. He was hungry and he had money in his pocket from the Adored One. He would have a good meal and then return to his hiding place by the old lady's RV and wait. "TRACKS!" Shouted his personal deity while Marvin ate his hamburger. Marvin nodded, grinning in delight at his God's boundless supply of wisdom. Of course! He would approach the hiding place by walking down the railroad tracks. No one would see him.

Feeling incredibly superior, he finished the hamburger and fries and walked his bike to the railroad tracks behind the shopping center. He rolled the bike on a path next to the tracks until the woods were on his right. He hid the bike behind some palmettos and lifted the machete out of the cardboard box in which he had hidden it.

## CHAPTER FOURTEEN: THE ATTACK

Marvin silently worked his way through the woods toward Canuck's Rest. He found his hiding place near Margaret's motor home, and sat on the pine needles leaning against the trunk of a tree. His belly was full and he had a couple of hours before darkness came. He closed his eyes and relaxed, musing happily on how the Adored One would reward him for this.

He wasn't sure how long he had been asleep, but he awoke to find it was dusk. He parted two palmetto fronds and looked at Margaret's RV. Her car wasn't in its gravel parking space. He hoped she would be coming home soon. He would love to get this done as soon as possible.

The shadows of the trees in which he sat loomed across Margaret's container garden and the steps to her home. Mosquitos began to plague him. They had returned with the increasing warmth of a Florida spring, but he was steadfast in his duty. He was the secret soldier—the knight in shining armor—after all. Nothing would cause him to disobey the Adored One.

When darkness finally settled over Canuck's Rest, Marvin was relieved to see that there were very few streetlights. Margaret's motor home sat in darkness. He was glad it was painted a light color. His target would show up as a silhouette against it. After what seemed to Marvin to be an eternity of waiting, sweating, and swatting mosquitos, the headlights of Margaret's car swung into the little gravel parking area. Marvin grasped the machete and crouched.

As she pulled into her parking spot, Margaret's brain seemed to suddenly be going crazy. A high-pitched whine began in her mind, as if a buzz saw was cutting through a thick log. Before she shut off the headlights, she thought she saw a movement in the palmettos near her home. Then everything seemed to slow down.

Without knowing why, she got out of her car and went immediately to the peavey pole leaning against the motor home. Even before she turned, she could hear the clapping of palmetto fronds as something burst through them. Margaret picked up the pole with a practiced motion and spun around facing the noise. She reflexively thrust the spike end of the pole in front of her, as a barrier to whatever it was. She could see a figure running at her waving something in its hand. It looked like a large spider, running on two legs.

The figure apparently did not see the spike in the darkness and collided with it. Margaret felt something swish by in front of her face. The man's weight forced the butt end of the pole to bang into the side of her motor home. This drove the spike deep into Marvin's upper right chest. The steel point broke through the rib and penetrated his right lung.

The pain was sudden and excruciating. Marvin let out a mixture of a grunt and a scream. Margaret wondered if she had impaled some kind of wild animal. After his initial swing, the machete fell forgotten from Marvin's hand. He was too busy trying not to die. The god with the British voice inside his head was strangely silent.

His pierced lung had collapsed and he was struggling to take in a breath. His panic at possibly suffocating was even greater than the pain he was feeling. He writhed around on the ground as Margaret continued to hold onto the other end of the pole sticking out of his chest. He was like an insect pinned to a board. He swatted feebly at the peavey pole sticking out of his chest.

Margaret held on firmly to the other end of the pole. She felt the sickening vibration of the pole in her hand as the point moved around inside Marvin's flesh. Margaret didn't want to kill the man. She simply wanted to keep him away from her.

Sally came running from her RV at the odd sound Marvin made. She had a flashlight.

"Maggie? Are you okay?" Sally shouted.

"Call the sheriff!" Margaret hollered. Sally ran back to her motor home to retrieve her cell phone. Marvin's breathing began making a strange whistling sound. A couple of minutes later, Sally returned with her flashlight. She pointed it at the man impaled on the ground.

"Why, that's Starvin' Marvin!" She exclaimed.

"Who is he?" Margaret asked. The sound of sirens could be heard in the distance.

"He's a homeless guy who has been around the town for a while now," Sally replied. She then swept the light around the immediate area. "What's this?" She said, stooping over and picking up the machete.

When Margaret saw the blade in the flashlight's beam it suddenly hit her how close she had come to being killed. She shook so suddenly that she almost let go of the pole. By the time the ambulance arrived, Marvin's tanned, dirty skin had a bluish tint to it.

A half hour later, Starvin' Marvin was being loaded into an ambulance. A burly sheriff's deputy got into the vehicle with him. Another deputy was taking statements from Margaret and Sally. Margaret's once quiet, secluded motor home was awash in flashing blue lights.


CHAPTER FIFTEEN: BIG PLANS

When she got news of Marvin's arrest, Sandra started smoking again. She had smoked as a college girl, but had stopped when she was pregnant with Clay Junior. Part of her carefully constructed social identity was to be a non-smoker and only a social drinker. But the Adored One felt that all bets were off now. She fancied herself as being like Noel Taylor crossing the wooden bridge. She understood that she was reaching the end of her life, so why bother with pretense?

Her freedom from restraint began with Clay. He came home from work one day to find a drunken Sandra sitting at the dining room table. As soon as she saw him she launched into a screaming tirade, listing all of his faults that she had been forced to live with for so long. The more she shouted, the angrier she seemed to become. Finally, she threw and empty bottle of bourbon at him, which bounced off the wall next to the kitchen door. Then she suddenly got quiet. She sat back down at the table, took a drag from her cigarette and smiled at her husband with dead eyes.

"If you don't get out of this house, Clay darling, I will kill you in your sleep."

Tired, confused, all Clay could do was ask her to let him pack a suitcase. Another drag, another empty smile, and Sandra purred: "Of course my husband." A half hour later, Clay had made a hasty exit and Sandra assumed he would run to one of the motels out on I-95. She laughed aloud at how easy it had been to claim this house as her own. All it took was a little cruelty. Noel Taylor would be proud of her.

For about a week after Marvin's arrest, Sandra remained housebound by choice. During this interval she only left her home to go to the store for more bourbon and cigarettes. Occasionally she would get something to eat. She needed time and space to think.

Her biggest upset over Marvin's capture was that he was still alive and under police guard at the hospital. She knew that in his addled state, he would eventually mention her. It was only a matter of time before they came to question her. If she was lucky, she might have a few days of freedom left before they pieced it all together.

The thought occurred to her to flee, but the idea seemed repugnant. She was sure that in this situation, Noel Taylor would simply embrace his fate and go out in a blaze of glory. She would do the same, she decided. It would be a testament of her undying love for him and all he stood for. But what form should it take? What one last act would punish the stodgy inhabitants of St. Ignacio for their weakness and small mindedness?

During the second week after Marvin's arrest, the idea came to her. She was driving home from a liquor store when she passed St. Ignacio Haven. Following an inspiration, she pulled into the parking area behind the building. She eased into a space, turned off the car and lit up a cigarette. She studied the layout of the building.

The structure was shaped like a capital H. It consisted of two parallel wings containing residents' rooms. The two wings were connected in the middle by a wider section. From her visits to Doris Hampton, Sandra knew that this middle part of the structure contained the dining area. She looked at the curb in front of her car and realized that a vehicle would have no trouble climbing it. She was almost gleeful as she started the engine and drove toward home.

Sandra found herself delighting in Clay's absence. It gave her free run of the place. She felt suddenly ebullient as she poured herself a drink in her kitchen and wandered out to the garage. Now that she had a plan, and she knew she would no longer exist soon, it felt as if a great weight had been lifted from her shoulders.

In the garage, she laughed aloud when she saw Clay's beloved ancient pickup truck. The man had loved this old monstrosity passionately and had steadfastly kept it running over the years. It seemed like the ultimate irony that she would use her husband's prized vehicle to bring ultimate sadness to the town she had grown to hate so virulently.

She wandered over and looked into the bed of the truck. The metal deck of the bed was rusty in several places, but still solid. She laughed aloud again when she saw the keys to the truck still hanging on their prescribed nail in one of the wall studs of the garage. In his haste to escape her, Clay had forgotten to take them. Her idiot husband was making this hilariously easy for her, she thought.

She found a half-filled five-gallon plastic container of gasoline next to his riding lawn mower and put it into the back of the truck. She would need more gasoline, she thought, as she sipped her drink and stared at the truck. She swayed slightly as she pivoted on one foot and went back into the house.

She poured herself another drink and sat at the kitchen table, smoking and thinking. From this point on, she reasoned, everything had to be done just right. It was difficult, keeping a train of thought going through the alcoholic haze in her brain, so she found a note pad and began writing things down:

1. Buy more gas cans.
2. Fill them.
3. Leave a statement.
4. Wait for suppertime at the Haven.

She looked at the list with great pride and satisfaction. Yes. This made sense. She rose unsteadily and went into her bathroom. There, she made a perfunctory attempt to look normal, washing her face and lightly brushing her hair. She grabbed her purse and stopped at the kitchen table to finish her glass of bourbon. She then went out to the garage and started up Clay's truck.

The man at the home improvement store looked puzzled at the five five-gallon plastic gas containers in her basket.

"Big project?" He asked as he rang her up. Sandra shook her head.

"No," She replied. "My husband wanted me to pick these up for his company." This apparently made sense to the cashier, and Sandra congratulated herself on her cleverness. She was surprised and pleased at how much fun this subterfuge was becoming.

It took her nearly an hour to drive up and down highway one, filling each container at a different gas station. She was convinced that doing this would prevent people from becoming suspicious. What *did* attract the attention of some customers, however, was the sloppy job she was doing of filling the jugs sitting in the bed of the pickup. In nearly every case, the pump kept running after the container was full and gas spilled into the truck bed.

She wasn't worried, however. The truck bed was open. There would be plenty of ventilation. There would be no dangerous buildup of fumes. She congratulated herself on her decision not to smoke while she was doing this. Once again she allowed herself to delight in her own slyness. Noel would be proud of her. As she was heading home, a sudden inspiration hit her and she swung off of the highway into the parking lot of St. Ignacio Haven.

## CHAPTER SIXTEEN: A SECOND SHORT VISIT WITH DORIS

Doris Hampton felt fear as she always did when she saw Sandra coming to visit her. Lunch had just ended and she was sitting in the dining hall, waiting for Alicia to wheel her back to her room for a nap. Doris had watched the younger woman unravel over the past few weeks. Today, Sandra looked especially strange. Her hair was a mess, and she had replaced her usually neat outfits with jeans and a tee shirt, both of which were dirty and reeked of gasoline. Sandra plopped down in the chair closest to Doris's wheelchair and smiled her insane, dead-eyed smile.

"I'm going to die today, Doris and so are you," Sandra whispered to the vacant eyes of the old woman. "I'm going to pull Clay's truck, loaded with gasoline right to this wall," she nodded her head at the north-facing wall behind them. "I'm going to do it at dinnertime when all of you are here." Sandra leaned in closer to the old woman, giggling. Her breath smelled of cigarettes and alcohol.

"Then we're all going to glory!" The younger woman exclaimed in an excited whisper.

"See you then!" Sandra said brightly. And with that she was gone, rising suddenly from the chair, swaying a moment and then marching out of the building.

Doris Hampton took out her journal and began writing furiously. It took her nearly ten minutes to get everything written in such a way that it made sense. She was suddenly exhausted. It was all she could do to beckon to Alicia to come to her.

## CHAPTER SEVENTEEN: CONFEDERATE MEMORIAL DAY

Sandra had not realized it was April 26th until she got back home and looked at the calendar. When she was a little girl living in Georgia, April 26th was celebrated in her small town as Confederate Memorial Day. If it fell on a weekday, children would be escorted from the school to a nearby cemetery where they would place plastic flowers on the graves of Confederate soldiers killed in the Civil War. When she realized that her coming sacrifice would occur on this propitious day, a satisfying sense of destiny flooded her. It was clear to her that divine providence was behind this beautiful synchronicity. She had a couple of hours to kill before the five o'clock dinnertime at the St. Ignacio Haven, so she sat at the kitchen table, smoking, drinking, and planning.

As she sat there, she realized that to truly honor Noel, she needed to leave a message behind. She found a piece of notepaper and a pen and printed in all capital letters: I LOVE NOEL TAYLOR! IN HIS HONOR I AM TAKING YOUR LOVED ONES FROM YOU, BECAUSE I CAN!

Sandra smiled grimly. "That will shock the bastards!" She muttered. "No apology here," she mused. "Noel will appreciate that."

She went into the bedroom and found her dog-eared copy of Doris Hampton's book. When she set it on the kitchen table it automatically opened to the picture of Noel Taylor.

"We'll be together soon now, baby," She purred and kissed the photograph. She dug in the junk drawer in the kitchen and found a roll of tape. Tearing off a piece, she taped her note to the page containing Noel's picture.

On the same page were the two pictures of Rolly Collingsworth. Her lip curled in a snarl when she thought of the dumpy little woman who now wore that hated visage.

"All my troubles started with that little bitch!" she hissed aloud to the empty kitchen, and finished off the bourbon left in her glass. The lady with Rolly's face would have to die—that's all there was to it. She glanced at her watch. It was a few minutes past three. She would have to find a way to kill Margaret quickly and then drive over to St. Ignacio Haven. Inspiration struck her.

Rising suddenly from the table, she experienced a brief head rush and steadied herself. Then she lurched into Clay's bedroom. She knew he kept a pistol in his nightstand and he would be just idiotic not to take it with him. To her dismay, however, she discovered that Clay had been more thorough than she had hoped. The gun was gone. She wandered dejectedly back into the kitchen and emptied the bottle of bourbon into the glass.

As she stared at the empty bottle, another inspiration struck her. Weren't there these bombs that you make from empty bottles? Her mind fought through the alcoholic fog to remember. Yes. You put gasoline in a bottle, and use a gas-soaked rag as the stopper. You light the rag and throw the bottle. The bottle shatters and the rag ignites the gas. There was a clever name for these bombs but she couldn't remember what it was. Sandra laughed aloud in the empty kitchen and kissed the empty bottle.

As she finished off the last glass of bourbon, Sandra also finished her last cigarette.

"No sense blowing myself up too early!" She giggled aloud. She then went into the bathroom and made a stab at putting on makeup. It crossed her mind that she wanted to look good for Noel. By the time she headed out to the garage, it was a few minutes before four o'clock.

As she walked through the garage to the pickup truck, she noticed Clay's large charcoal grill in one corner. She snorted when she though of how much he loved to cook steaks on that grill. He used to rave about how the charcoal flavor made the steaks wonderful. All she seemed to be able to taste was the charcoal lighter fluid he used to start the coals. That's when her eyes fell on the white plastic container of charcoal lighter fluid. She walked over and picked it up. It was nearly full.

"Hell, yeah," she slurred. "Join the party!" She tossed the white plastic bottle into the truck bed with the containers of gasoline. She did not notice that the flimsy red cap on the bottle come loose when it hit the truck bed.

The late afternoon sun was causing the shadows of the pine trees to fall across the road as she drove toward highway one. She found the strobe effect of the alternating bars of shadow and sunlight irritating. She was relieved when at about four thirty she pulled into Canuck's Rest RV Park. She took out the crumpled paper with Margaret's space number on it and began driving up and down the streets, reading lot numbers. After about ten minutes, she located Margaret's RV sitting on the last row. She was delighted to see Margaret's car parked next to it. The bitch was home. This would be fun.

She pulled the truck into an empty RV space located next to Margaret's vehicle. Margaret's door faced her. Sandra smiled in anticipation. After the bomb was thrown the bitch would have no escape. She picked up the empty bourbon bottle and the dry dishrag she had brought with her. She swayed against the hood of the truck as she walked around it.

Once on the other side, she picked up the half-filled gas container she had fished from her garage. She filled the bottle sloppily, gas pouring over her hand. She then poured gasoline onto the rag, soaking it thoroughly. She set the plastic gas can back into the truck, not noticing the slight splashing sound. She stuffed the rag into the neck of the bottle hastily. She remembered she had to be at the rest home by five o'clock. She fumbled with the lighter in the pocket of her jeans.

She lit the rag. Unfortunately, the spilled gasoline on her hand caught too. The sudden flash of light and pain caused her to reflexively pull her hand back, sending the Molotov cocktail into the truck bed.

Witnesses were to later describe it as a massive explosion. But there were actually three explosions within milliseconds of each other. The first was a kind of "WHUMP!' as the lit rag ignited the mixture of spilled charcoal lighter fluid and gasoline that had puddled in the truck bed. A second, louder explosion followed, as the open gas container from her garage sucked in the flames from the truck bed in a backdraft and blew up. This ignited the remaining gas containers.

Sandra's body was propelled through the air and smashed head first into the wall of Margaret's motor home. Her neck snapped on impact and she was dead. Margaret's car caught fire from the explosion and this in turn badly damaged her RV.

Margaret her self was not hurt. Since Marvin's attack, she had been staying next door at Sally's place. The attack had unnerved her badly and she had asked Sally if she could take refuge with her. Sally was more than happy to have the company.

The St. Ingnacio Fire Department did a good job of controlling the blaze and within an hour of answering the call, the fire was out. In the wreckage of the pickup truck, sheriff's deputies found the license plate of Clay's pickup.

Meanwhile, three miles up highway one, other deputies were puzzling over a note written by Doris Hampton that warned of an attack against St. Ignacio Haven. They weren't sure if the note should be taken seriously, but the teenaged girl who had called them assured them that Mrs. Hampton's mind was still sound even though her body was not. Just to be certain the officers had parked patrol cars blocking the open ends of the H-shaped building. When they received word of the exploding pickup truck at Canuck's Rest, they began to realize that the two incidents might be related.

It took a couple of weeks before the sheriff's department could tie everything together and figure out just what had happened. Sandra's husband Clay was not much help. He seemed to be permanently in a state of shock where his late wife was concerned. When Clay let officers into his home, he was as stunned as they were by the note Sandra had left taped to the book. Most of the people living in St. Ingnacio had no idea who Noel Taylor was.

## CHAPTER EIGHTEEN: AFTERMATH

Over a year and a half later, Margaret and Sally were sipping wine on the porch of the manufactured home they shared. It was at the far southern end of Canuck's Rest. They had lived together in Sally's RV for several months after the explosion, and although they got along well, they realized that if they were to continue sharing a home, they needed more space. Not willing to let go of their companionship, they decided to buy the more permanent structure together. The arrangement was working out well.

"We're mates," Margaret said simply. Sally gave her mischievous smile.

"I don't swing that way, lady," She grinned. Margaret chuckled.

"No, you idiot," she teased. "We're mates like the Australians."

"The Australians?" Sally asked.

"Yes," Margaret answered. "I get the impression that their concept of friendship means something stronger than ours." She took a sip of wine and continued. "In Australia, if someone is your mate, you are willing to do just about anything for them." Sally nodded with a smile.

"Yep. That sounds like us."

**THE END**

## CONDUIT

Quentin Cliburn had been addicted to coloring the designs long before the wreck that put his wife into a persistent vegetative state. He had developed the habit years earlier during the seemingly never-ending financial struggles involved in raising a family on the meager salaries of two public school teachers.  One day, while passing through a restaurant's gift shop, he had spied an adult coloring book. A memory had flashed into his mind from his childhood of spending hours in pleasant solitude, meticulously filling in designs with crayons. He recalled being totally absorbed in color and line and forgetting all else. Forgetting all else seemed very desirable to Quentin at the time, so he purchased the book and a set of fine-pointed markers.

He very quickly learned that staying inside the design felt like hiding out, protected from the rest of the world. Soon, he was buying adult coloring books with a wide variety of themes: mandalas, animals, plants, abstract designs, etc. Quentin was a worrier and a planner by nature, but in dealing with the designs and the colors with which to fill them, he relied more on instinct. He would simply look at a portion of a design and the first color that leapt into his mind was what he chose. When he finished completely coloring in a design, it was as if he was looking at the work of someone else. His concentration on each portion of the figure was so intense that he never really grasped the beauty of its entirety until it was done. This reliance on intuition is what led him to discovering the conduit.

Six months earlier, a drunk young man in a sports car had come roaring through a stop sign and T-boned their compact car on the passenger side. Janey's head had been slammed against the window and the impact had broken her right hip. Quentin's injuries were less serious. The airbag had cracked his sternum and his right ankle had become dislocated from being wedged under the brake pedal. When he became conscious enough to realize what had happened, he felt guilty for being pleased at the news that the idiot who caused this had been killed—his body mangled in the wreckage of his expensive little showpiece.

At the hospital, doctors performed surgery to relieve the swelling of Janey's brain and to repair the hip. Afterwards, as she lay in ICU, he sat next to her, staring at the slumbering face he had come to love after 38 years of marriage. On the other side of the bed, the heart monitor beeped a steady rhythm.

He felt as if nothing was quite real. It wasn't just the painkillers they had given him for the chest and the ankle. It was the total contrast in Janey before the accident with the person he was looking at now. Janey hiked and danced and bicycled and laughed...a lot. Quentin had always referred to her affectionately as "the light bringer." The pale figure sunken into the hospital bed in front of him seemed like someone else.

"I love you so much!" Quentin thought to himself. The heartbeat on the monitor sped up for a few seconds. Quentin had looked around the room carefully to see if she could be reacting to something else nearby. There was nothing.

"Can you hear me?" He wondered. Again the heartbeat sped up for a few seconds. He had laughed and cried at the same time. His best friend, the love of his life, was still in there! The other aspect of the conduit—*receiving* messages from Janey—came later.

Even after the swelling of the brain had subsided and her condition was stabilized, Janey had not regained full consciousness. She usually opened her eyes in response to being fed, and she could swallow, but the gaze was unfocused and glassy. After a week, it became clear to the doctors and Quentin that her condition was not going to change any time soon. Thus began the rapid alteration of their lives.

Their son—who was now a highly placed executive in a New York publishing house--had left his wife and kids at his home in Connecticut and had flown down to do what he could for his parents. It was not a comfortable visit. Robert was the product of Janey's first marriage and he and Quentin had never gotten past the awkwardness inherent in the stepfather-stepson relationship. The one thing the two men had in common was their love for the lady lying in the hospital bed.

As Robert and Quentin stood in silence, staring down at her, it was Robert who spoke first.

"When's the last time you were home, Quent?" he asked. Quentin honestly couldn't remember. Finally he answered.

"Two days ago, I think," he said. "The staff here lets me sleep in one of the armchairs in the waiting room."

"What are you going to do about the house?" Robert asked, his voice sounding like a teacher helping a befuddled student figure out the answer to a math problem. The house. Quentin had given no thought to anything. He shook his head slowly.

"I'm sorry, Rob," The old man said finally. "I'm like a ship that's dead in the water. I just can't think straight. I don't want to do anything but stay here with her."

So Robert took charge. He got a leave of absence from his job and undertook to re-arrange his parents' lives. First, he rented a motel room a block from the hospital where Quentin could stay when he wasn't with his wife. He had driven Quentin back to the house to pick up some clothes and personal belongings. It was a horrific visit. Without Janey there, the house was grim and empty.

After loading his clothes into the car, Quentin turned to his son with tears in his eyes.

"If she doesn't recover, I don't want to ever come back here," he managed. Robert nodded. The son then hired a moving company to pack up the rest of his parents' personal belongings and put them in storage. After that, he put their little cottage on the outskirts of Sydney, Florida, up for sale, furnished.

It was Robert who made the difficult decision to move his mother and her husband into assisted living in downtown Sydney. The little house had sold quickly as another elderly couple sought to grab a piece of the Florida retirement dream while they were still able. Robert used the profit to secure a place for his parents in the modern, high-rise facility whimsically named The Windward Towers. From their eighth floor rooms, Quentin had a wonderful view of the Indian River Lagoon, the barrier island and beyond it, the Atlantic Ocean.

Life at the Windward Towers quickly settled into a routine. Except for weekly trips aboard the facility's shuttle bus to the supermarket to buy food, Quentin stayed with his wife. He passed the time by cooking, watching television, and of course coloring the designs. He also read aloud to her, and would talk to her about what he had just read. Janey was no longer hooked up to a heart monitor and so the first two weeks at the facility were frustrating for Quentin because without the beeping of the machine, he could no longer be sure she was listening to him.

Then one evening, he was coloring a particularly complicated design. For what seemed like the millionth time, he was lamenting being so cut off from her. He was working on a portion of the design shaped like a flower. He reached for the blue marker, when the word "RED" popped into his mind. When he had looked at the flower, his intuition had told him to color it pale blue. But this change to red seemed to come from somewhere else.

"Is that you?" He wondered silently.

"RED," The word popped into his mind again. He picked up the red pen, but his hand was shaking so badly he didn't try to color.

"Are you in pain?" he thought to himself.

"BLACK," The word suddenly appearing in his thoughts.

"Black is no?" He wondered.

"RED."

His intuition told him that "red" meant yes and "black" meant no. He rose from his bedside perch and kissed his wife on her forehead and cheek, his tears falling onto her face.

"RED! RED! RED!" Came the response.

The doctor who attended Janey was a handsome Hispanic man in his forties. He was small but powerfully built, with graying temples. He was soft-spoken and shy, but he exuded warmth and caring with his patients. Quentin had seen some young female staff members looking at the man longingly, but he seemed oblivious to these attentions.

The person who had the most consistent contact with the old couple, however, was a young nursing assistant named Jennifer. She was a beautiful young black girl who was working her way through night classes at Sydney University. Like the doctor, she was quiet and shy, but she honestly cared about Janey and Quentin. Jennifer was one of those people who made Quentin feel better just by seeing her each day.

One morning, during Janey's fifth month at the facility, the doctor and Jennifer were at her bedside together. The doctor looked across the bed at the old man, his face a mask of concern.

"We've had some complaints about the night nursing staff not doing a good job of cleaning patients," he explained. "We want to check your wife for pressure ulcers."

"Pressure ulcers?" Quentin asked.

"Bedsores," Jennifer explained. Then she and the doctor proceeded to gently roll Janey's body to one side. In doing this, their bare arms touched and each of them drew back as if they had experienced electrical shock.

"RED!" Flashed into Quentin's brain. This puzzled him. He looked at the doctor and the nurse's aide who now seemed very disconcerted.

"Is it about them?" Quenting wondered.

"RED!" The old man looked at the two younger people who moved to the other side of the bed to roll Janey the other way. This time they were obviously taking great pains to not touch each other.

"Are they in love?" Quentin mused.

"RED!" He thought for a moment about the discomfort the two young people seemed to be experiencing.

"Have they told each other?" he wondered.

"BLACK!"

The doctor and Jennifer found no evidence of bedsores on Janey, but Quentin noticed that they lingered at her bedside longer than was needed. Both of them looked at his wife fondly before leaving. Quentin was not surprised by this affection. Janey had always drawn people to her—even strangers. All her life, she had been a bringer of energy into the lives of those around her. That energy never stopped radiating from her, even in her present state.

A few days later, Quentin awoke to the realization that it was Valentine's Day. He had slept late and so did not bother with breakfast. He barely made it downstairs in time to catch the shuttle to the supermarket. It was one of those unseasonably hot days that sometimes occur in the middle of a Florida winter. The air was heavy with humidity and it did not take much movement to work up a sweat.

Quentin fretted as he bought a week's supply of groceries because he wanted to make sure that he got something especially nice for Janey's Valentine's Day gift. Janey was an outdoor person. She had never cared for the usual "girly-girl gifts," such as chocolates or jewelry, or a night out on the town. They loved hiking through the Florida woods and Janey thrived on photographing wildlife. She had a superb eye for color, setting and framing a shot. She gloried in nature. The only gift Quentin could think of was a dozen red roses from the floral section of the market.

The place was crowded and the lines at the checkout stands were very long. By the time Quentin made it to the register, he was feeling very tired. When they had moved into the nursing home, he had purchased a collapsible cart to put bags of groceries in. At the checkout stand, he put the bagged groceries in it, but held the rose bouquet in his hand.

The shuttle bus was late picking them up and the crowd from the nursing home was forced to stand in the unrelenting sun for over a half hour. Quentin and the more ambulatory residents stood, while frailer people sat on the one bench that was available. Quentin was sweating profusely and he leaned on the upright handcart for support.

The shuttle finally came, and Arthur, the driver apologized and explained something about a wreck tying up traffic. Quentin struggled to get his handcart up the steps of the bus, and by the time he settled into his seat, he was feeling dizzy.

The next thing he knew, he was staring up at the face of the doctor and Jennifer, who were standing over him, concern wreathing their faces.

"You okay?" Jennifer was asking.

"Yeah," Quentin answered, shaking his head to clear it. "What happened?"

"You passed out on the bus ride home," the doctor replied.

"I did?" The old man asked. He sat up straighter and looked around. The bus was empty except for the three of them and it was parked by the front door of the facility.

"Yes you did," Jennifer replied. "Did you have any breakfast this morning?" She asked.

"No," Quentin answered. "I had to rush downstairs to get the shuttle. It's Valentine's Day and I wanted to get something for Janey." He looked around for the roses and saw that they had fallen into the aisle of the bus and had been trampled. "Oh, Janey!" He moaned with disappointment.

The doctor and Jennifer helped the old man off the bus and into a waiting wheelchair.

Jennifer took charge of the chair and the doctor followed with the handcart full of groceries. A couple of minutes later, the three of them were alone in the elevator when it dawned on Quentin what he should give to Janey in place of the roses.

"Talk to each other," He flung over his shoulder to the two people standing behind him.

"What do you mean?" The doctor asked.

"You know what I mean," Quentin answered. He heard a sudden intake of breath from Jennifer.

In Quentin's apartment, the doctor had Quentin drink glasses of water while Jennifer cooked some instant oatmeal in the microwave. They asked questions about how he and Janey had met, and what had kept them together for so long. Quentin could feel his energy gradually returning and he enjoyed telling them about he and his love. At one point, the doctor went over to Janey and used his stethoscope to listen to her heart. Quentin was busy eating his oatmeal and didn't see the doctor's face, but he saw Jennifer's worried glance at the doctor.

"What?" Quentin asked, the spoon halfway to his mouth. The doctor came around Janey's bed to face Quentin.

"Her body seems to be shutting itself down." the doctor said. He looked down at a clipboard. "I see she has a DNR form here?" Jennifer nodded sadly. The doctor then put his hand on Quentin's shoulder. "I think her time is coming." Jennifer was at Quentin's side immediately. She bent down and hugged him, her eyes tearing.

"I'm so sorry," she whispered brokenly. When she straightened, the doctor put his hand on her shoulder and his eyes were full of sad fondness. "I have some other patients to check on, but I'll be back in a few minutes. You stay with them, okay Jennifer?" Jennifer smiled in spite of herself when he mentioned her name.

"Of course," she said, patting his hand on her shoulder. The doctor left and Jennifer went to the other side of Janey's bed and sat looking sadly at her patient. Occasionally she would stand and listen with her stethoscope.

Quentin left the blank design he had just pulled out to color on the table and moved his chair next to the bed. He held his wife's hand and stroked her forehead.

The heartache he was feeling was unimaginable. It was as if something deep within him was tearing loose. Janey's breathing was shallow and her skin was cool to the touch. In an effort to distract him self from the pain he was feeling, Quentin looked back at the blank design on the table. It was an abstract piece that resembled a path winding through some hills. As he looked at it, no colors came to mind. It was as if his intuitive selection of colors was blocked. This puzzled him. The color selection reflex had been his companion for years. An idea occurred to him.

"Are you doing this?" he wondered to himself.

"RED!"

Quentin looked at the love of his life. He knew he couldn't ask her why. The answer must be in the diagram. He looked back at it. It was simply an empty figure, devoid of color. Empty. Janey's life had been all about color, light, laughter and movement.

"Is where you are now empty?" He thought to himself.

"RED!"

And suddenly he understood. More than the roses, more than seeing young love blossom, there was a much greater gift his wife wanted for Valentine's Day. He looked at the colorless design again and then looked into the face of the woman he loved beyond all measure.

"Is it dark where you are right now?"

"RED!" It tore him apart inside to ask the next question, but he knew he had to.

"And so you want to be free?" He wondered.

"RED!"

"You know I will always love you, don't you?" He asked silently.

"RED!" He felt the conduit close. Jennifer stood and listened intently through the stethoscope, but Quentin knew Janey was gone before Jennifer nodded at him sadly. His stomach muscles clinched and the sobs came pouring out.

It was three months after Janey's death before Quentin could bring himself to return to his addiction of coloring the designs. He had stayed on at the assisted living facility, but transferred to a smaller apartment. This one lacked the beautiful view of the lagoon and the ocean, but that did not matter to him. Those three months following the funeral passed in a daze. It was as if Quentin was standing outside of his body, watching himself go through the motions of daily life.

Then one morning, just before being fully awake, the word "BLACK!" flashed into his mind. He understood immediately what it meant: it was time to begin the laborious process of climbing up out of his grief. That's when he picked up the design he had opened the day Janey died. This time, colors flooded into his mind like they never had before, and he began working on the design rapidly. He could feel the knots inside of him gradually untying. When he was finished, he was astounded by what he had done. He had never seen such vivid hues that fit together so startlingly well. A few minutes after he had finished, Jennifer stopped by to check on him and saw the piece.

"Wow, Quentin!" She exclaimed, picking up the paper. "This is *really* good! Can I post this on the bulletin board?" Quentin shrugged.

"Okay."

Jennifer hung the drawing on the board with an explanatory sign, giving Quentin credit for the coloring. By the end of the day, two people had stopped by his apartment offering to pay him if he would color one for them. The more drawings he colored, the more the demand seemed to grow among the residents. He didn't charge them anything for the pieces because the designs came from a book. All he did was color them. To sell them would violate copyright law.

One evening, just before turning in, Quentin was looking at his most recent coloring job. The design was of a kind of wreath composed of birds and leafy branches. The birds were so lifelike they looked as if they would launch into flight at any second. He sighed contentedly.

"You and I make a good team," He thought to himself.

"RED!"

THE END




## HAPPY BIRTHDAY, MARY ANNE


Drake Blodgett hated being in Florida as much as his wife loved it.  She loved the fact that it was cool and sunny in January, but not cold. He preferred the cold and snow of Michigan. He liked wrapping up in heavy winter clothing. He believed that it successfully hid his ponderous gut. Every January, however, he accompanied her to the little bungalow they had purchased in Sydney Beach, Florida.

They had bought the place several years ago at her insistence. They had visited friends living in a gated senior development. The development sat on a barrier Island with the Indian River lagoon to the west and the Atlantic Ocean to the east. Mary Anne seemed to become instantly intoxicated with the balmy weather and the easy pace of life in the senior complex. To Drake the whole setup looked crushingly boring, but he went along with buying it. Back then, he wasn't as morbidly obese as he was now, and was still physically capable of having a mistress. So he saw buying the Florida winter home as a clever way to keep Mary Anne happy and away from him for a while.

They had therefore fallen into a predictable routine over the years. She spent the Months from January to May there, playing pickle ball and doing water aerobics. She delighted in draping their Florida home with what seemed to Drake, ridiculously tacky beach-themed artifacts. He would come down with her each year during the first week of January, but could only stand the boredom for about a week or two. He would then fly back to Ypsilanti. Although his last mistress had drifted away a few years earlier to a younger more attractive wealthy man, he still preferred life in Michigan to life in Florida.

He relished the power he exercised as president of the Ford Lake Bank and Trust Company. Besides, he was more comfortable in the large house just off Huron River Drive. That house, the bank and Ypsilanti itself were, to Drake, his personal fiefdom. He was respected there and sometimes feared. It excited him to know that he held in his hands, the financial destinies of some of the town's most prominent citizens—and many of its poorer ones.

As a result, these yearly sojourns to Florida with his wife were occasions of great frustration and irritability for Drake. People here did not appreciate his lofty status back home. In Florida, he was forced to mix with people he wouldn't give the time of day to in

Ypsilanti. He was always relieved when his obligation ended and he could return to the familiar chill of the north.

Then, he and Mary Anne would resume what seemed to Drake, comfortably separate lives until the spring. This year, he had agreed to stay on a couple of weeks longer, because she had pleaded with him to be with her on her birthday in late January. He had reluctantly agreed, but was secretly (he thought) chomping at the bit to return to Michigan. His behavior during these self-imposed "duty visits" would become increasingly irritable and abrupt as the days wore on. Mary Anne was usually as relieved to see him return to Ypsilanti as he was to leave.

This year, Mary Anne's birthday wish was for him to accompany her on a weekend trip to St. Augustine. As it happened the city's annual pirate festival fell on the weekend that included her birthday. She thought it would be fun to see the festivities. Drake secretly grumped to himself about having to see tourists dressed in stupid pirate outfits. But he agreed to the trip with as much equanimity as he could muster. Thus it was that they left the bungalow in the early morning and drove three hours up I-95 to the "oldest continuously inhabited European settlement in the United States."

They checked into the most expensive hotel on the Avenida Menendez, facing the bay. It was a modern affair, and their room had a great view of yachts bobbing at anchor in the harbor and the Bridge of Lions. He was disturbed somewhat by the décor of the bathroom. The walls were mirrored, so that one could not escape one's own reflection. He had read somewhere that this was a popular decorating idea—that people liked nothing better than looking at themselves. Given his huge girth, Drake did not share in this view.

Once they were unpacked and settled into the room, Mary Anne said she did not want to waste any time and wanted to begin sightseeing immediately. Drake thought he did a masterful job of pretending to share her enthusiasm. Mary Anne suggested that their first stop should be the fort that dominated the old section of the city—the Castillo de San Marcos.

Drake had figured there would be a lot of walking on this trip, so the day before he had purchased some very expensive and very thick-soled athletic shoes. For the walk to the fort, they were proving a wise purchase. Walking didn't come easily to Drake. He was so obese that he could not put his feet in front of his torso, but had to rock side-to-side as he walked. Mary Anne and several of his friends had suggested he use a cane, but he was too proud. So he waddled behind his much thinner and trimmer wife.

As they proceeded down the avenue toward the fort, a trolley came by, loaded with tourists. The young man driving was also narrating over a loudspeaker. He was telling his passengers about how the Avenida Menendez was named for a Spanish military leader who oversaw the massacre of French Protestants a few miles south of St. Augustine.

Rather than be horrified by the story, Drake admired the Spanish commander's direct approach: Have some people nearby you don't like? Get rid of them! Bam! Problem solved! It appealed to Drake's love of simple solutions to complex problems. He could visualize the effectiveness of such a policy in dealing with today's minorities that he viewed as dangerous.

He and Mary Anne crossed Avenida Menendez and entered the National

Monument.  Drake was panting by the time they mounted the low hill to the Ranger's office. He paid the admission fee and followed Mary Anne across the drawbridge. She insisted on stopping on the bridge and having Drake take her picture with the empty grass-covered moat in the background. He waited until his breathing returned to normal and took the picture.

Mary Anne's first stop of course was the gift shop. Drake sighed heavily and growled to her he would wait for her outside and found a bench on the edge of the fort's interior parade ground. He sat and pulled a handkerchief out of his XXL sized walking shorts and mopped his florid, sweating brow. His knees seemed especially grateful for the respite.

Drake knew he was a little heavy, but saw nothing wrong with that. After all, he didn't smoke and didn't drink much, so except for the weight, he assumed he was not in bad shape for a man about to turn sixty. Since his interest in sex had dried up over the years, his love of food was his one vice. He kept intending to exercise more, but it simply was too painful. He was convinced that the infernal Florida heat was the culprit behind his current distress (even though the temperature this late January day was in the low sixties). He couldn't wait to be free of the Sunshine State and wondered Irritably why Mary Anne always dawdled so long in museum gift shops.

For her part, Mary Anne could feel Drake's pouting like a familiar black cloud that seemed to follow them everywhere. As she walked about the tiny gift shop, she questioned her own sanity in asking him to share her birthday trip with her. After all, she had known about the mistresses, and how much he loved playing lord of the manor in Ypsilanti. She had resigned herself years ago to living parallel lives with her husband.

So she ruefully wondered what had prompted her to ask him to stay on for her birthday? She should not have been surprised when he treated the trip to St. Augustine as a kind of martyrdom. Had she expected Drake to magically revert to the handsome, attentive young man she had fallen in love with forty years ago? She shook her head at her own foolishness as she pretended to look at some souvenir tee shirts. "Well, we're here now," Mary Anne thought to herself, "and today is my birthday, and I will make the best of it." Years ago, Mary Anne had given up on ever pleasing Drake.

Twenty minutes later she exited the gift shop empty-handed, Drake looked disturbed. "You didn't buy anything?" He asked, pretending concern, but the accusatory undertone wasn't lost on Mary Anne. He clearly could not understand how she could be in the tiny gift shop for so long with nothing to show for it.

"I looked, but nothing jumped out at me," she said dismissively then walked up the stairs to the ramparts. Those stairs nearly did Drake in. It isn't that they were steep. Each step was not very tall, but there were a lot of them. He held onto the handrail and waddled up to the flat area of the rampart.

"Oooh, look at the view of the city!" Mary Anne exclaimed. Drake leaned against the interior wall and stared out at the collection of spires.

"Very...nice..." he managed between gasps. Again the handkerchief came out and was used to mop his brow. He scanned the skyline briefly and then turned his attention to the enclosed parade ground he had just climbed up from.

That's when he saw the girl. He started to dismiss her as just another stupid tourist dressed in a pirate costume, but there was something not quite right about the young woman. For one thing, she was staring directly up at him. She had long dark hair and deep olive skin. She was wearing a simple dress that wasn't white so much as a dingy gray. The top of the dress was gathered under a loosely laced bodice. Her amazing breasts seemed to be free under the thin cloth. There was a tattoo of some kind high up on her left breast. She was smoking a thin cigar and as she looked at him, she smiled and exhaled a plume of smoke. She then stepped out of sight into the archway leading to the drawbridge.

Mary Anne was alarmed to see Drake waddle quickly across the rampart to the part of the wall overlooking the drawbridge. To Drake's profound disappointment, the girl never came out onto the bridge. After a few moments, he decided she must have gone into the gift shop in the archway.

"What is it, Drake?" Mary Anne asked, concerned at this strange behavior.

"Nothing, " He answered absently. "I thought I saw someone I knew...it was nothing."

Mary Anne resumed her tour of the ramparts, taking pictures with her phone of the cannons and the watchtowers. She took a picture of the two small cannons that still worked. A sign said that the cannons would be fired again that day at 3:30PM. Drake followed her about, often glancing down into the parade ground and at the drawbridge arch, but not seeing the girl. It had been years since he had felt any sexual attraction, but something about that strange young woman aroused him. The odd thing is, he did not approve of tattoos or of women smoking, but she seemed to represent the forbidden. As Mary Anne led them back to the stairway, something else occurred to Drake that mystified him: as amazing as the girl's appearance was, no one else seemed to take any notice of her.

After nearly a half hour of touring the ramparts during which time Drake continually checked the archway leading to the drawbridge, Mary Anne decided she had seen enough. Drake was relieved to descend the stairway and as luck would have it, Mary Anne became distracted by a display inside the archway. It was the barrack room of Spanish soldiers whose job was to monitor the drawbridge. She wandered into the room snapping pictures with her phone. This gave Drake the opportunity to waddle back to the door of the gift shop and peek inside. To his great disappointment, the girl was nowhere to be seen.

After leaving the Castillo de San Marcos, they re-crossed Avenida Menendez and began walking down St. George's Street—a pedestrian walkway lined with shops and restaurants that ran the length of the old part of the city. In spite of his discomfort, Drake had to admit that St. Augustine had done a good job of preserving its old buildings and its heritage. There was no graffiti, and no loudmouthed, combative drunks. The streets were clean and delightful smells emanated from the shops.

Drake followed Mary Anne dutifully and grumpily as she made her way slowly past the enticements of each little store. If a particular shop did not involve food, he would find a nearby bench to sit on in righteous indignation. He watched the foolishly dressed masses pass him by, grateful that he was not one of them. When Mary Anne emerged from each store, he would heave a great sigh and stand up to resume the excursion.

If a shop involved food, however, he would follow his wife inside. There was a fancy chocolate shop and a wine shop that specialized in exotic cheeses—two of his favorites. When he emerged from these two stores, he was carrying bags of his own. His mouth watered at the thought of diving into these treasures when they returned to the hotel room. He suddenly realized how very hungry he was.

To his relief, Mary Anne stopped in front of a restaurant inside of a lovely whitewashed, two-story building. There was a tiny courtyard replete with fountain and lush tropical plants. A sign said, "Bayamo Norte Restaurant." Underneath the large letters of the name was the phrase, "Specializing in the tastes of Cuba." Drake immediately felt his usual suspicion and disdain for ethnic food of any kind, but he was hungry, so he accompanied Mary Anne through the heavy wooden door. A young lady greeted them and ushered them to a table in the main dining room.

The area was flooded in natural light that came in via a large skylight overhead. Even

Drake had to admit that the place was tastefully done. A four-foot tall strip of beautifully colored, tile ran from the flagstone floor up each wall. Above that, autographed snapshots of famous visitors were interspersed with expertly done tile mosaics of various tropical images—parrots, palm fronds, etc. Perhaps it was the relaxing effect of the daylight, but Drake's initial concern about eating at a foreign-themed restaurant seemed to ebb away.

The menu, however, was something of a disappointment. It featured a lot of dishes he could not pronounce, and the fact that the food was reasonably priced made him suspicious of its quality. Mary Anne was excited to find chicken and yellow rice and that's what she ordered. Drake settled on a steak of some kind and hoped for the best. Mary Anne excused herself and retreated to the ladies room. Drake was relieved not to have to make conversation and looked around the room. Across the sunlit room, there was a window looking out onto the street. Crowds of tourists shuffled by and he regarded them absently.

He saw the plume of smoke before he saw her. The next thing he saw was sunlight reflecting off of shiny black hair. She was shuffling past the window among the crowd, her head down. Suddenly she paused and turning her head, her gaze pierced the window, shot through the sunlit atrium in which Drake sat, and looked directly into his eyes. Again, the smile. Again, the exhalation of smoke. Again, she moved out of sight.

Mary Anne took an extra long time in the rest room. She postponed returning to the awkward silence of their table as long as possible. When she did return she was relieved to see that the food arrived just as she did. This would keep Drake busy for a while and she could enjoy her meal. The food was delicious and she sipped her wine as she ate. She *loved* this restaurant! The sunlit space seemed to revive her spirits. She felt she could survive anything—even Drake.

For his part, Drake was torn between two strong desires—the steak in front of him and the girl outside. He opted for the steak and found it was good. He had to scrape some kind of ethnic topping off of it first that looked like a mixture of onions and lime. But the meat itself was very tasty. He couldn't gobble it up fast enough. The steak came with a portion of yellow rice, which he regarded suspiciously. He was amazed to find that the rice had a very pleasant nut-like flavor. For desert, Mary Anne had flan and Drake enjoyed a kind of white cake, filled with chocolate and covered with chocolate. When he emerged from the restaurant, he was pleasantly full and was beginning to feel sleepy. In the street, he glanced about hopefully for the girl, but she was nowhere to be seen.  He asked Mary Anne what she wanted to do next, and she said she wanted to continue looking into shops on St. George's Street. Drake frowned.

"Well, I'm really tired," he said. "If it's okay with you, I'm going to go back to the hotel and take a nap. Do you have your room key?" Secretly relieved, Mary Anne nodded and bid her husband goodbye.

As he made his way back toward the bay front, Drake paused at every street corner and looked in all directions for the girl. But his search was in vain. The closer he got to the hotel, the more exhausted he felt. As he entered the lobby, he began to experience double vision. He had trouble punching the right floor button on the elevator and had difficulty seeing clearly enough to get his key card into the door slot.

Once inside the room, he was seized by the sudden desire to defecate. As he waddled into the mirrored bathroom, he wondered angrily if the Cuban food had given him diarrhea. He settled onto the toilet. He suddenly smelled the faint odor of cigar smoke. Glancing up, his double vision had cleared and he saw the girl in the mirror standing behind him, smiling.  That was Drake Blodgett's last conscious image. The aneurysm in his brain stem that had been gradually swelling for several days finally burst. He died instantly sitting on the toilet in mid-shit.

An hour later, Mary Anne returned to the room to find him there, slumped to one side, his massive bulk kept upright, supported by the bathroom sink. She called the front desk. The clerk there dialed 911. While she waited for help to arrive, she covered her husband as best she could with a sheet from the bed. She sat on the edge of the disheveled bed and wept. Mary Anne wept for the young man she had married years ago, who had become buried under layers of fat and arrogance. She wept for the knowledge that any chance that the young man could somehow re-emerge was now lost.  From the fort came the distant sound of the 3:30 cannon. Beneath her pain and grief, Mary Anne sensed that the sharp report also signaled her freedom.

THE END




## FOSTER CELEBRATES THE NEW YEAR

Foster Delac decided to go to the party because his dead brother had visited him in a dream. Brian had died at age fourteen of cystic fibrosis, so whenever he appeared in Foster's dreams he was as he was when he died—thin, with pale skin bordering on a bluish tint. Brian's attitude during these visits was as it had been while he was alive— calm, humorous, and upbeat. Foster had long puzzled over how Brian seemed to know from the outset that his time on earth was limited, and yet seemed to feel no bitterness or depression.

Just before Brian's death, Foster had asked his brother about his unshakeable positivity in the face of what was coming. Brian had shrugged with that secretive smile he had.

"It is what it is, Foss," he had replied using his pet name for his brother. "Getting upset over it won't help anything. I want to enjoy what I can, when I can." Two months later, Foster was attending Brian's funeral.

Brian only visited Foster in dreams, and there had been only two other visits before this one. The first visit occurred a few days after the funeral. In the dream, Foster and Brian were sitting on the edge of Foster's bed, talking casually. Foster's sleeping body lay on the bed behind them. Foster couldn't remember all of the conversation except that he had called it to Brian's attention that he was supposed to be dead. Again the secretive smile.

"Yeah," Brian had said. "It's not like you expect it to be. It's not bad at all, really."

Those were the only words from the encounter Foster could remember. He did remember that somehow he managed to express to Brian how very much he loved him and missed him. Brian seemed to be pleased by this.

The second visit came the night before Foster had submitted his doctoral dissertation for review. He was a nervous wreck and his sleep was fitful. He was having a nightmare about being adrift in the ocean at night. The lights of a city were nearby, but as he swam toward them, they seemed to get farther and farther away. His arms were beginning to feel like lead, when suddenly he and Brian were sitting on the edge of his bed again. "You've got to stop this, Foss," Brian had told him in the dream. "You're going to give yourself a heart attack."

"But my whole future depends on this!" Foster had exclaimed, all the anxiety he was feeling coming out in his voice. Again the secretive smile.

"No it doesn't," came the reply. "If the paper isn't accepted, you'll find some other course of action." At that point in the dream, Brian turned to look at him and the look in his dead brother's eyes was one of absolute love. "Whatever happens, Foss, you're going to be okay."

The most recent visit happened Christmas Eve. Once again, the two brothers sat on the edge of the bed, while the body of the living brother lay behind them. "There's a faculty party coming up on New Year's Eve," Brian had told him. "And I want you to go." Foster shook his head.

"I hate things like that!" The living brother exclaimed. "I never know what to say to people!"

"I know you do, Foss, but I want you to do this for me."

"But why?" Foster asked.

"Something wonderful will happen," Brian said and was gone.

As for the submission of his dissertation three years before, the review was more than okay. The paper described some little-known, isolated communities in the Southern United States, which had actually opposed the Confederacy. It examined their effect on post-Civil war history. The groundbreaking work was applauded widely in academic communities around the country. A publisher, hearing of the grassroots response, tailored the dissertation into a best-selling volume.

Foster's alma mater, Sydney University, quickly hired him as a resident scholar, requiring him to teach only one class—a small circle of the best and brightest graduate students. The university did this in hopes that Foster would produce another best-selling publication that would enhance its reputation. Foster used the money from the book sales to buy a modest cottage in the residential neighborhood surrounding the university.

Before the college was built, it had been a poor neighborhood. The paychecks of professors and administrators had "gentrified" the area and the increasing property taxes drove the less fortunate inhabitants out. Its newest inhabitants viewed their little enclave as an island of enlightenment in the redneck wasteland of Central Florida's Atlantic Coast. Although Foster had bought property in the precious tiny academic compound, he had very little to do with his neighbors.

Foster had a large birthmark that began at his left collarbone and proceeded up the left side of his neck and ended just below his left eye. He had gone through his childhood enduring a series of insults and nicknames, such as "Freaky Foster, Devil Child, Blotchy, Pinto, Pizza Face, etc."

Even as an adult, he never got used to the sight of people's eyes regarding the mark and then looking away in slight distaste. So he was relieved when the University offered him a chance to make a living with minimal human contact. He kept to himself in his little cottage and settled into the quiet life of an academic at a small college. He threw himself into his latest research: the influence of runaway slaves on the Seminole tribes who took them in.

Those runaway slaves and free blacks that sought refuge with the Native Americans went by several names, but a popular one was "Seminole Maroons." According to what he was able to find, the blacks and the Seminoles usually lived in adjacent but cooperative communities. Maroons and Native Americans often intermarried. Some of the Maroons paid for the protection of the tribe by giving a percentage of their crops to the local bands.

During the three Seminole Wars against the United States Army, the Maroons became known for their ferocity and strategy in battle. Foster was fascinated by the rapidity with which these refugees swore allegiance to a people they had only recently come to know. He wondered what had led them to be willing to put their lives on the line for their adopted home.

Foster loved the fact that this research involved a certain amount of fieldwork. He would wait until the cooler days of the Florida winter would come about. Then he could wear collared shirts or hooded sweatshirts, which hid the birthmark. He would drive west, heading inland from Sydney, Florida on the Atlantic coast. The temperatures this time of year were always pleasant, the mosquitoes were practically non-existent, and the snakes were underground.

His research into old public records had shown him the location of various communities in which Seminoles and ex-slaves had coexisted. He would then tramp around in the woods of various state parks and nature preserves with his camera, looking for any traces of these long disappeared settlements. Often, all he found were midden mounds and occasional pottery shards, but these were evidence of habitation that he carefully documented.

One of Foster's favorite days to explore was Christmas Day. His parents were dead and any relatives he had lived far away, so he always spent the day alone. He found it an ideal time to take to the roadways and the woods, looking for Seminole Maroon sites. Traffic on the highways was practically non-existent, and people were inside with their families. Almost no one was tramping around the woods on a Christmas morning. He liked not having to explain to people what he was up to, or have them suddenly notice the scarlet mark on his face. Most of all, he enjoyed the solitude and the silence of the woods.

On the Christmas morning after his dead brother's visit, he was heading to a location in the middle of the state on what was euphemistically referred to as "The Mid-Florida Ridge." This is a strip of high, sandy ground that runs down the spine of the Florida Peninsula. Its highest point is only a little over 300 feet, but in the otherwise flat expanse of the state, it stands out. His research had indicated that there might have been Maroon settlements located just north of what is now the city of Lake Wales.

He had driven about ninety miles west of Sydney when he came to a crossroads where two state highways connected. According to a sign, the crossroads apparently had a name: Cloverfield. It seemed the sole reason for Cloverfield's existence was the intersection that he now drove through.  The settlement consisted of a gas station/minimarket, and an old motel that looked like a holdover from the 1950's.

It was a long, single-story building composed of cinderblock, painted a deep red that was fading in the Florida sun. The neatly crafted, hand-painted sign out front read "Seminole Maroon Motel." Intrigued, Foster pulled into the gravel parking area. He just *had* to know the basis for the motel's unusual name.

There were no other cars in the parking lot, but there was a Jeep parked by the office, which was at the end of the building closest to the intersection. Foster got out of his c ar and entered the office. He found it empty. Stepping back outside, he saw a woman exiting the farthest room pushing a housekeeping cart.  As he looked down the covered walkway that protected the doorways of all four rooms, he could only see a dark silhouette against the sunlit palmetto thicket behind her. A low, smooth voice floated toward him the length of the walkway,

"You want a room, hon?"

The woman began pushing the housekeeping cart up the walkway toward him, and she gradually emerged from silhouette. She was the most remarkable woman Foster had ever seen. She was short and plump, with a riot of salt and pepper hair that seemed to have a mind of its own. It seemed to Foster that her skin was a luminous caramel. He suddenly realized she had asked him a question and he jarred himself to answer.

"Uh, yes," he replied, wondering what prompted him to make such a sudden decision. "If you have one available." He had no idea why he had said that. The woman smiled and gestured at the empty parking lot.

"As you see, no one here but you." She pushed past him with the housekeeping cart and parked it outside the office door.

"C'mon in," she said.

Inside the office, she walked around the little reception counter and put a registration form in front of him. As he filled it out, he was very conscious of her studying him. When she spoke, her voice was soft.

"You keep the hood pulled up to hide the mark?" she asked. Her tone was gentle.

Foster was aware that he was blushing. He glanced up to see warm brown eyes regarding him. He instinctively pushed the hood back, revealing all of his face.

"Yes," he replied, looking at her face for signs of distaste or ridicule. Instead, he was greeted with a sad smile.

"We all have things we don't like about ourselves, hon." She sighed. "You've got your birthmark and I've got my fat and some unfortunate tattoos." She stuck her hand across the counter.

"I'm Serena," She said. Foster shook the hand gently.

"Foster."

"I don't think I've ever met someone whose first name was Foster," Serena said. "So what brings you to the thriving metropolis of Cloverfield?" He was conscious of her studying him again. He was sure she would think him a hopeless nerd when he answered.

"Well, I am researching runaway slaves and free blacks who lived with the Seminoles in the nineteenth century." He said it quickly and waited for a snort of derision or a shrug of boredom.

"You mean Seminole Maroons," Serena suggested.

"Exactly," Foster answered, now excited by the fact that she seemed to know what he was talking about. "It's why I pulled into your motel—because of the name. I was curious."

"Yeah. Most people think it has something to do with Florida State University," Serena replied. "I'm descended from one of the maroons," She added. Foster was instantly intrigued.

"Really? If you have the time I would love to talk to you about that." Serena filed his registration paper and returned his credit card to him. Then she studied him carefully again. She seemed to reach some sort of decision.

"Okay, professor," she smiled. I will be your historical source, but you have to have a cup of coffee with me."

"Sure," Foster agreed. "But I don't want to intrude on your work." At this, Serena laughed. "Well you do see how very busy this place is!" she said incredulously. Foster really liked the sound of her laughter.

"C'mon around here," Serena invited, gesturing around the counter. "Step into my little hovel," she said, leading him through a doorway into a tiny apartment. As he followed her, Foster was very conscious of the fact that he had never felt this at ease around an adult female in his entire life. Serena motioned to a chair at a Formica-topped table in what was the kitchen area. Foster sat down and watched Serena putter with a coffee maker.

" So how long are you staying?" She asked over her shoulder.

"I'm not sure," Foster answered. "I wasn't intending to stop for the night," he shrugged with a wry smile. "I'm kind of following an impulse here." Serena nodded.

"Me too," she replied, turning to the table holding two cups of coffee. "I don't usually invite guests to have coffee in my apartment." Foster flushed with pleasure and had no idea how to respond to that.

"I have milk, sugar, and sweetener," Serena said, covering the silence of Foster's confusion. She set the cups on the table.

"Just milk for me," Foster said.

"Ah…" Serena said, retrieving a gallon of milk from the refrigerator and pouring some carefully into both cups. "A man who watches his health." She put the milk back and sat down across from Foster. Grinning mischievously, she spooned sugar from a ceramic bowl into her cup. "I however, lack your dedication." Foster had never seen anything as delightful as her naughty grin. Serena took a sip, leaned back in her chair and regarded Foster with a smile.

"So what do you want to know, Foss—can I call you that?" she asked. Foster felt his heart leap at the sound of the nickname only his brother had used—until now.

"Sure," he replied. "Why don't we start by you telling me who your ancestor was?"

"Billy Two Hats," Serena replied. "That's him over there." She said gesturing at a painting across the room. It was of a man who was obviously black, but was wearing the traditional orange-patterned tunic and headband of a Seminole warrior. Foster was astounded. He had come across the name of Billy Two Hats a couple of times while researching the Seminole Wars.

"He was famous as a kind of unofficial diplomat and translator, wasn't he?" Foster asked. "From what I read, he was constantly trying to forge peaceful relations between the whites and the Seminoles." A look of cold bitterness crossed Serena's face.

"Yeah, that ended a few years after 1842."

"The *Armed Occupation Act?*" Foster asked. Serena nodded.

"Yep. The US Government offered 160 acres of free land in Florida to any whites who could bear arms and defend themselves against the Seminoles."

"But those settlers were told to avoid any Native American lands, nor were they allowed to claim land in any community already settled." Foster said. The bitter expression stayed on Serena's face.

"Not all armed occupants abided by that," she replied. "Have you ever heard of Wylieville?" she continued. Foster shook his head.

"Was it a Maroon settlement?" he asked.

"Yes," Serena answered. "You're sitting where it used to be. "Before the whites named this crossroads Cloverfield, it was a little village of blacks and their Seminole spouses quietly working farms. They called it Wylieville."

"Is this where Billy Two Hats lived?" Serena nodded.

"Have you ever heard of the Wylieville Massacre?" She asked. Foster had never come across any mention of the village in his research.

"No," he responded. "I have found nothing about that."

"You probably won't. It was successfully hushed up."

"What happened?" Foster was intrigued. To him, researching historical events was like detective work, and he sensed he was onto something fascinating. He wasn't wrong.

"Sometime in 1856, a mob of about a dozen heavily armed whites rode in from the north. Their intent was to wipe out the Wylieville settlement and take over the land." All kinds of questions flashed into Foster's mind, but he wisely held his tongue.

"Billy knew they were coming. The warning came to him through a network of slaves and free blacks in the area." Serena sipped her coffee and continued.

"Billy rode to the nearby Seminole settlement of Black Water as the whites called it or Lysteowy in the Seminole language, and recruited some of the men from there. They joined the men from Wylieville and waited. The next day, when a lookout rode into town ahead of the whites, Billy organized an ambush at the crossroads," she gestured at the intersection

Foster had driven through a few minutes earlier.

"When it was over, all the whites were dead. Their bodies were buried around here somewhere and their horses and belongings were transported farther south. Word has it that they were handed over to the bands that were following Billy Bowlegs in his raids around Fort Meyers." Foster nodded in comprehension. His research had revealed that those raids were in retaliation for a US Government "surveying" party destroying part of a Seminole farm. The raids and the retaliations were referred to as the Third Seminole War.

"So no trace of the white raiders was left?" He asked. Serena nodded.

"That's right. A few days later the sheriff from up in Orlando passed through, looking for them. Billy told him the men had passed through the settlement and had continued south toward Lake Okeechobee. The sheriff had no reason not to believe him, so he continued his search." Foster nodded in comprehension.

"That would have been during the Third Seminole War," He mused. "The sheriff probably figured the men got involved in that and were killed."

"It worked," Serena said. "After that, Billy stopped trying to bring peace with the whites and just worked his farm until his death."

"How did this motel come about?" Foster asked.

"The land was passed down through the generations," Serena replied. "My momma eventually ended up owning it." Serena's eyes grew sad. "She married a typical white cracker farmer—a nice man named Whitfield." Serena stared off into space for a moment. "I am the result."

"So you don't work the farm any more?" Serena shook her head and smiled ruefully.

"No." My dad ate a typical cracker diet—fried everything. He smoked like a stove and drank way too much. So he died in his late forties." Again the sad expression returned to Serena's eyes. Foster wanted very badly to do something to console her.

"The farm was too much for my momma to work, so she sold off most of the land and used the money to build this little place."

"Have you lived here all your life?" Foster asked.

"Except for a period in my twenties when I sowed my wild oats," Serena smiled conspiratorially. "When I graduated from high school, I moved to Orlando." She shook her head ruefully. I drank too much, partied too much and had a good old time. I worked as a waitress and took some art and history classes at a community college." Foster glanced at the painting of Billy Two Hats and rose from his seat to get a closer look.

"Did you do this?" he asked, gesturing at the painting.

"Yes," Serena replied, her tone guarded.

"This is really good!" Foster exclaimed leaning in closer. Not only were the complex patterns on the woven tunic clearly visible, but also the creases in the leathery skin looked as if you could touch them. He returned to his seat.

"You must have had some really good teachers," he said sitting down. Serena's expression became animated.

"I did." There was one in particular—Mr. Fisher—who inspired me to find my own style. I learned a lot from him about balancing technique and emotion." Foster nodded.

"There's a lot of affection for Billy Two Hats in that painting," He said. Serena looked at him carefully, smiling.

"Yes there is," she said after a few minutes.

"So what brought you back home?" He asked.

"Momma got sick during my third year in Orlando and I came home to care for her and take over running this place." She finished her cup of coffee and looked at her hands. "When Momma died, I didn't feel like going back to the city, so I just kept on working here." Foster hesitated before asking his next question. He was not usually this bold, but something about the instant familiarity that had grown between them prompted him to take a chance.

"You never married?" He asked. Serena smiled as if she had expected this.

"No, Foss." She answered. "C'mon," she said, rising from her chair, still smiling. "Let's get you settled in your room." Serena led him back into the office and retrieved a key from a rack of keys behind the counter.

"I'm giving you number one," she said handing the key to him. "It's right next to the office so you can tap into my Internet service if you'd like to." Foster thanked her and began unloading what few belongings he had brought with him into the room. Serena went back into the office for a few minutes. She came back out of the office with her purse and locked the door behind her. She put a "Be Back in an Hour" sign on the office door.

"Foss, I'm going to run into Kissimmee for groceries," Serena said. "There's a supermarket there that opened at noon today. Except for Mr. Mack at the mini-mart having some God-awful hot dogs and cold sandwiches, there's no place to eat around here. Do you want me to pick something up for you while I'm at it?" Foster had not even thought about food. As he hesitated, Serena seemed to have come to another decision.

"Look," she began. "Why don't you just eat with me? You're the only one here and I will just get some extra stuff."

"That would be great!" Foster exclaimed. "But let me pay for the food." Serena thought a moment.

"Tell you what. When I get back, I'll show you what I bought and you decide how much it's worth to you I could add that amount onto your bill." She stuck out her hand. "Deal?" Foster shook the warm, smooth hand and found it exciting.

"Deal!" he said.

Foster spent the afternoon typing on his computer in his room. He wanted to transcribe all Serena had told him while it was still fresh in his mind. After an hour staring at the screen, he walked across the empty intersection to the mini mart. Mr. Mack turned out to be a thin, bent leathery old white man with a ruddy complexion and a permanently startled expression on his face. Foster bought some potato chips and a diet soda.

"You stayin' at the motel?" Mr. Mack rasped.

"Yessir," Foster answered.

"That Serena's like a daughter to me," Mack stated his eyes narrowing as he regarded Foster. It dawned on Foster that this was actually a disguised warning. "She's good people." Mack asserted as he handed Foster his change Foster nodded.

"Yessir, she is," he said and walked back across to the motel. Serena's Jeep was back and she was unloading bags of groceries.

"Here, let me help," he said grabbing some bags out of the back of the Jeep. Serena smiled impishly. "Hell, Foss, if you keep this up, I may have to force you to stay on here." Foster shrugged.

"I could think of worse things," he smiled. It dawned on him that this was the closest he had ever come to flirting with someone.

About an hour later, Serena knocked on his door to let him know that supper was ready. He followed her into her tiny apartment behind the office. Foster noticed that Serena had done some straightening of the tiny living space and she was wearing a nice-looking dress and gold hoop earrings. Foster felt underdressed in his jeans and plaid shirt. He apologized for not dressing up more, and Serena waved his apology away.

"I don't get a chance to dress up much any more," Serena said. "I did this for me, but if you like it, all the better." They sat down to a dinner of fried chicken, green beans, and rice with white gravy. Foster had smelled it cooking and was ravenous. It was delicious, and both of them wasted no time on conversation as they dug in. At one point, both of them looked up suddenly conscious of the silence brought on by the enjoyment of the food. They laughed simultaneously. When they had finished, Serena picked up their plates and put them in the kitchen sink.

The rest of the evening was spent in pleasant conversation over coffee at the

Formica table. Serena asked him about his research and his family. He told her of the deaths of his parents and his brother. And how doing research in the relative isolation of his university office appealed to him

"But don't you get lonely Foss?" She asked.

"I could ask you the same thing," he replied. Serena smiled guiltily.

"Touche'" She said softly.

"We know why I isolate myself," Foster began. "But I don't understand why you do." He gestured across the table at Serena. "You're beautiful, you're brilliant, you're obviously talented, so why do you pen yourself up here?" Serena sipped her coffee and thought a moment. She looked across the table flirtatiously.

"Beautiful?" She asked. Foster covered his embarrassment by pursuing his question.

"Don't change the subject," he teased. "Why do you stay here alone?" Serena kept her insinuating smile and shrugged.

"What you see as a prison, I see as a refuge." Another pause. "I know it doesn't look like much, but except for the occasional customer, I am left alone here to paint and to explore the nearby countryside." Foster thought of the joy he felt when he was alone in the woods and he believed he understood what she meant.

"The motel brings in enough to support me," she continued. "Most of my customers are truck drivers hauling phosphate or they're road maintenance crews. Both of them operate on predictable schedules and I am one of the stops on their routes. So it's a steady income."

Foster envisioned handsome, rugged, suntanned men in jeans and felt a surge of jealousy. This was followed immediately by the realization that he was thinking like an adolescent. He involuntarily shook his head to erase these thoughts.

"What is it, Foss?" Serena asked, leaning across the table and placing her hand on his arm. He was too embarrassed to answer, but Serena seemed to figure it out for herself. She smiled at him fondly.

"Most of those guys are married," she began. "The ones who *are* single are full of swagger and bullshit." She squeezed his arm. "I want more."

That was the tipping point. As he thought back over the evening, Foster could not remember what was said after that, or how they ended up in each other's arms. All he could focus on was her incredible skin and her delicious mouth. The lovemaking was gentle and sweet and extremely powerful for both of them. Afterwards, both of them slept long and deeply.

When they awoke, sunlight was streaming in through the windows. They instinctively rolled toward each other and grinned into each other's eyes.

"You are distracting me from my duties as innkeeper," Serena teased.

"You are distracting me from being a recluse," he replied.

"Good!" She said and got to her feet. "Here's the deal," she said putting her hands on her hips and assuming a mock dictatorial stance. "I am going to bathe here and you are going to bathe in your as-yet-barely-used room."

"Yes ma'am."

"Then you are to report back here for breakfast!" She barked. Foster rose from the bed and struggled into his jeans.

"I live to serve," he said. He swept her into his arms and kissed her passionately before stumbling out of the office to his room. He did not see Serena watching him leave with a grin and then exhaling with a soft "Whoo!"

The next five days were a blur to Foster. After breakfast on the day after Christmas, Serena took him around behind the motel to one of those aluminum sheds one can buy at home improvement stores. Foster expected it to be loaded with maintenance tools. Instead, he found himself in a homemade artist's studio. A hole had been cut in the corrugated metal of one wall and a small air conditioner had been installed. Looking up at the ceiling, he could see that half of one side of the roof had been cut out and replaced by a sheet of glass. An easel stood in the middle of the small space, bathed in daylight. It held a blank canvas.

"I've been stuck for a long time," Serena explained sheepishly, standing next to the easel. Foster glanced at a row of finished paintings leaning against each other in a corner. He walked over to them and began leafing through them. They were all about the Florida he had come to know and love— the old Florida, eternally baking in the unrelenting sun. There was a white sand road winding through a palmetto prairie, a weathered barn with a fading "Hadacol" ad painted on its side, a rusting tractor parked in the shade of a huge oak tree. There was also a delightful rendering of Mr. Mack from the convenience store, with his permanently surprised expression.

"These are wonderful," he said. Serena came and stood next to him and took his arm. She pushed her breast against it.

"Flattery will get you anywhere," she murmured and lightly bit his earlobe. They made love again on the floor of the studio. Afterwards, they retrieved their clothes from the helter-skelter locations in which they had been thrown. At one point, as Foster, still naked, picked up his pants, he glanced up to see Serena staring at him fondly.

The next four days followed a wonderfully relaxing pattern. There were absolutely no customers during that time for the Seminole Maroon Motel. Serena got into the habit of leaving signs on the office door explaining that she would be back at such-and-such a time. Then she and Foster would hop into her Jeep and drive so some isolated spot in the area that contained something she thought he might find interesting. There was a hidden spring in which they skinny-dipped, and the ruins of what was once a turpentine mill in the middle of the jungle. After each expedition they returned to the motel around noon.  The afternoons and evenings were spent talking, laughing, and making love.

On the evening before New Year's Eve day, the first customers showed up—a very tired-looking family driving back to their home in Tennessee from what was apparently an exhausting family Christmas in Miami. Foster enjoyed watching Serena deal with them. He sat in the office in a chair in the corner, pretending to read a magazine. Serena was tender, funny and welcoming. Foster could see the tension quickly work its way out of the shoulders of the two adults. Serena showed them to their rooms adjoining each other. The two kids—a pair of twin boys--were delighted to see they had their own room with their own TV. When Serena returned to the office, she was smiling.

"That's a part of the job I enjoy," she said. "People come in here as if they've been beaten up by the road. Then they find rest and refuge inside these cinder block walls."

"It's not the walls, Serena," Foster said holding her gently.

"It's you."

Leaving the Seminole Maroon Motel the next day was one of the hardest things Foster ever had to do. It was New Year's Eve morning, and he explained to Serena about his promise to Brian. He expected her to step away from him in fright, certain she had been with a mad man the past few days. But Serena surprised him again.

"I see," she said, even though tears were forming in her eyes. "But I want you to do something for me."

"Anything," Foster said.

"At the party, I want you to look at everything very carefully," she pleaded. Foster kissed the tears rolling down her cheeks and told her he would return as soon as he could. He left hastily, aware that his own eyes were filling up.

Foster drove back to his house in Sydney and prepared for the New Year's Eve party. He bathed put on clean clothes and this time he wore a shirt with the collar unbuttoned. He didn't even bother to hide the birthmark.

He wasn't familiar with party etiquette and so he arrived on time at nine o'clock. The host and hostess—two young chemistry professors—appeared to be startled by his prompt arrival. As the young man led him into the living room, Foster noticed that the fellow was making a concerted effort NOT to look at the birthmark. He would glance in Foster's direction and then flick his eyes away. For the first time in his life, nothing about this behavior bothered Foster. On the contrary, he seemed to find it amusing. The man poured Foster a glass of wine and then he seemed to be hit by inspiration.

"Come with me, Dr. Delac," he said. "I want to show you my baby!"

Foster was led through the house to what he assumed would be a nursery. Instead the two men entered the garage, where the host turned on the lights. Foster found himself looking at what he recognized as a Ford Mustang model from several years ago.

"Isn't she a beaut?" The fellow gushed. Out of politeness, Foster pretended interest.

"She sure is," he agreed.

The host then launched into a long explanation of all the work he had done on the car. There were statistics about engine size, fuel to oxygen ratio, and something called struts that Foster could not make heads or tails of. But he would nod and grunt affably when appropriate. The fellow seemed flushed with relief to have something to talk about that interested him. He seemed even more relieved when the doorbell rang. He and Foster returned to the living room.

The next people to arrive were the head of the History Department, Dr. Andrew Wood, and his tiny wife, Penelope. Foster had only seen Penelope once before, when she was leaving her husband's office at the university. Her face wore a permanent mixture of anger and fear. On this particular evening, Penelope's visage had a glazed look as if she had fortified herself with something before coming to the party.

Dr. Wood was his usual bombastic self. He was one of those men who talked AT you, not WITH you. His idea of conversation was to make an endless series of pronouncements. He shook Foster's hand when introduced, frowning at the birthmark.

"You're the fellow that wrote the best-seller?" He asked, envy disguised as contempt was in his voice.

"Yes, I am," Foster replied, unapologetically.

"Well, more power to you my friend," Wood shrugged. "But in all honesty I must tell you that, in my opinion, anything that happened after the Renaissance isn't really history. It is only journalism."

"The men who died in World War Two will be amazed to hear that," Foster said. Wood arched his prodigiously hairy eyebrows and shuffled away.

The room gradually filled with other academic types. Each of them made an effort to acknowledge Foster's presence, but it was clearly an effort. He realized that at least being acquainted with the guy that wrote the bestseller might seem like a wise career move to them. For most of the evening he was left alone to watch.

He had walked past a dog park a few weeks earlier and he had noticed the animals sniffing each other's butts in an effort to establish some kind of hierarchy. He felt he was observing the same behavior here. As the wine flowed and things became louder, he notice inhibitions begin to fall.

At one point, Dr. Wood was holding forth at great length and volume about medieval tapestries. A group of professors and their wives were dutifully standing around him, hoping to curry favor by pretending to be fascinated. Foster noticed that Penelope Wood was standing nearby, her face toward a window. He could see her reflection in the glass. He was amazed to see that she was sneering and silently mouthing the words that her husband was saying.

At one point a bitter looking, plump little woman with a mop of brown hair topping her chubby face came and stood next to him. She was smoking some kind of exotic brown cigarette. She began pointing out to him all that seemed wrong with the occasion: the wine was cheap, the hors d'oeuvres were store bought, and her husband was drinking too much again.

"I will probably have to drive him home and put him to bed in a few minutes," she said, swaying against Foster slightly.

"After that, I will have the whole evening free," she murmured in his ear.

"Enjoy yourself," Foster said simply and walked away. He then thanked the shocked host and hostess for inviting him, and left the party. As he drove home, he wondered aloud to his empty car, why Brian had wanted him to attend such a dreadful occasion.

"I don't belong there, Brian!" He exclaimed, and that's when the realization hit him: THAT WAS THE POINT! That's what Brian wanted him to see. Foster shook his head, in disbelief.

"THAT was the wonderful thing that was supposed to happen?" He asked the empty car incredulously. "I knew before now that I didn't belong with those people!" Then came the logical next thought: "So where DO I belong?" His mind was flooded with the memory of caramel skin and laughter. When he pulled into the driveway of his cottage, he picked up his cell phone. Serena's voice did not sound sleepy when she answered.

"You up?" Foster asked her.

"Of course," said the low velvet voice he had come to love. "Are you drunk?

"Stone cold sober, " Foster answered, then continued. "I've had the most wonderful realization..."

A few minutes later, Serena set her cell phone down on a small table in her studio. She was excited by the prospect of Foster rejoining her the next day. She smiled fondly at the rough sketch she had been working on. The previously blank canvas now contained the figure of a middle-aged man with a birthmark standing naked and holding a pair of pants.

THE END

# MARIA'S JOURNEY

*Dorothy...*

Dorothy took a long drag on her cigarette as she watched her next meal ticket drive away in his tow truck. She could see him glance back at her in his rear view mirror and so she put on her most affectionate smile and waved happily. When Rick had turned out of the motel's gravel parking area and onto the highway, she went back inside and poured herself some coffee from the coffee maker. She sat at the table in the tiny room and considered what was about to happen.

It had taken about three months to get Rick into the position she had him now. She had singled him out the first night she had visited Bud's Hideout in Oscar—a little Florida farming community. The town sat on the edge of the marshes that bordered the headwaters of the St. Johns River.

Her predatory eye had noticed several things about Rick. First of all, he was not very bright. She noticed he had trouble figuring out which bill he should pull from his wad of cash to pay for his beer. Secondly, he smelled bad—a mixture of gasoline, grease, and body odor. And finally, he had a violent temper. While she was striking up a conversation with him, a man accidentally bumped into him and Rick lunged at him, hollering at the top of his lungs. Several men who bore a family resemblance to Rick immediately restrained him and convinced him to calm down.

Dorothy discovered that these were Rick's brothers—four of them in all. They all seemed to be slightly saner than he was (they were certainly *cleaner)*, and they seemed very protective of him. Once they had calmed him down, Dorothy was able to continue working on him.

It wasn't hard to get Rick to talk about himself, and she learned a lot about her potential prey that first evening. He was part of a large family—the Smeltons—who practically ran the town of Oscar, Florida. They had their hand in several businesses, including the auto junkyard that Rick managed. This puzzled her at first. How did an auto junkyard owner come by the large amount of cash he was flashing around that evening? Later, she found out about the illegal "chop shop" operation he had going at the back end of the yard.

She got the impression that the family had put Rick in charge of the junkyard because he was a good mechanic and they figured he couldn't mess that up. According to Rick, they had also put him in charge of their mother, who was very old and very ill. As Rick described his mother's illness to her, Dorothy could tell it was probably congestive heart failure. One of her previous husbands had died of that (with her help), so she was familiar with it. She knew Rick's mother didn't have much longer to live.

She led him back to her motel room that night and he enjoyed the sex tremendously. It called on Dorothy's considerable acting talents to make him believe that she was equally enthusiastic. Even though Rick did not wear a ring, she was not surprised to learn that he was married. It amused her to find out that his wife was a much younger Filipina woman who, Rick said, spoke almost no English.

According to Rick, the girl had had been literally *sold* to him when she was sixteen by one of her relatives. It was clear to Dorothy, listening to the pride in Rick's voice as he described the purchase, that he fancied himself a man of the world. When they discovered what Rick had done, the Smelton family put pressure on him to elope with the girl to Georgia where the age of consent was sixteen. So he drove her in his tow truck across the state line where they were married in Kingsland.

Rick bragged to Dorothy about the fact that as soon as he got his new bride home late that evening, he had raped her. He was very proud of the fact that the girl—Maria—had become pregnant almost immediately. Dorothy made the required remarks aimed at praising Rick's virility. He was visibly pleased.

He added that since the birth, Maria had gotten fat and unappealing. Dorothy was pleased that her competition was so weak. He told her that the only reason he kept the girl around was that she did a good job of taking care of the house and his mother.

Rick told her that the result of the pregnancy was a little boy—Rick Junior, or Ricardo as Maria called him---who had something wrong with him. He was nearly six years old now, and Rick had never heard his son speak a single word. All the boy did was make animal sounds, and carry around a little shapeless doll Maria had fashioned for him out of one of Rick's old socks. He said the kid spooked him a little because he had big brown eyes that seemed to somehow look through him.

When he had left that first morning, Dorothy began the ritual that characterized each of her encounters with Rick: she took a long hot shower, getting the smell of him off of her. She had met Rick only three short months ago. Now, things were coming to a head and Dorothy was very pleased with herself. She had gotten Rick to pay her rent at the motel and give her some cash to live on. This enabled her to keep the money she had taken from that truck driver in Kissimmee who had awoken one morning to find Dorothy and his wallet gone.

Her door was always open for Rick and he appeared at her room three or four nights each week. About a month after they had met, Dorothy had tearfully professed her love for him and her sadness that they could not be together permanently. She told him that sneaking around made her feel "dirty," and that she "wanted to shout their love from the rooftops." She could tell that he bought the whole performance, hook, line, and sinker.

In the past two weeks, he had begun discussing ways in which he could get rid of Maria and the boy. He had immediately ruled out divorce, and Dorothy knew she had to be very careful here. So she pretended alarm initially when he discussed murdering them and disposing of their bodies. But as he began to ruminate about methods for doing so, she would occasionally chime in quietly with reasons why this or that plan wouldn't work.

Last night, Rick seemed especially agitated. He had found the little boy's sock doll in the doorway of the chop shop at the back of the junkyard. Because Maria never let Ricardo go anywhere outside alone, this meant that she now knew about the operation.

"But as dumb as she is," Dorothy had cautioned, "She probably did not understand what she was looking at." But Rick continued to be upset.

"Yeah, but if she ever did say somethin' to somebody, my brothers and I could end up in jail," he warned. "Right now, we got a late model Mercedes we're choppin' up for parts. She might be bright enough to figure out it don't belong there." Dorothy shrugged.

"I see," she put a hand on his arm supportively. "Whatever you think is best, darlin'." He had then picked up his cell phone and had called each of his brothers. They were to meet at the yard late the following afternoon and discuss what was to be done about Maria and the boy.

As she dried her hair, Dorothy contemplated what would probably happen next. She knew Rick would not get away with it. Idiots like him always got caught and that would work to her advantage. Once Maria was out of the way, she could move in with him, speed up the old lady's demise and pretend shock when he was arrested for murder. There had to be cash or stuff that could be converted to cash lying around the place. This could be a major score for her and then she could move on with an even bigger stash.

After her bath, Dorothy put on her shiny green blouse. It was St. Patrick's Day after all, and she felt like celebrating. She knew that Rick and his brothers would be tied up today with their ridiculous plans, so she was free to celebrate. She thought she would go back to the Bud's Hideout Bar, and get an early start on the day.

*Rick*

Rick drove slowly along the grid of dirt roads that lay between the motel in the heart of Oscar and his junkyard just off the main county road into town. The county apparently figured this part of central Florida would be swept up in the land boom fueled by retirees seeking warmth. It had laid out a series of roadbeds that could easily be converted into suburban streets. A deep drainage canal bordered each road—the system by which the former swamps had been converted into dry land. Sadly, the expected influx of new residents had not yet occurred. The result was a network of roads and canals through what amounted to stretches of Florida jungle and occasional large pastures.

Rick was driving slowly because he needed to think—something that was painful for him. All he knew for sure was that he *had* to have Dorothy with him, at all costs. The idea of divorce seemed messy and complicated to him. Besides, wasn't there something in the law that said Maria would get half of everything? To keep a woman like Dorothy interested would require all the income he could generate, but she was worth it.

No. To Rick, simple solutions were the best. He would just have to make Maria and that weird little boy disappear. He had felt no kinship whatsoever to his son. The boy looked nothing like him, and even at five years old, his attitude toward Rick seemed contemptuous. At the thought of removing those spooky brown eyes from his life, Rick felt a surge of relief.

Killing them wouldn't be a problem. They lived far enough from their nearest neighbors that gun shots would not be heard. Rick could foresee two problems after that: disposing of the bodies and the old lady. It had dawned on him that the ground of the junkyard was so soaked with oil from the wrecks that were stored there, that even if the sheriff's department became suspicious and used search dogs, they wouldn't smell anything. He would simply use the forklift to raise a wrecked car up, bury the bodies, and then set it back down on top of the graves. He congratulated himself on his brilliance.

Then there was the old lady. He had to be careful there. She was dying—anybody could see that—but her mind was still as sharp as ever. She still handled the bookkeeping for the junkyard (and the chop shop), and lately her attitude toward him had become more and more angry. He wondered if she somehow had figured out he was seeing another woman and disapproved. As far as he knew, he had been smoothly covering his tracks.

Whatever he and his brothers decided to do, it might have to wait until the old lady was dead. He speculated on whether Dorothy would be smart enough to be the bookkeeper once his mother was out of the picture. He wondered if there was a way he and his brothers could speed that up. They were smarter than he was and he had always counted on that. Maybe they could come up with a way to solve all these problems. He began to rub his forehead as he drove. All this thinking was painful. He suddenly realized he was hungry. He headed the tow truck in the direction of Jenkins Road. There was a diner there at the entrance to I-95.

*Cleo.*

That afternoon, Cleo Smelton watched Maria as she cleaned the bedroom in which the old woman had become imprisoned by her failing health. As her condition had worsened, her appreciation of the quiet younger woman and her strange little boy had increased. Six years ago, when Rick had first brought the poor girl home with him, Cleo had tried to warn him that what he was doing would backfire on him some day. But he of course refused to listen.

It wasn't that she was a religious person—she wasn't. In fact, as part of the redneck criminal family that was the Smeltons, Cleo had done her share of criminal dealings over her long life. But as her condition worsened and she was forced to move into the back bedroom of Rick's house, her regret over how much of her life had been wasted in money grubbing began to eat at her.

Over the months of her gradually increasing lack of mobility, she had begun to view Maria as a fellow prisoner. Cleo was imprisoned by heart disease. Maria's jailer was Rick. He never took his young wife anywhere except to the supermarket once a week, on Mondays. Cleo imagined her son stayed close by his wife as she procured groceries.

Every few months, Rick would grudgingly take his wife and son to a local thrift store. There he would pay for whatever clothing they had picked out, grumbling about the expense as he did so. It appealed to his sense of superiority that the woman and her little boy seemed so excited about a few bits of used cloth. If his ego had been massaged enough by the experience, he might treat them to lunch at the drive-thru of a burger place.

Each Monday morning Cleo would give Rick a deposit envelope that he would stick into the night deposit slot at the bank. On those market days the boy, Ricardo, would be left at home in Cleo's care. The old woman assumed he would be no trouble, because he spent every waking moment in front of the television in the living room.

The first time Cleo had taken care of the boy, however, he turned off the television and came into the bedroom. Then he did the most remarkable thing. He crossed to the bed, picked up the old woman's hand and looked into Cleo's eyes tenderly. He said nothing, but she could see that he was honestly concerned. It was clear to her, that in spite of his seeming inability to speak, Ricardo understood *everything.*

She felt oddly comforted by the presence of the five year old. It was at that moment Cleo began working on what she called "her project." When they were alone again on the following Monday, she explained "the project" to Ricardo. She could see that he understood completely. From that point on, she began to look forward to market days.

Cleo spent most of the day propped up on pillows with a lap desk across her middle. Often she would have books, papers, and piles of money spread about her on the bed and she would be working with a calculator and ledgers.

On those days, Ricardo would wait until his father and mother pulled away in the truck, then he would turn off the television and join her in her room. He would stand in the doorway, looking at her questioningly. If Cleo needed something, she would simply ask him. Apparently, his months of staring at the television screen had given him some understanding of English. But there was something else as well.

On their second Monday together, Cleo found herself craving a cup of coffee. The doctor had told her to avoid stimulants, but her addiction to caffeine was too strong. She knew that Maria always prepared a pot of coffee for Rick each morning. Cleo started to call for Ricardo, but he appeared in the doorway looking at her.

"Coffee," she had said. Ricardo uncharacteristically looked puzzled. Cleo's craving was so strong she could see a cup of the elixir in her imagination. Ricardo suddenly nodded and was gone. He returned a couple of minutes later with a full cup. Cleo sipped it gratefully. Then the thought struck her: he hadn't understood until she had imagined a cup of coffee. She then tried an experiment. She visualized a piece of the chocolate candy Maria had bought for her. It was stored in the pantry. Even though no words were said, Ricardo nodded and was gone. He returned after a few moments with the box of candy. Cleo had never believed in the supernatural and she thought anyone who did was an idiot. But it was obvious to her that this little boy had a talent that could be very useful some day.

She had known about Rick's involvement with a woman at the Oscar Motel as soon as it had started. Her son was dumb enough to use his charge card at the motel and as the bookkeeper she had come across the receipts. She watched his involvement deepen over the weeks, and she could practically hear his slow mind grinding to the inevitable conclusion that Maria and the boy would have to go.

She also knew her son did not have the mental capacity to deal with the legalities of divorce. Cleo correctly figured that Rick would not make his move to eliminate Maria and the boy as long as she was still alive to witness it. In the past month or so, however, she could feel herself beginning to spiral downward. Even the slightest effort seemed to exhaust her. Maria would have to help her out of bed to use the bathroom, and on Mondays, Ricardo did so without complaint. It was clear to Cleo that things were coming to a head.

As part of her "project," Cleo had begun to teach Maria some Basic English. She was pleased by how fast the younger woman seemed to learn. The new knowledge came in particularly handy this afternoon. The house that Rick had built near the junkyard was on a slight rise. From the bedroom window, one could look out over the field of rusted, oily hulks baking in the Florida sun. Maria was cleaning the windows in the room when Cleo heard her give a sharp intake of breath.

"*Kuya*!" Maria muttered.

"English?" Cleo suggested. Maria seemed to struggle for a moment to find the right word.

"Brother," the younger woman said finally.

"One?" Cleo asked. Maria shook her head.

"Many," she answered. Cleo slumped back against her pillows. So it was beginning. She suddenly felt extremely weary. But she knew she needed to focus now more than ever. She was about to shout Ricardo's name, but the boy appeared in the doorway before she could, his face a mask of concern.

"Help me up," Cleo said. Maria and the boy helped the old woman out of her bed, but instead of leading her to the bathroom, she impatiently pointed at the window. When she was able to look out, she saw the vehicles of her five sons all parked in front of the office at the far end of the junkyard. This was very troubling. It was St. Patrick's Day, after all. That was usually an occasion for her sons to get wildly drunk and raise hell. For them to forego the pleasures of green beer was not a good sign. Cleo pointed at the closest section of the metal fencing that surrounded the property. Beyond it was a tangle of pine trees, palmetto, and thick brush.

"You must leave through there as soon as possible," she said. She realized she was talking mainly to the boy. He nodded gravely. Cleo stretched her arm in a northwesterly direction. She was panting heavily now and had difficulty speaking.

"Head that way," she rasped. "Stay off the roads—they will be looking for you. It's about four miles." She leaned her head against the wall next to the window as she collected her breath for a few seconds. "There's a Greyhound Bus stop where Jenkins road hits I-95."

She motioned for them to help her back to the bed. When she was settled again, she waited for her breath to return. Meanwhile, she visualized a backpack that was hanging in her son's closet. Ricardo disappeared. She then motioned at the dresser across the room.

"Look in there," she said, her voice was practically a whisper. Maria went to the dresser and put her hand on the handle of the top drawer and looked questioningly at Cleo.

"Bottom," the old woman sighed pointing her index finger downward. Maria opened the bottom drawer. It was full of Cleo's underwear. Maria looked up, puzzled.

"Look!" the old woman rasped desperately. Maria rummaged around in the garments and fished out a large, overstuffed envelope.

"Inside!" Cleo managed. Maria opened the envelope.

*"Hesokristo!"* the younger woman exclaimed. The envelope was crammed with money—twenties mainly with some other denominations, including a few hundreds. Reaching into the envelope, Maria pulled out a stamped and sealed letter and looked at Cleo questioningly. At that moment Ricardo returned with the empty backpack.

"Mail!" Cleo said and pointed to the letter. Maria still looked puzzled. Cleo imagined a red and blue mailbox. Ricardo nodded. The old woman's breathing was shallow and rapid now. She fought against the fog of drowsiness that seemed to be creeping into every part of her. There was a little more to do. Leaning back on her pillows, she began to imagine things: a can of insect repellant, bottles of water, and a flashlight. As she did this, the boy scuttled about the house collecting those things. With what little strength she had left she looked at Maria.

"That letter is to the sheriff's department," she said. "Mailing it will rid you of Rick and his brothers." Maria still looked puzzled, but by this time, Ricardo had re-entered the room. He nodded vigorously at Cleo. At this point, Cleo surrendered. She slumped back onto her pillows with her eyes closed. In spite of herself, she felt a surge of fear at what was coming. She felt someone lift her hand. It was the boy. He then spoke the first words she had ever heard him speak.

"You okay," he said in an unusually low voice for a five year old. It wasn't a question; it was a statement. Cleo sensed that the boy knew what he was talking about. Whatever was coming for her would be okay. Cleo felt relief flood through her just ahead of the darkness. She did not feel Maria kiss her forehead. By the time Maria and Ricardo had walked through the back door, Cleo was dead and she was smiling.

*Exodus...*

Maria and Ricardo walked along the fence for about fifteen yards until they found a place where the ground had subsided under the bottom of the barrier. There was enough room for a person to crawl through. The subsided ground was wet and muddy, but Ricardo did not hesitate. He wriggled through the opening easily and beckoned to his mother. Maria's plump body caused the back of her jeans to snag momentarily on the bottom of the fence. Ricardo leaned over and unhooked her.

When they stood up again, Maria could see that they were facing a wall of greenery. She hesitated, not sure where to go next. Ricardo took her hand and looked up at her. Maria's breath caught in her throat. The brown eyes looking up at her did not seem to belong to a little boy. She got the impression that she was looking at love for her tinged with ancient knowledge. Ricardo tugged on her hand and led her through a break in the palmettos that she had not noticed. A moment later, they were completely out of sight of the house and the junkyard.

After more brushing through narrow openings in palmetto thickets, Ricardo found a trail heading roughly northwest. It was a pleasant trail. A forest of pine trees shaded the palmettos and the surface of the trail was covered with pine needles. To Maria, it was like walking on plush carpeting. Every now and then the pine needles gave way to bare patches of earth. Maria saw many animal footprints there in the soft earth and one kind gave her a surge of fear: pig tracks. She had been raised on a small farm on the island of Luzon, and her neighbors had kept pigs. She was very familiar with the dual sharp impressions of their hooves. She also knew that the pigs roaming these woods were feral and had been known to attack humans. She looked about anxiously. Ricardo apparently sensed her fear and gave her hand a gentle squeeze.

It was a late afternoon in March. The good news was, the temperature was fairly comfortable and the mosquitoes were not as plentiful as during the Florida summer. Maria was glad they had taken the time to spray themselves with repellant before leaving the house. But the bad news was, the approach of spring would mean the snakes were emerging and they would be hungry.

Every hundred yards or so, Ricardo would pause, listening. He would close his eyes, his head erect, as if hearing something. After a few seconds, he would nod and begin walking again. Maria found herself more than content to let her little boy lead the way. After what she had witnessed in her son's eyes just outside the fence, she sensed that something more powerful than her was in charge.

When they had gone a little over half a mile, Ricardo stopped suddenly and pointed ahead on the trail. A large rattlesnake was crossing the open area leisurely, beginning its nightly hunt for rodents. Ricardo waited until it had disappeared into the palmettos before moving on.

It was getting dark when they came to the first road. A deep canal separated them from the white sandy expanse of roadway. Ricardo led them along the bank of the canal, looking for a way to cross. They had gone a few steps when he suddenly pulled his mother into a copse of pine trees. A few seconds later, a pickup truck roared by on the road. Maria recognized the truck as belonging to one of Rick's brothers. It was clear to her that the hunt was on.

A quarter of a mile along the canal, they came across a huge pine tree that had fallen across the canal. Ricardo climbed up onto the trunk, which was about two feet in diameter, and beckoned to his mother to follow. Maria hesitated, but her son's insistent gesturing won her over. She hoisted her round body up onto the trunk.

When she looked across the canal at the other bank a long, dark shape was lying next to the water. At first she thought it was another large tree trunk. Ricardo bowed his head again, as if listening for instructions. After a few moments, he nodded and made the strangest sound Maria had ever heard. It was as if her son had swallowed an explosion. It was a loud, muffled "WHUMP!" that seemed to reverberate from the boy. The long dark shape on the other bank flung itself into the water with a loud splash.

Ricardo walked easily across the trunk to the other bank and stood waiting for his mother on the roadbed. Maria could not trust her balance to walk on the tree trunk, so she straddled it and scooted along on her bottom.

When they crossed the road, they stepped gingerly through a barbed wire fence into an open field. In the fading light, they could make out huge shapes dotting the landscape.

Maria took out a flashlight and trained it on the nearest hulk. It was a rolled up mass of hay, as tall as she was. Ricardo motioned for her to turn off the flashlight.

This field had apparently been recently harvested. At first, she was relieved at the openness of the terrain. When they were only a few hundred yards into the field however, she heard the pickup truck coming back along the road behind them. Ricardo tugged on her hand and led her behind the nearest hay roll. There they crouched.

The truck was going slowly now, and a bright light was being played across the field. It swept past the bale that hid the woman and her son, and kept moving. When the vehicle was out of sight, Ricardo stood and the two began walking rapidly across the open space.

Maria only used the flashlight every now and then and relied on her strange son and his gift to lead them. The open space seemed to stretch on forever and Ricardo frequently had to lead them around low, marshy places with standing water. There was no moon, but a cloud layer hung over everything. This helped visibility. As light from nearby communities like Oscar and Sydney reflected off the clouds, it provided some faint illumination.

After nearly an hour of walking, they could see a line of trees in the distance. Ricardo stopped suddenly and cocked his head as if listening again. He suddenly grabbed his mother's hand and whispered, "Bilisan!" in his unusually low voice. Obeying her son's urging to speed up, Maria began to walk as rapidly as she could. Ricardo was leading them straight toward the line of trees and he was not bothering to avoid marshy places now. They had to wade through occasional mucky depressions. At one point, Maria stumbled to her knees. Ricardo helped her up, whispering "bilisan!" again.

After a few minutes of this furious pace, a large shape began to appear before them in the distance. Maria could see it was some kind of farm machinery parked near the beginning of the woods. She suspected it was the machine responsible for the neat rolls of hay that dotted the landscape. Now Ricardo was nearly running toward the machine. They arrived at the metal monolith sweaty, dirty and out of breath. Ricardo climbed up the metal steps on the side of the machine and tried the door to the cockpit. It was unlocked. He climbed down and helped his mother manage the steps and climb inside. He slammed the door firmly behind them.

Maria had just settled into the driver's seat and pulled her son up onto her lap, when she heard the grunts and the hoof beats. Looking through the windows of the cockpit, she saw what Ricardo had been racing: a group of about thirty wild pigs. They milled around the hay baler for a while, then became distracted by other possible prey and wandered away.

Maria and Ricardo drank the two bottles of water and ate the bag of potato chips she had grabbed as they left the house. They ate and drank silently in the safety of the enclosure and began to relax. Just before she nodded off to sleep, Maria marveled at how light her son's weight was on her lap. "So much authority in such a little body," she thought as she drifted off. The two slept that way for hours—a lonely Madonna and child in a hay baler.

Angel came to work early. There was a lot of cleaning up to do. Yesterday had been St. Patrick's Day and the truck drivers and farm hands had nearly bought up his entire stock of cold beer. The parking area of his convenience store/gas station was littered with cans and cardboard. When he got out of his car, he didn't even bother to go inside, he began picking up the litter and carried an armload of it to the dumpster behind the store. He tossed it into the large metal container and when he turned around he was amazed to see a woman and a small boy sitting against the back wall of the store. The young woman was asleep, but the boy was looking at him.

"We need help," the boy said in Tagalog. Angel was surprised and pleased by hearing his native language from one so young. At the sound of the boy's low voice, the woman began to stir.

"Where have you come from?" Angel asked. Now awake, the woman began to relate to Angel, the nature of their escape. When Maria told him about her uncle selling her into virtual slavery, he spat on the ground in disgust. In the Philippines, family meant everything. For a man to turn on his own family like that was unforgiveable.

"Your uncle is an animal," Angel growled and Maria nodded at the older man. Angel then became worried. He wondered if this was a sob story intended to bleed money out of him. The two people in front of him were filthy and bug bitten and certainly looked homeless.

"What are you going to do now?" He asked. The woman looked stunned for a moment, so the boy answered.

"We want to buy a bus ticket and leave this place," Ricardo said matter-of-factly.

"Where do you want to go?" Angel inquired. Ricardo looked at his mother, who shrugged.

"It doesn't matter," the boy answered. "When does the bus get here?"

"The next bus will be here in about three hours. It will be heading north toward Jacksonville." Maria nodded.

"Do you have money for the ticket?" Angel asked, suspiciously. He felt sympathy for the pair, but he wasn't running a charity, after all.

"We have money," Maria answered. "But my husband is looking for us. He wants to kill us." Angel scratched his head. This was a tricky situation. It had taken years for the local rednecks to get around to trusting the little brown-skinned man who ran the mini-mart/gas station. He didn't want to endanger that by getting involved in a domestic dispute. On the other hand, these two fellow countrymen had obviously been through a lot. He reached a decision.

"There is a Filipino church in Jacksonville," he began. "I will give you the address. If you can get to them, they will be able to help you." He then turned and unlocked the back door.

"Follow me," he said and let them into the store through the back door. "There is a bathroom there," he said pointing to a small room off the storage area. "Get yourselves cleaned up as best you can and stay back here out of sight until the bus comes."

The next three hours were like a game of cat and mouse for Maria and Ricardo. First, they cleaned themselves up in the bathroom. They used up all the paper towels in the dispenser getting the dirt and grime off of themselves. Angel brought them more paper towels, along with some donuts and coffee for Maria. Ricardo was overjoyed to get a cup of hot chocolate.

Whenever the store and the gas pumps out front were empty of customers, Angel would knock on the storage room door and Maria and Ricardo would emerge from hiding to shop. First, the bus tickets were purchased, and Angel handed Maria a piece of paper with the church's address on it. Maria then purchased more snacks and some brightly colored tee shirts for her and the boy, with "Florida" emblazoned across the front. Whenever a car pulled into the lot, they retreated to the storage room.

About an hour later, another lull occurred and Angel knocked on the door again. This time, Maria and Ricardo emerged dressed in their new tee shirts. Maria purchased a sun visor and sunglasses for each of them, as well as toothbrushes and toothpaste before retreating again to the back room.

The third time they emerged was about forty-five minutes after that. Maria bought some hot dogs and cold drinks for them and headed for the back room, just as another vehicle pulled into the parking lot. Her heart sank when she saw it was Rick's tow truck. On the other side of the closed storeroom door, she listened as Rick entered the store.

"You seen a woman and a little boy?" Rick asked Angel.

"Yes, I have," Angel answered. "Both of them dark haired—the little boy about six?"

"Yeah, that's them!" Excitement was in Rick's voice. "You seen 'em?" Maria's blood seemed to freeze in her veins she measured the distance from where she and Ricardo stood to the back door.

Then Angel spoke

"Yes. I saw them bum a ride off a truck driver I had just sold some beer to." Ricardo smiled up at his mother.

"Where was he headin'?" Rick asked.

"South, I think," Angel answered. "I think he said something about a delivery to Fort Lauderdale Airport."

"Thanks," Rick said. A few moments later, Maria heard the door to the convenience store open and close. She opened the storage room door a little and saw her jailer backing out of the parking space. A few moments later, he was gone. It was the last time she was ever to see Rick Smelton.

A little over an hour later, Angel watched the woman and the little boy climb aboard the bus. He looked down at the letter she had given him to mail. It was addressed to the county sheriff's office. He smiled and set it on the tray with the other outgoing mail.

THE END

# BLOCK HOUSE

## CHAPTER ONE: GERALD

Gerald saw the Florida gopher tortoise when he was about ten yards away. It isn't that his eyes were sharp; they weren't. But he had lived on the barrier island for so long, he knew what shapes to look for in the roadside grass. This looked like a huge gray helmet moving slowly toward busy highway A1A. He pedaled faster down the paved bike/jogging path that paralleled the road. He arrived at the reptile when it was still a couple of feet from getting flattened by traffic. He got off the bike as nimbly as his 67-year-old body would let him and came up behind it. As soon as he touched the front part of its shell, it pulled in its head and sat still as he hoped it would.

He waited for a break in the traffic and then picking it up with his hands just below the middle of the shell, he carried it across the asphalt to the grass on the other side of the highway. During this portage, the tortoise instinctively flailed its front flippers and its back legs in an effort to claw his hands loose, but experience had taught him where to place his hands to avoid this. He set the tortoise down in the roadside grass, pointed in the direction it had been heading. He awaited another break in traffic before re-crossing the highway, He looked back to see the reptile grumpily speeding up to find cover in the palmettos farther away from the road.

"You're welcome," Gerald muttered at the tortoise, a grim smile on his face.

When another traffic break occurred he hurried back across the highway to his three-wheeled bike with its load of groceries in the basket behind the seat. It was late June and the heat of a Florida summer was in full swing. He wanted to get the milk and the frozen stuff home. Fortunately, he didn't have much farther to go.

Up to this point, his ride home from the supermarket had been very pleasant. The paved bike/jogging path had passed by scrublands—low, sandy mounds covered with palmettos, sea grass, palm trees, gumbo-limbo trees, scrub oaks, sea grape trees, and an occasional pine. These undeveloped stretches of the barrier island seemed older than time itself to Gerald, and he had grown to love them.

When he and Sadie had moved to the barrier island nearly fifty years earlier, it was almost all scrubland. Theirs was one of the few houses along this stretch of beach. There were no streetlights around them back then and so on a clear night, the stars looked as if one could touch them. They didn't mind driving fifteen miles to the nearest supermarket on the mainland in Sydney, FL. It was worth the extra effort to live their solitary lives.

Gerald didn't mind commuting into Sydney to his job as an electrician either, because at the end of the day he got to come back to Sadie and his little "blockhouse" as he called their home. After supper he and Sadie would walk along the beach. Every day, the Atlantic seemed to offer some new sight, some new experience.

All he and Sadie had needed was each other. Then the cancer had come and he watched the love of his life waste away. Gerald felt the peculiar tugging at his insides that occurred whenever he thought about Sadie—which was several times each day. It had been five years since she had passed away, and he still missed her terribly. Some nights, he would sleep with one of her nightgowns next to him in the bed.

Now his ride home took an unpleasant turn. He was passing what he had nicknamed "The Babbitt Block." A row of modern, unattractive "mega-mansions" bordered the highway and the biking path. It was a development prosaically named, " Flamingo Meadows Estates." Gerald always sneered when he saw the sign. It was obvious to him that whoever picked out this idiotic name had never been here. There were no meadows, only jungle and scrub land, and although flamingoes were making a comeback of sorts in the area, they were still a rare sight.

This stretch of uninspired suburban housing symbolized everything that Gerald found repugnant about the eradication of the scrublands and jungle of the barrier island. It was clear to Gerald that over the years, Americans had become so urbanized they were out of touch with the planet they inhabited. Nature was something to be tamed and paved over, not enjoyed and embraced. And lately, the trend seemed to be big houses and small yards. Gerald wondered, as he pedaled toward the bland stretch of houses, what these people would do if some calamity forced them to try to live off the land as their ancestors had done.

The last house in the development was the largest and the ugliest. It belonged to the founder of the boring enclave—Artie Schenkler. Artie was an aggressive loudmouth who had become Gerald's biggest antagonist in recent years. Artie apparently considered Flamingo Meadows Estates his personal fiefdom and like any good medieval lord, he hungered to expand his holdings and make more money. Gerald realized that the undeveloped land he owned right across the fence from Artie's place was like a bloody steak in front of a lion.

As he approached the house, his nemesis was rolling his garbage bin out to the curb. Artie wore no shirt and his huge belly protruded over his shorts like a tidal wave surmounting a seawall.

"When you gonna sell that goddamn wreck of yours?" Artie shouted at Gerald as he pedaled by.

"When you lose that gut of yours, Artie!" Gerald shouted in return.

"It's a goddamned eyesore!" Artie shouted to Gerald's back.

"So are you!" Gerald responded over his shoulder. He could hear Artie shouting something else, but the fat man was so out of breath by now, none of it made any sense. Gerald was always relieved when he passed the chain link fence that separated his property from the Babbit Block.

Gerald's land was one long forest of sea grape trees, and it ran for almost a half mile along the highway. The only clearing was in the middle, where his house sat. He had purchased the house and property for a song back in the 1950's and he and Sadie had paid off the mortgage a decade before she passed away. He realized that to money-hungry developers like Artie Schenkler, his land was worth millions.

Whenever Gerald considered selling his land, his stomach turned sour. He knew every inch of it, and loved it. He knew of at least two burrows inhabited by Florida gopher tortoises on the property. He had named them Alley and Oop. The thought of bulldozers crashing into that world was more than he could bear.

A few minutes and a quarter of a mile later, Gerald arrived at the building that made Artie froth at the mouth—his home. It looked for all the world to Gerald like a blockhouse one might find in an old fort or at a missile testing facility. It was a two-story cinder block cube, painted off-white. It occupied an open space in the midst of the grape tree forest that covered his strip of oceanfront.

Out of sight of the road, a stairway ran up the back of the structure to the upper floor where he lived. The lower floor had been a garage at one time, but when Gerald's eyesight began to fail, he had stopped driving and sold his car. Now the bottom floor contained a small workshop and not much else.

A cracked, asphalt apron led from the garage door to the highway. Gerald pulled onto this and dismounted. He walked the bike around to the back of the building. He knew better than to try to ride it through the soft sand that surrounded his home. He began the laborious task of transferring the groceries from the basket in the bike to the refrigerator and pantry upstairs. After a few trips up and down the stairs, he was breathing hard and sweating. When the last bag was brought up, he walked down the stairs one last time and moved his bike farther around behind the building, out of sight of the highway. He was just getting ready to go back upstairs and turn on the air conditioner when he heard the truck.

## CHAPTER TWO: CHAD (WHO WILL LATER BECOME DAN)

He walked around the corner of the building to see an old pickup truck with a young man getting out of it. It took him a few seconds to realize he was looking at his nephew, Chad. The young man stood over six feet tall. The boy gave Gerald a sad smile, and said, "Hi, Uncle Jerry."

Gerald didn't know what to do. He had always been awkward when relating to others, even those people he loved. He debated hugging the young man, but offered his hand instead. Chad shook the hand, looking puzzled at this response. An awkward silence fell between them. Gerald realized he had not seen his nephew in over five years.

He had last seen the boy on one of the rare occasions when his brother and his wife deigned to visit Gerald. They had dutifully come to pay their respects after learning of Sadie's death. His brother Rodney was ten years younger than Gerald, but from early childhood had seemed more like an unhappy old man. As a child, Rodney had collected baseball cards but never played the game himself. He loved compiling statistics on each player and had organized them into a complex filing system. He had kept the thousands of figures in a loose-leaf binder filled with graph paper.

When home computers started to become common, Rodney was in his element. The younger brother apparently found it much easier to relate to a machine than to humans, and quickly became an expert programmer and software designer. The whole family felt it was something akin to a miracle when Rodney actually found a woman willing to live with him as his wife. Betty had come from a "good family" in Boston and apparently was smart enough to see in Rodney a good provider.

Even though Rodney was nearing retirement age, Gerald sensed that his brother would never retire. Being a computer whiz kid had fed Rodney's self-absorption for years, and now he was a respected—and feared—executive with a major corporation. The older brother knew that his younger sibling could not let go of that which had massaged his ego so long and so well.

Rodney and Betty and their sullen teenaged kids had attended the memorial service for Sadie, and seemed extremely uncomfortable when Gerald chose to release his beloved's ashes into the surf near their home. It was clear to Gerald that they did not think much of his home, the barrier-island, or Sydney Beach. As an act of noblesse oblige toward a poorer relative, they "treated" Gerald to a post-funeral dinner at a beachside restaurant. If Gerald's brother and sister-in-law were truly distraught at the loss of Sadie, they hid it remarkably well.

Among locals the place they took him to dinner had the reputation of featuring poor quality seafood at outrageous prices. It had a large bar and like many of its kind, it was festooned with fishing nets, plastic starfish, and replicas of old ships' lanterns. But tourists and some "snowbirds" (people who only lived in Florida during the winter) fancied it as a true tropical experience.

It had been a terribly uncomfortable meal. His brother Rodney's face wore a vaguely irritated expression as if he was being forced to smell something unpleasant. He had become beefy and red-faced in his middle years, and he drank a lot of alcohol which only seemed to sour his mood further. Rodney's contribution to the table talk was to bluster about the heavy responsibilities of his job.

His wife Betty kept up with him in consuming martinis and blathered on about their lives in Boston, and the important people they knew. Both of them seemed to be trying to portray a golden existence in Massachusetts. As he listened to them, it dawned on Gerald listening that, they were trying to contrast their lives with what they saw as his pathetic existence.

Chad and his younger sister said almost nothing during the entire visit. They spent the time checking their cell phones and broadcasting boredom and impatience. Gerald had been relieved when it was over, and was grateful to return to the sanctuary of his "blockhouse." So, given their last time together, Gerald could not figure out why his nephew had suddenly appeared on his doorstep.

"I flunked out of college over in St. Petersburg, Uncle Jerry," Chad explained. "Mom and dad are totally pissed at me and I need a place to stay until I can figure out what to do." With his usual awkwardness, Gerald did not know how to respond to this, so he didn't. He changed the subject instead.

"Where did you get the truck?" He asked, nodding at the vehicle. Chad looked down at his feet with a sheepish grin.

"I figured dad and mom were going to cut me off when they found out," he explained. "So I used the credit card dad gave me to get some cash and buy this before I told them what I had done."

Gerald nodded, impressed with the boy's resourcefulness even though he had clearly been irresponsible. Gerald had never gotten along with his younger brother Rodney, and he took secret delight in Chad's getting what he could from his stodgy, judgmental parent. The older man walked around the vehicle. It was hard to tell what color the truck had been originally. Weathering and sun damage had taken its toll. At present it was a cross between a charcoal gray and a reddish-brown.

"'76 Ford," Gerald mused. "One of the last ones to not have any computerized parts." He glanced into the bed, where he saw a suitcase, a duffel bag, and a backpack. He turned to his nephew.

"So how long you planning to stay?" Gerald asked. The boy shrugged.

"I don't know, Uncle Jerry," Chad began. "I've really screwed up and I don't know what to do next." Jerry thought for a moment and once again retreated to the safe subject of the truck. He pulled a ring of keys out of his pocket and walked over to the garage door. He opened the padlock and swung the two doors outward.

"Let's get your truck inside," Gerald said. "This salt sea air will corrode metal pretty fast." Gerald pulled the suitcase and the backpack out of the truck bed and left the duffel bag for his nephew.

While Chad parked the truck, Gerald went upstairs and tried to think about what he should do. Should he call his brother and tell him to come get his kid? Something inside of him rebelled at this thought. He wasn't sure why. Perhaps it was the memory of his brother's cold, expressionless face that made him reluctant to surrender Chad to his parents. His thoughts were interrupted by Chad entering the apartment, lugging his duffel bag.

"I'm going to call my folks," Chad said, "But if it's okay with you, I'd rather not go back to Massachusetts."

"You can't just hide out here forever," Gerald said, and instantly regretted the harsh tone he had taken. Chad nodded.

"I know, I know, Uncle Jerry," The boy said apologetically. "But if I could have a few weeks—say this summer—to figure things out, that would be great."

"You'll have to get a job of some kind," Gerald warned. He just couldn't seem to keep the defensive tone out of his voice. "My pension isn't going to be enough to feed both of us." Chad nodded again.

"I will, Uncle Jerry," He said. "And I can help out around here, as well. For example I can take you places in my truck." Gerald nodded at this, and then turned his attention to where Chad would sleep.

The apartment took up the whole top floor of the building. It consisted of a large living room, at each end of which stood a bedroom.

There was a kitchen/dining area, and a bathroom. The second bedroom had been used as a sewing room by Sadie, and after her passing, had become a kind of storage space, with cardboard boxes stacked along one wall. It did contain a small single bed, however. When Chad had mounted the stairs with his duffel bag, Gerald showed him the room.

"This will be fine, Uncle Jerry," the boy said and set his duffel bag down on the bed. "Can I use your phone?"

"You don't have your cell phone?" Gerald asked.

"Dad cut me off the family plan for phone service," Chad admitted sheepishly. Gerald nodded. That was his brother all right. He motioned to the old landline wall phone near the kitchen. Chad paused in front of the relic.

"Wow!" I don't think I've ever used a dial phone!" The boy exclaimed. Chuckling, he dialed the number. He stopped chuckling when someone answered.

"Hi, Dad," Chad began. "I just wanted you to know I am safe and I am staying with Uncle Jerry for now." Gerald couldn't hear his brother's response, but he could guess.

"I know, Dad," Chad replied to the voice on the phone.

"That's what I'm trying to do, Dad," Chad responded. After listening some more, Chad turned and handed Gerald the phone.

"He wants to talk to you," The boy said, looking worried.

"Hello, Rodney," Gerald said, resignedly.

"So you're going to enable him?" His brother asked. Gerald felt his anger rising.

"Rodney, does that cob up your ass hurt when you sit on it?" Chad tried to stifle a guffaw.

"You deserve each other," His younger brother sneered. "You're both losers."

"Coming from you, that's a compliment, Rodney."

"He couldn't hack it in college and you chose to live on the redneck Riviera." Roger taunted, his voice rising.

"Rodney, you have always been a pretentious little prick," Gerald replied calmly. "I could kick your ass when we were kids and I can still do it."

"GO TO HELL!" Rodney hollered and hung up. Gerald replaced the receiver on its hook and turned to find Chad almost shaking with gratitude.

"I think that went splendidly," Gerald smiled grimly.

"Thanks, Uncle Jerry," The boy said, his voice choked with emotion.

"No problem," Gerald smiled. "That actually felt good. Oh! One other thing!"

"Anything," Chad answered.

"Nobody calls me Jerry any more. My name is Gerald."

## CHAPTER THREE:  HENRY, MARTHA, ALLEY, AND OOP

Chad awoke the next morning to the smell of bacon. When he came out of his room, he found his uncle in the kitchen area, making breakfast.

"There's coffee in the coffee-maker," Gerald said over his shoulder.

"Thanks, Uncle Jer—Gerald," Chad replied sleepily.

When breakfast was over, Chad offered to do the dishes and Gerald took him up on it. Before abandoning the kitchen, however, the older man picked up a large metal pot with a lid on it, and started to carry it outside.

"What is that?" Chad asked, nodding at the pot.

"Vegetable kitchen waste," Gerald answered. "I'm trying to make the sandy soil out back fertile. It was always Sadie's dream to find a way to grow vegetables here."

When Chad finished the dishes, he joined his uncle down the stairs and into the sandy area that comprised the back yard. About forty feet beyond this open area, the land dropped down to the beach. On either side of the open area, the sea grape forest began. He found his uncle burying the smelly contents of the kitchen waste pot in a mound of sandy soil.

"I've tried everything I can think of," the older man said resignedly, "but the sand just doesn't hold onto nutrients for very long. Everything dries out and what fertilizer there is percolates away."

Chad was staring at the mound when he saw the snake. It was about four feet long, black and shiny, with a small head. Chad reached for the shovel to kill it. Gerald refused to let go of the shovel.

"Leave it alone," the older man warned. "That's Henry."

"Henry?"

"Yep," the old man explained. "It's a black racer that lives under the house." Gerald gestured at the smooth, shiny black ribbon that was gliding effortlessly around the base of the building. "It eats mice, roaches, and sometimes other snakes. It is basically free pest control."

"Is Henry poisonous?" Chad asked.

"Not at all," Gerald answered. "The key is the shape of the head. If the head is large and triangular, then you should worry."

Chad returned his attention to his uncle's frustrating attempt at putting in a vegetable garden in what is basically, coarse beach sand.

"Do you have just regular dirt anywhere on your property?" he asked. "Maybe we could mix it in with the sand."

Gerald thought for a moment.

"That's a good question," he answered. "Let's go see." And with that, he led Chad on a tour of his land. The truth is, Gerald knew that there was no dirt—just sand on the property, but he saw it as a good excuse to get the young man acquainted with where he lived now. Also, Gerald simply enjoyed walking through the sea grape forest.

The wide, shiny leaves formed a cooling canopy over head and the shade prevented much of the undergrowth found elsewhere on the barrier island. The contorted trunks never failed to fascinate Gerald with their wind-designed shapes. A sandy path—worn by Gerald and Sadie's feet over the decades, wandered through the copse.

"Wow! This is really cool, Uncle Gerald," Chad muttered, looking around. Occasionally the path would wander close to the beach and the sea grape trees would part, giving a wonderfully framed view of the surf.

"Are you a surfer" Gerald asked. Chad shook his head.

"Not much surfing in Boston," the younger man grinned.

As they resumed the stroll, Gerald asked the question that he felt had to be asked.

"So why did you flunk out of college?" Chad looked downcast. He had obviously been expecting this. When he spoke, it was in a tone full of embarrassment.

"I've always had a problem sitting still and reading, Uncle Gerald." He shook his head. "I barely graduated high school, and the only reason I got into that private college was because of Dad's influence." The boy seemed to be struggling to find the right words. "I need to *move*! I need to do stuff with my *hands*! I'm good with machines and I'm good at working outdoors. Back home I would hike in the hills all the time. I hiked all ninety miles of the Appalachian Trail in Massachusetts!" Chad exclaimed. Gerald nodded. The boy reminded him so much of himself at that age. It made the old man very grateful he had stumbled onto his interest in electronics.

They walked to the end of the property, which was delineated by a wooden fence. That's the Richard Rackland Nature Preserve," Gerald said. "Its property runs for a mile beyond mine. There are hiking trails, and some freshwater ponds on it. I have seen some good-sized alligators in those ponds. Sometimes I will spend a day hiking the trails and clearing brush off of them."

"Do you get paid for that?" Chad asked.

"No," Gerald replied. "I just like being out in the woods." Gerald turned left along the fence and led them toward the beach.

"It drives developers crazy that they can't get their hands on either my property or the nature preserve." the older man grinned as they emerged onto the sand of the beach.

The tide was out and so they could walk easily along the hard-packed sand just inland from the water. Gerald could see that Chad found the shells he was passing too fascinating to ignore. Occasionally, the young man would stoop and pick one up and examine it more closely. He put a couple into the pocket of his shorts. Gerald grinned in understanding at the sight of this. He had lived on this shore for almost half a century and he still found something new and different each time he walked the beach.

"Your aunt and I used to walk this stretch every evening after supper except when it rained." The younger man noticed the dreamy, fond expression in the older man's eyes. "The sea never disappoints," Gerald said. "There is always something interesting to notice on the beach." Chad nodded. Gerald was pleased to see that the younger man was appreciating what he was seeing as much as he did.

They had passed the house and were continuing up the beach, when they came across a peculiar set of tracks. It looked to Chad as if a small tracked vehicle like a tiny tank had come out of the surf and proceeded inland. Another set of the same tracks seemed to lead back into the surf. Gerald pointed at the tracks.

"That's Martha," he said. "She is a Kemp's Ridley sea turtle." Gerald motioned for Chad to follow him, walking alongside the tracks. The marks in the sand led up off the beach and into the sea grape trees.

"Martha's weird," Gerald said.

"What do you mean?" Chad asked as Gerald stopped them several feet away from a small mound set inside of a crater. The crater stood in a small, sunbaked opening in the trees.

"Well, what Kemp's there are in Florida usually lay eggs over on the Gulf side of the state. Martha keeps coming back all the way over here each year and nests in this same place." He motioned at the mound in the crater. "Also, I have never heard of a sea turtle crawling all the way off the beach and into the trees to lay eggs. They usually nest in the soft sand above the tide line."

Chad took out his phone and took a picture of the crater in the hole.

"I thought your phone service was cut off," Gerald said.

"Don't need the service to take a picture," Chad responded.

They continued on north until they came to what was obviously the end of Gerald's property. A chain link fence poked out of the sea grape trees, delineating the beginning of the "Babbitt Block." A path ran next to the fence and Gerald led them on it. As they re-entered the sea grape forest, Chad noticed that the trees closest to the beach were shorter than the ones a few yards inland. He wondered if salt spray had stunted the growth of the closer trees, causing this gradual rise in the canopy. Another well-worn path led south, back toward the house. After a few yards, Gerald stopped and pointed off to the right, at a large hole in the ground.

"That's Alley's home," Gerald said.

"Alley?"

"A Florida gopher tortoise," Gerald responded. "It has lived here as long as I have." He motioned off to the left of the burrow. "There's another, younger tortoise living off in the trees over there. I call it 'Oop.'" Chad took out his phone and took a picture of the burrow.

# CHAPTER FOUR: JACKIE AND THE DAWN CAFÉ

The next morning found Gerald and Chad eating at the Dawn Café in Sydney Beach. It had been Gerald and Sadie's favorite local hangout when she was alive. Since she had died and Gerald had given up his car, he had not been back there more than a couple of times.

Gerald had awakened Chad early with the promise of a delicious breakfast if the boy drove them to the café. Chad sleepily agreed. He had slipped on some shorts and a tee shirt and sandals, ran a comb through his hair and followed his uncle down the stairs.

At the restaurant, Magda, the manager broke into a wide smile when she saw Gerald coming through the door.

"I thought you had dropped off the face of the earth!" She said, rushing to hug him. She showed Gerald and Chad to a table in the corner. The place, as usual, was full of regulars—nearly all of them locals. It being summer, most of the "snowbirds" were up north at this time of year. It was a testament to the notoriety of how good the place was that it was still full during the off season.

The excellent food and reasonable prices comprised an ideal business model that had worked successfully for years.

Besides the food and the prices, there was the service. Magda's adorable daughters circulated like ballerinas among the crowded tables, serving, joking, and laughing. Magda had taught her daughters to show an interest in their customers as people. They had learned to memorize details about their customers' lives, and this made their patrons feel like family. Gerald was surprised to see a new girl approach their table.

She was tiny, with short black, shiny hair and incredible olive skin.

"I'm Jackie," She grinned, her gaze staying a little longer on Chad.
"Coffee?" She asked. Chad seemed unable to speak, so Gerald nodded. Jackie spun, still smiling and hurried away. Chad's eyes followed her until Gerald handed him a menu.

A couple of minutes later, Jackie returned with cups and a pitcher of coffee. She poured them and then brought the carafe back to the coffee maker behind the counter. She was back a moment later, her ordering pad and pen in her hand. She grinned at Chad.

"So what's your pleasure?" she asked, chuckling. Again, Chad seemed dumbstruck, looking at Jackie. Once again, Gerald felt the need to cover for him.

"You're not one of Magda's daughters, are you?' He asked. Jackie shook her head.

"Nope," she answered. "I just look like them. Magda took me in a few months back when my dad died and my mom went off on a bender." What amazed Gerald about Jackie was that her voice was totally without drama or self-pity. The girl projected an attitude of "it is what it is, so let's move on." Gerald liked her immediately and apparently so did Chad, who continued to be speechless, gazing at Jackie in obvious awe. Again, Gerald came to the rescue.

"The blueberry pancakes here are to die for," the older man told Chad, hoping to jar him out of his trance.

"That's true!" Jackie exclaimed. "I've eaten them and have died several times, but I keep coming back for more."

"So...blueberry pancakes, Chad?" Gerald said, nudging the dazed young man with his menu. Chad seemed to awake from a dream.

"Uh, yeah, Uncle Jer—Gerald. Blueberry pancakes." Jackie smiled at Chad with a happy gleam in her eye, spun on her heel and pranced away.

The blueberry pancakes were as wonderful as Gerald had remembered them. Even Chad stopped watching Jackie long enough to dig in. Something in the pancakes seemed to have suddenly restored Chad's ability to speak. When Jackie returned to refill their coffees, the young man spoke up.

Look...uh Jackie..." He began. Gerald could see that Chad liked saying her name and Jackie liked hearing him say it. "I need a job really bad. Do you know anybody that's hiring?" Jackie cocked her head in thought for a second.

"I'll be right back," she said and pranced away once again. She went behind the counter and spoke to Magda. Magda nodded and looked over at Chad and Gerald. Then the older woman smiled a wise smile and shrugged. Jackie broke into a delighted grin and came back to their table.

"You mind getting your hands dirty...Chad?" She asked.

"Not at all," Chad said.

"We need a busboy," she said, watching his reaction carefully. "When can you start?" She asked. Chad smiled in disbelief.

"As soon as I finish my pancakes and give my uncle a ride home!" He said.

After breakfast, Chad drove Gerald home and literally ran up the back stairs. Gerald was amused to see the boy quickly bathe and comb his hair to begin his first day as a busboy.

Gerald was surprise to feel regret as he watched Chad's old pickup truck turn onto the highway. In the brief time they had been together, he had grown to like the young man. It had been nice having someone else in the house.

Gerald spent the day cleaning. He found some extra bed linens in a closet and put fresh sheets on the bed in Chad's room. It wasn't easy to do so, since he had to edge around stacks of cardboard boxes lining one wall.

He swept the hardwood floor of the old place thoroughly, herding the sand that was always present toward the door to the back stairs. He even swept the stairs themselves. Before going back into the house, he glared at the offending mound of sand intended for the garden that refused to be anything but sterile.

Chad was late getting home from work that first day. When he pulled onto the cracked asphalt driveway, Gerald glanced out the window to see that the bed of the truck was loaded with broken tiles and small chunks of concrete. Gerald went down the stairs as rapidly as he could without falling.

"What's in the truck?" He asked as he approached Chad, who had taken the shovel from around the back of the house, and was lowering the tailgate.

"Some stuff for the garden," the young man answered. "Do you have a wheelbarrow?" Gerald shook his head. Chad scratched his head looking at the loaded pickup.

"I can't drive around back in this soft sand," the boy said, thinking out loud. Then, he seemed to reach a decision.

"Uncle Gerald, can I dump the load here next to the driveway?" He asked. "Then over the next few ways, I will find a way to get it around back." Gerald nodded.

"You're welcome to dump the load, but what are you going to do with all this?" Chad grinned.

You're going to think I'm nuts," The boy said "But my plan is to use this stuff as a base for your garden."

"A base?"

"Yes. I am going to dig out a plot at least two feet deep and line the bottom with some garden cloth. Then I'm going to put this stuff on top of that to hold the cloth in place." The boy gestured excitedly, making leveling motions with his hands, palms down. "And then I was thinking of putting down a layer of those dead leaves that are all over the ground under the sea grape trees." Gerald was able to follow the boy's explanation and was impressed by how the boy envisioned doing the project mostly using what was available at little or no cost.

"Where did you get this stuff?" Gerald asked, nodding at the truck.

"Further up the highway there is a remodeling job going on," Chad explained. "This was in their waste pile by the highway. The foreman let me use a shovel to load the truck."

With that, the boy climbed into the cab and started the engine. He deftly maneuvered the vehicle to where the tailgate hung over the sand next to the driveway. Gerald shrugged, found a second shovel in the garage and joined the boy in the truck bed. Together, they began pushing the tiles and concrete chunks off the end of the tailgate and onto the sand. Twenty minutes later, both of them were sweating profusely and panting hard, but the truck was empty. Chad grinned at his uncle.

"I know it's a crazy idea, Uncle Gerald," The boy said. "Thanks for giving it a try." Gerald shrugged, smiling.

"Hell, nothing else has worked. Why not?"


## CHAPTER FIVE: HAPPY MONTHS

And so the summer of Gerald and Chad began. Chad would leave early in the morning to go to the café and Gerald would put in an hour or so working on the garden project. He would stop when the heat of the day started to become unbearable. He would quit and go inside to clean up and cool off. When Chad got home from work, he also spent some time before Gerald had dinner ready, working on the garden. It did not take long for Gerald to realize that, whatever Chad's difficulty was at college, it had nothing to do with laziness. The young man seemed tireless, once his mind locked onto a project.

Their shared labor began to show results. The garden plot began to look as if they were going to put in a very long, narrow wading pool. After receiving his first paycheck, Chad stopped at a home improvement store and bought some 2" x 12" boards and some black garden cloth. He used the boards to make a frame that bordered the trench and prevented the sand from caving back into the opening. He lined the bottom of the trench with the garden cloth.

The boy found a battered old wheelbarrow at a yard sale one Saturday afternoon and began using it to haul debris from the front yard to the back. Fortunately the barrow had wide, fat tires and could manage the sand. Gerald could not get over the boy's seemingly boundless energy. After a full day at work, he would put in at least an hour of hard labor working on the garden. It took several days, but at last the base of the garden was done. The broken tile and concrete was spread evenly over the garden cloth. On top of that, was a thick layer of sea grape leafs.

"Uncle Gerald, should we buy some fertilizer?" Chad asked over supper one evening.

"Definitely not," Gerald replied firmly. "That crap is full of chemicals that leach into the ocean." Gerald shook his head for emphasis. "I want to build up nutrients in the soil without using chemicals." Chad nodded.

"I understand, Uncle Gerald," the boy said. "We'll take our time and do it right."

Meanwhile, Chad seemed to be thoroughly enjoying his job at the Dawn Café. Gerald suspected this sudden embracing of menial labor had a lot to do with Jackie's dancing dark eyes. The café was only open from 6AM to 3PM. It normally took an hour to clean the place up and get it ready for opening the next morning. After that, Chad was free. Twice a week, he would drive Gerald to his favorite supermarket in Sydney Beach. Gerald would pick up what was necessary for meals for the next few days.

On those days when he didn't have to drive Gerald to the grocery, Chad worked on the garden project.

It cost less to feed Chad than Gerald had anticipated. The boy ate breakfasts and lunches at the café. The only meal Gerald had to provide for the boy was supper each night. Chad started out giving Gerald half of his weekly paycheck, but Gerald soon realized that was more than was necessary. He told the boy to reduce his contribution to the household to one fourth of his pay. This enabled Chad to buy insurance on his truck and finance his own cell phone plan. The boy also spent way too much (in Gerald's opinion) buying materials like organic topsoil to treat the dirt to be used in the garden. Gerald insisted on paying for much of this.

Chad could have had Mondays and Tuesdays off, but he elected to work all seven days of the week. The boy got permission to start work a couple of hours later on Monday mornings, however. That was the morning each week he brought his uncle to breakfast at the café. On those occasions, Magda repeatedly told Gerald how impressed she was with Chad's work habits. Gerald voiced his suspicions that Chad's constant presence at the café had a lot to do with Jackie.

But it turned out he was only partially right. This became evident to Gerald when he and Chad would walk on the beach after supper. The cooling breeze coming off the Atlantic seemed to break the hold of the oppressive summer mugginess. On these walks Chad would chatter to Gerald about how intelligently the restaurant was run. The young man seemed to be as obsessed with the café as he was with the garden.

"It's brilliant!" Chad exclaimed one evening. "Think about it, Uncle Gerald: they don't need to advertise, they have a steady clientele, and in winter the place is so packed, they have to turn people away." Gerald enjoyed the excitement in the younger man's voice. Chad might not have paid attention to his collegiate studies, but he seemed to be majoring in the Dawn Café now.

"And Frank, the cook!" Chad exclaimed. "Have you ever watched him in the kitchen?" Gerald shook his head. "The man is everywhere at once!" Chad waved his arm for emphasis. "He's practically a blur in the kitchen! And the stuff he turns out is *phenomenal*!" Gerald saw a chance to comment.

"It *is* good food," Gerald offered.

"*Exactly!* If the food sucked, nobody would eat there! Frank is actually the heart of the operation!"

Chad and Jackie began dating after his third week at the restaurant. Gerald watched his nephew nervously prepare for the first date, and wisely stepped in when Chad picked up a bottle of cologne from the bathroom counter.

"Go easy on that stuff," Gerald warned the younger man. "Sadie told me that if a guy reeks of too much cologne, it's as big a turn off as smelling of body odor." Chad nodded and used the liquid very sparingly. Several hours later, Chad returned from the date starry-eyed. After that evening, Jackie and Chad seemed to be inseparable. Jackie even began spending some time helping Chad in the garden after work. Gerald liked having the girl around. She was smart, funny, and not afraid to voice her opinion. She reminded him a lot of Sadie.

After supper, she would join them in their walks on the beach. The conversation between the three of them flowed easily. It would always cause a twinge of regret when Chad would drive Jackie home each night. It dawned on the old man that the three of them had become a kind of family. They were thrown together by circumstance, but were instantly comfortable with each other. With Chad and Jackie around, the old blockhouse was full of life again.

Every summer, the Dawn Café would close down for two weeks in late July and the entire staff would go somewhere on vacation together. Magda would foot the bill. Chad was ecstatic when they invited him and Jackie to go with them. This year, the destination was Key West. Gerald was amused at how excited the younger man was at the prospect of spending time with the family that employed him. It dawned on the older man that it was extremely rare for an employee to actually like his employers.

Chad returned from the trip to Key West sunburned and engaged. The younger man related to Gerald how it had occurred. The group had taken the ferry from Key West to Dry Tortugas National Park—an island with a Civil War era fort on it. The island lay out in the Gulf of Mexico, seventy miles west of Key West. There, they spent the day snorkeling in the clear water, and picnicking in the shade of the few trees next to the campground.

During his underwater searching, Chad had spied the core of what had once been a medium-sized spiral seashell. The remnant made a perfect finger ring. A few minutes later, he and Jackie were sitting on the beach, catching their breath, when Chad took her hand and slipped the seashell ring on her finger. He explained to her that at present, it was all he could afford, but he just could not imagine living the rest of his life without her. According to Chad, she grabbed him saying, "Yes!" over and over. Then she pulled away from him for a moment and admitted that she didn't like his first name.

"It sounds like one of those snotty preppy guys," she had said. "And you are nothing like that." So she decreed from here on out, Chad would be called by his middle name—Daniel or Dan." Chad grinned as he related all of this to his uncle.

"I never did care for the name Chad," his nephew admitted to Gerald. "So I guess I'm Dan now."

When Chad/Dan returned to the blockhouse, Gerald began to feel guilty about the boy's cramped living quarters, so he announced to Dan over supper one evening that he intended to tackle the painful job he had been postponing for five years: going through the boxes in the old sewing room that contained a lot of Sadie's possessions.

The next day after work, Dan and Jackie showed up at the blockhouse. With her characteristic directness she walked up to

Gerald who was putting the finishing touches on some spaghetti sauce.

"Mr. Gerald," The girl began, "Dan told me what you are planning to do, and I would like to help."

"Just call me Gerald please," The older man said. "Why do you want to get involved in this?"

"Two reasons," Jackie replied with unblinking honesty. "I want to live in this room with Dan until we get married and find a place of our own." Gerald glanced at his nephew who was grinning and nodding proudly. Jackie continued.

"This will ease the pressure on Magda and her family, whose house is already full of people."

"The other reason is, I am really good at spatial relationships. I know how to pack stuff." The thought of his brother Rodney exploding in rage because his son was going to marry a waitress pleased Gerald.

"I would be honored if you helped us," Gerald said gallantly. Jackie laughed in delight, stood on her tiptoes, hugged the old man and kissed him on the cheek.

"Now let me see how much stuff we are talking about," she said and marched to Dan's room

The next day after work, Dan drove Jackie to the store at which Gerald always shopped for groceries and household goods. There, under her direction, Dan bought an assortment of sealable plastic bins. After supper, the three of them began the difficult task of sorting through the remnants of Sadie's existence. As Gerald expected it was occasionally a very emotional and painful task. Jackie was wonderful. She seemed to sense what the older man was feeling and did not rush his decisions about what to keep and what to give to charity. At one point, she put her hand on his arm.

"Think about your wife," she said softly, her dark eyes serious. "What would she want you to keep?" Her words struck home. Sadie was all about enjoying life. She was not a possession-oriented person. "Hell," Gerald thought to himself. "She chose to live in a little square building in the middle of the jungle!" After that, the task became easier. He would only keep things that had meant a lot to Sadie or that helped him remember her.

The things worth keeping were sealed in the plastic bins and were stored downstairs. The articles to go to charity were loaded into the cardboard boxes and put into Chad's truck. When they were done, the amount of available space in the little room had nearly tripled. That was the first night Jackie had spent with Dan in the room. Gerald was very glad that the bedrooms were at opposite ends of the house and the central air conditioning allowed all parties to close their doors for privacy.

Jackie was tiny and young, but she had already been through so much in her life, that she possessed the kind of street smarts that only experience could provide. She seemed to delight in being a kind of mother to the two men. She would scold Gerald with a playful grin if she felt he wasn't taking proper care of himself. Even after working a full day at the café, she was a dynamo around the house, constantly cleaning.

Dan began taking over a lot of the cooking at the house because he was practicing for his job. Ever since the vacation trip to Key West, Magda was having Dan work in the kitchen with Frank, learning the fine art of high quality short order cooking.

And it *is* an art, according to Dan. Frank's eggs were always perfect, his pancakes were light and fluffy and specialty items like baked oatmeal were much sought after. Fruit and produce, which were used as garnish, were always fresh. Unlike many small cafes and diners, grease was never found on any of the plates Frank put up in the serving window.

Magda and her husband Tim were thinking of expanding the business by opening Dawn Café #2 across the Indian River in Sydney in a year or two. The plan was for her oldest daughter, Theresa, to manage the new place with her husband Frank as the cook. Dan was being groomed to replace Frank at the original Dawn Café. It would be up to him to see that there was no drop in the quality of the food when Frank left for the new restaurant. Dan felt the weight of this responsibility keenly. From what Gerald could tell from the taste of Dan's cooking, he was learning well.

## CHAPTER SIX: SINAPA

By the end of October, Gerald estimated that the garden was almost ready to plant.

This part of Florida has a year-round growing season, so planting in late October/early November was not impractical. This particular morning had dawned cool and dry. It felt as if the unrelenting summer heat was finally breaking and the beautiful days of Florida's fall and winter were coming.

Dan and Jackie had left for work, and Gerald was standing at the edge of the garden, sipping a cup of coffee. He was squinting with his failing vision at the ground. He was trying to visualize what he would plant and how the plants would be arranged. As he stood there, he got the distinct impression he wasn't alone. He glanced to his left at the sea grape forest, but nothing was there. He turned his attention back to the garden.

The mind that was observing Gerald was centuries old. When he was alive, his name had been Sinapa. He had belonged to the Ais Native American tribe that had inhabited these shores when the first Europeans showed up. When he was seventeen years old, his father and he had traveled to the Spanish fort at St. Augustine and traded dried fish to the soldiers there for knives and tobacco. Sinapa and his father did not know that one of the soldiers they dealt with was in the early stages of smallpox. Two months later Sinapa and his father were dead.

Like all souls, Sinapa had been pleasantly swept away into what he thought of as the Happy River. Sinapa was relieved to find that there were no alligators or sharks in this river, and even if there were, there was nothing for them to eat. He felt the weight of living inside of a body and dealing with human life fall away. Unlike being alive, time in the Happy River does not exist, so he does not know how long he enjoyed its peace, its completeness and its joy. All he was aware of was feeling safe, fulfilled and free.

At some point, however, he began to miss the land where he had lived. He longed for the sunshine and sand of the scrubland he had inhabited. He missed the daily surprises of dwelling next to the living giant that was the ocean. The Happy River is not a prison. Souls often leave its warm embrace to travel at will, knowing that they can always return to its safety. And that's what Sinapa had done. He had returned to the island where he had grown up and he found this funny looking square structure there, with the old man squinting at the ground.

He knew that Gerald had sensed his presence. Sinapa knew without knowing *how* he knew, that when some humans are getting near the time of their deaths, the curtain between the living and the after life begins to unravel for them. And so Sinapa knew without knowing *how* he knew, that the old white man would be dead soon. This saddened him, because he could tell the old man had the same reverence for this patch of ground that Sinapa did.

The wonderful thing about not having a body is that one can inhabit whatever one wanted. So Sinapa chose not only to be present *on* the patch of scrubland where he had grown up so many centuries ago. He chose to *become* the land on which the blockhouse sat. He infused the very ground with himself. He could feel every movement of each blue land crab in its hole. He witnessed the strange cohabitation of a large rat snake and Alley the gopher tortoise, sharing the same burrow. Whenever raccoons made it across the highway to forage for dead fish or turtle eggs on the beach, he watched their cautious, finicky progress through the sea grape forest.

He also became the air above the sea grape forest and the beach. He especially relished this new way of looking at his former home. When he had been alive, the greatest height he had achieved was climbing to the top of a tall pine tree that used to be where one of the homes in Flamingo Meadows now stood. From that vantage point, he could only see a few hundred yards in each direction, but he *could* see the inland shore of the Indian River in the distance. He spent a lot of his time in the air, watching and learning.

As he watched over the next few days, Sinapa observed that two other people lived in the strange square hut with the old white man: a young man and a beautiful girl. Sinapa fell in love with the girl. The white man's disease had taken his life when he was seventeen. He had not yet experienced falling in love with a woman. And so since he was destined to be an eternal teenager, he had become obsessed with Jackie. She looked so much like the girls with whom he had grown up, that loving her felt entirely natural.

Because his ego had died along with his body, he felt no jealousy toward Dan. He was pleased that the young white man was so protective of her. It did not take him long to realize that the young man and the girl shared the old man's love of the land. He sensed the unspoken fear all three of them were feeling about what would happen to the land when the old man was no longer around. Sinapa felt a strong kinship with the trio. So it was that, unbeknownst to Gerald, Dan, and Jackie, a fourth member joined their little family.

Sinapa shared their intense hatred of what was being done to the rest of the island. He despised the metal boxes with wheels that sped up and down the black ribbon that was highway A1A. He had tried to follow Dan and Jackie to work one day and simply could not stand the noise and pointless clutter of modern human existence. He especially disliked the large structures to the north that comprised Flamingo Meadows Estates. He found their tiny grass areas a ludicrous waste of water and space. He did not understand why they were not growing food on their land. It seemed ludicrous to him that such large structures sheltered so few people. It quickly became clear to Sinapa that the people in the large structures possessed no sense of tribe. The people in the small square structure did.

For his part, Gerald was aware that something in the background of his life had changed, but he wasn't sure what. One day after he returned from work, Dan drove the old man to a home improvement store where he purchased some sprouting tomato bushes, some sprouting eggplant, some cabbage seeds and some pole bean seeds.

The following morning, after Dan and Jackie had left for work, Gerald went down the stairs with his plants and seeds. He set them on a workbench he had constructed against the back of the house, and regarded his garden. The feeling he was no longer alone swept over him so suddenly and strongly, that he glanced quickly around, half expecting to see someone. No one was there, but then he knew how faulty his sight was becoming so he made the decision to explore his property just to be sure.

As he walked the familiar route he and Sadie had walked for years, the beauty of the place seemed to be especially vivid this morning. He was filled with such affection for *everything* he saw on that walk, that tears came to his eyes. The lumpy, twisted trunks of the sea grape trees were old friends. The carpet of large round, brown leaves seemed almost protective. Out on the beach, the tide was in, and the surf was high. He was forced to walk in the deep, soft sand above the tide line. The effort of doing so made him breathless

A sharp wind was coming off the water and as he looked out at the horizon, he could see one of those huge cruise ships—as big as several buildings—plowing its way south from Port Canaveral to the Caribbean. He paused at the north end of his property, to let his breathing return to normal. As he did so, he remembered videotape he had seen of the smog in such places a Los Angeles and Beijing. He was very grateful for the crystal clear air that filled his lungs.

When he reentered the sea grape forest, he noted with some satisfaction that the chain link fence Artie had erected to border Flamingo Estates was already starting to rust. Gerald grinned.

"Nature will always win in the end, Artie," he muttered to himself.

Halfway back to his house, his vision suddenly blurred and his arms felt as if they were made of lead. His mind went blank. He wasn't sure how long he had been leaning against a gnarled tree trunk but during that time, the image of a teenaged boy smiling fondly at him passed through his thoughts. When his mind cleared again, he had to take a few minutes to remember where he was and what he was doing. The TIA had only lasted a few seconds, but it shook Gerald to his core. He knew what it was, and he knew what he must do. He trudged back to his house and was conscious of being very tired. He struggled back up the stairs to his home. With fumbling fingers, he retrieved an address from his old metal card file box on the kitchen counter. He then dialed the number on the wall phone.

## CHAPTER SEVEN: HANRAHAN AND SONS

Old man Hanrahan elected to handle Gerald himself. The decision was prompted partially by affection and partially by guilt. Gerald, like Hanrahan himself, was "old Florida." Both had come here as young men from other parts of the country. The primitive beauty of the place had infected both of them and made them want to stay. Hanarahan's guilt came from the knowledge that he had made himself quite wealthy by working for the developers who were destroying that primitive beauty.

Since his two sons and his daughter had taken over the law practice, he had more time to play golf and reflect. As he walked the Sydney Beach Golf Course each day, he had become reacquainted with the fact that he lived in an exceptional place that was getting less and less exceptional each year thanks to overpopulation. People obviously wanted the "good life" in Florida and their version of that ideal meant destroying much of what made Florida exceptional in the first place.

The manicured lawns, like the one on which he used to play golf, leached chemical fertilizers into the Indian River Lagoon, causing algae blooms. These resulted in mass fish kills that one could smell some distance away. The chemical pollution also made any fish caught in the lagoon risky to eat. The paving of streets and driveways along with the concrete structures of buildings magnified the summer heat so that being outdoors in Sydney Beach on some summer days was like living in a convection oven. More and more of the beach areas—the main draw for tourists and new residents—were covered with litter.

The more time he had to think about what was happening, the more uncomfortable old man Hanrahan had become. As a weak form of protest, he had recently resigned his membership in the Sydney Beach Golf Club and had given his expensive clubs to his oldest son. And so it was that he was prepared to help Gerald in any way he could.

For his part, Gerald wanted to keep what he was doing a secret from Dan and Jackie. He knew they would be upset if they knew, and so he made sure to make his appointment with Hanrahan at a time when the two youngsters would be working at the café. The taxi ride from his house into Sydney Beach did not take long, but the fare seemed exorbitant to the old man. He was glad he had stashed enough cash away to cover it.

Hanrahan and Sons law offices were housed in a beautiful old Victorian home facing the Indian River Lagoon. The lovely receptionist walked him from what had been the living room, down a hallway into a refurbished library. Richard Hanrahan sat behind a large, highly polished mahogany desk.

"I haven't seen you since your wife passed away," Hanrahan said as he shook Gerald's hand. Gerald nodded and took a seat across the desk from the lawyer.

"I need help with a will," Gerald said. It was Hanrahan's turn to nod. He had suspected it was something like that.

The session with the lawyer lasted longer than Gerald had expected. When it was over, the beautiful receptionist phoned a cab for Gerald and he walked out of the building to find that it was late afternoon. He was afraid that Dan and Jackie would beat him home, and he would have some explaining to do. But he was able to keep his secret a little longer. By the time the two lovers got home, Gerald was already cooking pork chops for supper.

"You didn't plant yet?" Dan asked. Gerald shook his head.

"I brought them downstairs, but couldn't decide what to plant where," the old man explained. "If you don't mind, I'd rather you and Jackie do the planting." The two young people looked at each other nodding.

"Sure!" Jackie grinned. So after supper, while Gerald did the dishes, Dan and Jackie worked in the garden. Occasionally, as he was drying a dish or a pan, Gerald would step over to the kitchen window and watch them fondly. He wasn't the only one.

Sinapa could feel the richness of the soil that was receiving the seeds and sprouts. He could feel the potential life that had been carefully mixed in with the sand. He felt great affection for the white people that were treating his land with such loving care.

Because the Spanish had become such close allies of the Ais, the tribe members had been very suspicious of any Europeans that were not Spanish, even brutalizing and killing some shipwrecked sailors that fell into their hands. The Ais name for non-Spanish Europeans was "nickaleer." The white people in the little square structure were clearly nickaleer, but Sinapa could feel nothing but loyalty toward them.

He enjoyed watching the beautiful girl and the young man working in the garden. He particularly liked they way they laughed and talked together as they worked. Occasionally, Sinapa would find himself missing certain aspects of being alive, such as remembering how things tasted and felt. But the all-encompassing peace and pleasure that not having a body brought with it made these occasional twinges of loss fleeting. Listening to the boy and the girl bantering with each other brought back fond memories of playing with his brothers and sisters as children.

For *his* part, watching the two young lovers hard at work on a project they both enjoyed reminded Gerald of him and Sadie. Shared laughter with someone you love is a precious thing, and when that person is no longer with you, the shared laughter is what you miss the most. It was clear to Gerald that Dan and Jackie had something that would last.

They had decided to marry in January. It would be a simple ceremony on the beach by the blockhouse. Only the staff of the café would be invited. Dan and Jackie had been carefully saving portions of their paychecks to build up a fund with which to start their new lives. Jackie in her street wise, no-nonsense way had vetoed any plans for a large, expensive wedding.

"I can't see spending all that money for one afternoon of drama," she had told Dan. "Most of what we're saving should go toward starting our lives together."

This just caused Gerald to respect her even more. A justice of the peace had married him and Sadie, and their marriage had lasted for decades. He wondered what it would be like when his stuffy, pretentious younger brother and his wife met this new, no-bullshit daughter-in-law. He grinned at the thought of Jackie puncturing their inflated egos.

Gerald was not able to attend the wedding in person. On the morning of Thanksgiving Day, he simply did not wake up. Dan and Jackie held each other sobbing as the people from the mortuary carried the body down the back stairs to their waiting vehicle. For both of them, that old man was like this strange building—something they could count on for once in their lives. Gerald was a presence they could come home to; the loving parent neither of them had ever had. The sudden loss of him was like having their legs swept out from under them. But they had each other, and that would get them through this and what was to come.

There were no special preparations for a Thanksgiving meal. Neither Dan nor Jackie was in the mood to give thanks on this day.

That afternoon, Dan called his father in Boston. His mother answered the phone, and pretended happiness at hearing from him. Dan thanked her and asked to speak to his father.

"I'm not sending you any money," Rodney said when he took the phone from Betty.

"This is going to be easier than I thought," Dan mused to himself, feeling his anger rising.

"I don't want your goddamned money," Dan said. "I'm calling to tell you your brother died." There was silence for a moment at the other end. When his father spoke, there was no sadness in his voice, just the usual arrogance.

"So I guess you'll want some place to live now?" Rodney asked.

"All I want from you is your promise not to come to the memorial service or to my wedding," the younger man said and hung up.

Sinapa observed the old man's passing. He watched as a female spirit left the Happy River to be with the old fellow when he died. He watched their happy reunion, and saw her escort his spirit back to the Happy River. He sensed, however, that he would see them again. He had been slightly alarmed to observe that the nickaleer burned the bodies of their dead and spread the ashes in the surf. His tribe had buried their dead in mounds, constructed for that purpose. With the old man's passing, Sinapa was overcome with a sense of dread. This patch of ground had been protected by the old man's presence. Sinapa sensed that with the old fellow gone, his land was in danger.

## CHAPTER EIGHT: THE BATTLE FOR THE FOREST

One evening two weeks after the memorial service, Dan and Jackie were amazed to see a large, late model sedan pull into the driveway and park behind Dan's truck. The driver got out and quickly stepped to the back of the vehicle and helped a well-dressed elderly man exit the vehicle. Seeing that the old fellow might have difficulty climbing the stairs, Dan and Jackie went down to greet him. It was an unseasonably chilly day in early December, with a blustery wind coming off the Atlantic.

"Richard Hanrahan," the old man said, extending his hand. "You must be Chad and Jackie.

"His name is Dan now," Jackie said. Hanrahan grinned. "I see. But on legal documents, we have to use his full name."

"Legal documents?" Dan asked, a worried look on his face.

"I have your uncle's will here," Hanrahan said. "Is there a place we can talk?" Dan looked doubtful.

"We live upstairs," he responded. "The only thing downstairs is an empty garage." As usual, Jackie's quick mind came to the rescue.

"Why don't we just sit in your car?" she asked. "It will be warm and you won't have to climb the stairs." Hanrahan smiled again. He really liked this girl. With some relief the old man retreated to the warmth of the sedan. Dan sat next to him in the back seat, and Jackie sat next to the driver. Hanrahan opened the folder he had been carrying.

"Basically, Gerald left everything to you two," Hanrahan began. Again, Jackie's quick mind sliced through to the core.

"What exactly does that mean?" She asked.

"It means you two now own this house and this property," Hanrahan responded. "But there's a caveat."

"A caveat?" Dan asked, still in shock at his uncle's generosity.

"A catch," Hanrahan explained. "The will states that you cannot sell the property to developers. If you do, I am to take legal action to stop the sale." Dan and Jackie looked at each other and shrugged.

"Why would we want to sell?" She asked.

"You might not realize it," Hanrahan said. "But this property is literally worth millions of dollars."

After Hanrahan had left, Dan and Jackie went back upstairs and had supper. They were silent for most of the meal as each of them pondered this new development and what it meant. Afterwards, when the dishes were done, they put on jackets and went down the stairs for their evening walk. It being early December, they walked through the sea grape forest in twilight gloom, which seemed to match their mood. When they got to the southern boundary, Dan paused, letting his hand rest on the weathered wooden fence that bordered the Richard

Rackland Nature Preserve. He glanced at Jackie and she smiled and nodded.

When Dan and Jackie got to the northern end of the property, they thought a large bear was approaching them in the half-light. It was actually Artie Schenkler, dressed in an overcoat. He waved at them to get their attention. They stopped just short of the chain link fence to their left.

"Sorry to hear about Gerald," Schenkler began, breathing hard. Jackie could see there was no grief at all in the man's voice.

"What do you want?" She asked, frowning at the large glob of a man. Schenkler seemed momentarily thrown by this, but decided to continue. He decided to avoid the suspicious dark eyes of the girl and address Dan instead.

"Who owns the property now?" Artie asked.

"We do," Dan replied.

"Well, I represent some people who would like to buy the property," Schenkler explained. "We could make you a very wealthy man!"

"According to the will, we cannot sell the property to developers," Jackie interjected. Schenkler snorted derisively.

"Wills can be contested, sweetheart," The large man said, smirking condescendingly. "The people I work with can hire the best lawyers available. One way or another, we can free this property up for sale." Jackie stepped closer to Schenkler her face a mask of contempt.

"Bring it, *sweetheart*," She snapped and then turned toward the sea grape forest. Schenkler looked both stunned and angry. Dan grinned at him.

"You heard the lady," he said and followed Jackie. Artie watched the two young people disappear into the sea grape forest. The doctor had warned him about his blood pressure and at this point the large man felt he was about to explode. When he had heard about Gerald's death, he had figured the nephew would be more than willing to sell. He had not counted on the young man being as stubborn as his uncle. And where did that obnoxious little bitch get off challenging him? He turned and waddled back toward his house, cursing the deep sand he had to walk through and cursing tree-hugging bastards like Gerald. He would show them.

Later that night, Sinapa observed one of the metal boxes with wheels stop at the north end of Gerald's property. A lone figure stumbled out of the box and shouted at the box as it pulled away. Sinapa could smell the colored water the Spanish used to drink that drove men crazy.

The man who had exited the car stood wavering in apparent confusion in the roadside grass. He was mumbling incoherently to himself. In the moonlight, Sinapa could observe that the man's skin and eyes looked yellow. He could feel the life rapidly ebbing from the man. The ragged creature lurched into the sea grape trees and collapsed on the ground.

Six hours later, at first light, Harvey and his brother in law Martin were unloading the bulldozer from the flatbed truck parked on the roadside grass. Both of them were hung-over, but they simply could not pass up this job. That asshole Schenkler had promised them two thousand apiece for clearing some sea grape trees on someone else's land.

Harvey and Martin had done this kind of thing before. It was a common ploy used by developers in the area who had a lot of financial backing. They would bulldoze part of a property they wanted, and claim it was a simple mistake. If the property owner sued, the developers had the resources to either defeat the suit or keep it tied up in court indefinitely. In most cases, the property owner settled out of court for a generous payoff and the developer got the property he wanted. The money to be made from the land far outweighed the cost of grabbing it.

When the dozer was unloaded, Harvey lined it up with the edge of the chain link fence and attacked the nearest sea grape tree. He pushed at the trunk until part of the root system worked loose and tilted up. He would then position the edge of the blade under the roots and push the tree over. No sooner had he knocked over the first tree than the rising sun, filtering through the tree trunks, hit him square in the face. His alcohol poisoned brain screamed in pain at the intrusion of bright light. Harvey fished in his pocket for his work sunglasses. He prided himself on how dark they were.

"Practically welder's glasses," he used to brag to coworkers. His eyes now carefully shielded against the annoying sun, he continued clearing. Each time he backed the dozer up, he noted with some irritation that his lazy brother in law was sitting in the cab of the flatbed, playing with his cell phone.

"Worthless as tits on a boar hog," Harvey muttered to himself.

He had destroyed about a ten-yard square patch of trees when a pretty dark haired girl and very large young man appeared in the trees in front of him, hollering at him furiously. He shut down the dozer and prepared to go into his "Gosh-I-didn't-realize-this-was-the-wrong-property" act, when he heard Martin screaming incoherently behind him. His brother in law was so hysterical that it silenced the young man and woman. Turning in his seat, Harvey saw Martin pointing at what he at first thought was a pile of rags lying in one of the track prints of the dozer. Then he saw the blood and the head.

## CHAPTER NINE: MELVYN'S MARTYRDOM

The dead man had no identification on him other than a tattoo on one arm that said, "MELVYN." The body was kept in the county morgue for several weeks but was never claimed by any next of kin. Harvey and his brother in law were arrested on charges of trespassing and negligent homicide. They quickly told sheriff's deputies that they had been hired by Artie Schenkler to illegally begin clearing land he didn't own. The local papers got hold of the story and ran pictures of the cloth-covered body lying in the track of the bulldozer. The story attracted the attention of the nationwide television networks, and prompted an angry backlash against developers in Florida.

As a result of this publicity, the Flamingo Meadows development became a symbol of greed all over the country. Late night talk show hosts incorporated Flamingo Meadows into their monologues as a symbol of hilariously inept criminal activity. In the face of this blizzard of public hostility, most of the residents of the development put their homes up for sale and quietly moved away. Artie Schenkler's fiefdom was falling apart and the associates in his real estate consortium abandoned him. His obesity and his high blood pressure provided blessed relief from his almost daily court appearances, however. He died suddenly of cardiac arrest as he was climbing the steps to the Sydney County Courthouse one more time.

Dan and Jackie moved their wedding date up to mid-December. They realized that they needed to act quickly as a couple if they were going to end all future designs on Gerald's property. Sinapa observed the strange little gathering on the beach and understood it was some kind of ceremony. The young man and young woman were apparently being joined. A small gathering of people witnessed the event. The person performing the ceremony was an older woman dressed in robes of some kind.

Two weeks later, Dan, Jackie and another man were sitting in Hanrahan's office in Sydney Beach. Dennis Rackland was nothing like Dan had expected. He was young, suntanned, dressed in shorts and a Hawaiian shirt. His mustache and beard were trimmed in such a way that he seemed to have a permanent smile on his face.

"It's called a conservation easement," Hanrahan was explaining. "Basically, it means that you sell all rights to your property to the Richard Rackland Nature Preserve, but you are allowed to place any stipulations on that sale that you want."

"Like what?" Jackie asked.

"Well, for example if you wanted to still live on the property," Hanrahan explained. Jackie and Dan looked at each other and nodded.

"We do," They chorused.

"Well then," Hanrahan began, leaning forward in his armchair, his elbows resting on the desk and his hands clasped together. "That just leaves the job of negotiating." Jackie stood suddenly as if she had been waiting for a cue, and handed a paper across the desk to Hanrahan.

"We had the property appraised," she said. "According to this report, it is worth at least 1.7 million dollars." Dennis Rackland sat up straight in his chair and started to speak, but Jackie waved him off. "We have decided to sell the property to the Rackland Nature Preserve for three hundred thousand dollars." Hanrahan looked at Rackland, who leaned back in his chair. The lawyer could see the young man was doing some quick calculating. Finally Rackland spoke.

"You wouldn't consider donating the land?" He asked.

"We thought of that at first," Dan replied. "But as we looked around the house, we could see that it needed a lot of work." Dan shrugged slightly. "We are not rich people, and we want to stay in Uncle Gerald's house for now, but it's going to take some remodeling to bring it up to code."

"It's the best home Dan and I have ever known," Jackie said, her voice trembling with emotion. "Uncle Gerald was the heart and soul of that home and we can't bear the thought of living anywhere else." Hanrahan felt the need to speak up.

"Can the Rackland Foundation afford that price?" He asked Dennis. The young man thought for a moment then nodded in resignation.

"I would have to get it approved by the board but yes, I think they would be willing to spend that amount of money to almost double the size of the preserve."

A month later, a crew of volunteers from the Rackland Foundation spent a morning destroying the fence separating the preserve from Gerald's former property. They spent the afternoon constructing a new fence that paralleled the chain link fence bordering Flamingo Meadows. The following day, the same crew returned and fenced in the area around the blockhouse, including the garden, which was showing signs of flourishing.

Over the next few years, Dan and Jackie would be able to look out of their windows and see visitors to the preserve walking the same sandy path that Gerald and Sadie had walked. Their favorite time of day however was in the evening when the gates of the preserve were locked. They would retrace the walk they had done with Gerald each day. Like him, they always found something remarkable to look at and talk about.

For his part, Sinapa could feel the land sigh in relief. When he was alive, he had been taught that everything has a spirit—every rock, every tree, every animal. In the afterlife, he had found this to be true, and so he felt the spirits of the sea grapes, the tortoises, even the sand, sense that they were safe from those who were not aware of them. Nickaleers seemed especially blind and deaf to the existence of these life forces around them, but Sinapa took satisfaction in knowing that the young man and woman walking the land of his home appreciated all they saw and touched.

Now that it owned the property, the Rackland Foundation took a few unusual and very dramatic steps to bring home its message about preserving the wild environment of the barrier island. First, it paid for the cremation of Melvyn's body. In a small, quiet ceremony attended by volunteers as well as Dan and Jackie, the ashes were mixed in the sand of the torn up patch of land where he had died. Then the foundation purchased the bulldozer that had killed him and parked it in the middle of the torn up sea grape trees. Volunteers planted new trees around the dozer. The Foundation christened the area "Melvyn's Grove." A bench and an explanatory plaque were installed, explaining the story of Melvyn's unwitting martyrdom for the cause of conservation.

Over the years, as the dozer rusted away, the sea grape trees would grow. It would be clear evidence of what Gerald had said months before: "Nature always wins in the end."


THE END

# DAISY AND THE EXISTENTIAL GOAT

## CHAPTER ONE: ARTHUR

Daisy first met Arthur on one of the spoil islands in the Indian River. When the boating channel was dredged in the 1930's, the mud from the bottom was dumped into large mounds on the western side of the channel. These mounds became islands in the shallow, brackish waterway. Within a few years they were covered with trees, palmettoes and jungle.

Daisy was plump, blonde, blue-eyed, and she wore glasses. She had convinced herself, however that she was actually Native American. Because she lived on the Atlantic coast of central Florida, it was only natural that she thought of herself as a Seminole. She had gone online to look up Native American girl names and picked the appellation "Catori." It meant *spirit*, and it appealed to her. She ignored the fact that the name was Hopi in origin and not Seminole.

On this beautiful Florida morning in November, she had rented a kayak from

Captain Eddie's Fun Port in the town of St. Ignacio. Carrying herself like the Seminole princess she imagined herself to be, she paddled out to a spoil island that stood by itself. There was no wind and so the paddling didn't take a lot out of her. In her happily fractured mind, this was an obvious omen that the gods were clearing her path. When she got to the island, she dragged the plastic kayak ashore and tied it to a tree stump at the water's edge.

She stepped into the shade of the pine trees that coated the island and looked back at the land. The shore looked to be a half-mile away and she realized she could not be seen from it. Laughing, she took off her bathing suit and the loose-fitting sundress that had covered it. Leaving her sandals on, she stood chubby and naked under the pines.

First, she listened. The only sounds were the wind in the pines and the soft lapping of wavelets against the shore. The thrill of being naked and alone swept over her, causing her to feel giddy and more than a little horny. She took a deep breath of the pine-scented air and started exploring her realm.

She had landed on the narrower, northern end of the island and the land extended to the south for a quarter of a mile in the shape of a slipper. As she walked south on the carpet of pine needles, she relished the thought that like her imagined Native American ancestors, she was moving silently through the forest. She was surprised to find that the island possessed a small hill at the southern end. She climbed the fifteen-foot high knoll with some difficulty. The pine needles were slippery and her sandals did not offer much traction. She arrived at the top, panting with droplets of sweat trickling down between her large breasts. That's when she met Arthur.

Lying at the top of the hill was a large goat, watching her. Most of his coat was off white, with a streak of black running down the middle of his back, which enlarged to a kind of dark bib below his face. Two large gray horns crowned the intelligent eyes.

"You've got to get me off this island," the goat said. His lips didn't move, but Daisy/Catori could hear him clearly in her mind.

"How did you get here?" She asked. Arthur was amazed by the fact that she did not seem alarmed at all. Apparently a sentient, communicative goat was an expected part of her reality. He was intrigued.

"Some teenaged boys stole me from the farm where I lived and brought me here as a joke," Arthur explained. "I believe their plan was to return the next day with friends and barbecue me." Arthur waggled his horns in disgust. "That was three days ago. I've run out of what little grass there was to eat, and all the mud puddles have dried up."

"Why didn't you just swim back to the shore?" Daisy asked.

"Are you crazy?" Arthur asked incredulously. "There are bull sharks in this lagoon!"

"DON 'T CALL ME CRAZY!" Daisy exploded. "PEOPLE ARE ALWAYS CALLING ME CRAZY AND I'M NOT!" She paused trying to regain control. When she spoke again her voice was making an attempt at composure. "I'm brilliant and I don't do things like everyone else," she explained.

"But you're naked and you're talking to a goat," Arthur pointed out. He could see immediately this was a mistake. The girl's face got red again.

"DO YOU WANT TO GET OFF THIS ISLAND OR NOT?" She shouted. Arthur nodded his horns apologetically.

"Forgive me," he said quietly. "Your reality is your reality, and it's not my place to judge."

Arthur had some difficulty getting into the kayak. His hooves kept slipping on the smooth plastic. At Daisy's suggestion he did not try to stand for the voyage back to the shore. Instead he decided to lie down in front of her.

"Where should we go?" Daisy asked as she shoved the craft off the sand of the island and into the four-foot deep water.

"For now, let's just head toward land," Arthur responded. Once again, the gods seemed to be favoring Daisy's quest. A following breeze had sprung up. Coming out of the east, it was pushing her gently toward the shore. Once again, the gods seemed to be favoring her. When they were about twenty yards away from the muddy bank, she turned north and they paddled parallel to it. To their surprise, they came to a half-mile stretch of shoreline that appeared to be empty of all development except for a multi-storied shell of a building that was clearly abandoned.

"Here!" Arthur exclaimed in her mind. "Let me off here!"

"Calm down," Daisy ordered. "I'm looking for a safe place to land." Arthur could see her problem. In front of the abandoned building the shore presented a barrier of jagged rusting metal, broken boards, and shattered concrete chunks with rusting rods of rebar sticking out of them.

"This place must have been under construction when the 2004 hurricanes hit," Daisy surmised. "The storm surge must have gutted it."

Daisy spotted an opening in the debris about four feet wide. Dipping the left paddle deeply into the water, she successfully turned the kayak sharply. The water became very shallow and she poled her way into the narrow slot. Arthur excitedly got to his feet and promptly slipped off the smooth plastic into the water, but it was only a couple of inches deep and he quickly scrambled ashore. Daisy tied the craft to a piece of rebar and followed him.

Arthur raised his snout and sniffed the air then he took off running around the building to the other side. Daisy followed him, being careful to look for snakes in the weeds and tall grass. When she got around the building, she found Arthur standing in what was once a decorative fountain. The tiled enclosure was surrounded by a low wall and contained about six inches of scummy looking rainwater. Arthur was drinking thirstily.

"How can you drink that crap?" Daisy asked, frowning in revulsion.

"Great immune system," Arthur replied without pausing for breath. When he had slaked his thirst, Arthur jumped up on the wall of the fountain and surveyed his surroundings.

"This is perfect!" The goat exclaimed. They were standing in what had once been intended as a landscaped area in front of the building. A lawn had been planted, along with decorative flowering bushes, both of which now grew wonderfully out of control.

"There's plenty of food, and a water supply that gets refilled with each rain!" Arthur said excitedly. "And best of all, old man Winslow is not here to pen me up!" Then the goat dropped its head in momentary regret. "I do miss the nannies, however."

"The nannies?" Daisy asked.

"Female goats. My job was to get them pregnant," The horizontal pupils in Arthur's eyes looked wistful for a moment. "I really *liked* my job." Always the romantic, Daisy had to ask.

"Was there one nanny you liked best?" Arthur sighed, looking off into the distance.

"Clarissa," He said lovingly. "She was beautiful. She was an alpine like me, but she was a lovely light brown with white markings, and she had these adorable black legs. It looked like she was wearing stockings." Arthur waggled his head as if to shake the memory and hopped down from the wall of the fountain. He sauntered over to an area of tall grass and began munching.

"I'm sorry," He apologized. "But I'm really hungry."

"That's okay," Daisy said. "I've got to get this kayak back to Captain Eddie's. Glad you're okay now." She turned to leave but Arthur looked up at her from his feeding.

"What is your name?" The goat asked.

"My white name is Daisy," She answered. "But my Indian name is Catori." Arthur thought of pointing out the obvious, but wisely elected not to.

"I am Arthur. You saved my life, Daisy/Catori," Arthur said. "If you ever need my help, I'm here."

## CHAPTER TWO: DAISY, MOLLIE, AND MISTER STODDARD

Old man Stoddard owned the last non-chain supermarket in St. Ignacio. Over the decades, he had built up a steady clientele made up mostly of locals. He had made it a point to only hire long-time residents of St. Ignacio as employees. He had also earned the loyalty of the community by quietly starting a tab program for those on limited incomes, often widows living on tiny pensions.

He would allow each of them to run a tab during the month and then when the pension checks came in, the tab would be paid off. This allowed them to keep some pocket money during the month for bus fares, etc. He would keep track of the tabs himself and knew the financial circumstances of each customer. If a customer were in danger of charging too much, he would find a way to courteously warn them of this in private.

Mollie, Daisy's mother, had worked for him for decades, ever since the worthless man she had married deserted her and her child. Mollie was a good-looking woman when she was younger and Stoddard had taken her as his mistress. People in the town, including Mrs. Stoddard, had suspected as much. But the same small town loyalty that had been the foundation of the market's success insured that the affair would simply be winked at in private. Eventually, age and impotence had altered Stoddard's relationship with Mollie to that of a loving friend.

He took a particular interest in Mollie's struggles with her very different little girl. As soon as the youngster was able to talk, it became clear that she was not like anyone else. When Daisy was five Stoddard was visiting her mother at their tiny apartment when he saw something remarkable. While he was there, Daisy dumped a plastic container of alphabet blocks out on the living room floor. She looked at the array for a moment and then went into the kitchen to get a glass of juice. Her mother winked at Mr. Stoddard and asked the girl in the kitchen, "Daisy, which blocks are on the floor in here?"

Without leaving the kitchen, or even looking in the direction of the living room, the little girl proceeded to name every single block that had spilled onto the floor. Stoddard was dumfounded and never forgot the incident. When Daisy graduated from high school, he realized that her mother's lack of resources and Daisy's strange behavior might cancel any hope of going to college. But he wisely understood that she would be ideal for stocking the shelves in his store and keeping track of inventory. He was right.

This kept her behind the scenes in the operation and so her flights of fancy would not estrange the customers. He needn't have worried, however. Small towns like St. Ignacio have a way of including their local odd characters in the daily life of the community. It seemed that everybody in the village knew of Daisy's eccentricities just as they had knows of Mr. Stoddard's liaison with her mother. They accepted her as she was. Stoddard had judged correctly about Daisy. She turned out to be a hard and consistent worker like her mother and she was soon earning enough to support her self.

It had worried her mother when Daisy rented her own little apartment a block away from the market. Mollie wasn't sure if Daisy could handle living alone. That was a year ago, and so far Daisy seemed to be adjusting well to life on her own.

Although the grownups in St. Ignacio had accepted Daisy as she was some of the people her age were not as nice. It was from them that she had been taunted as "crazy." One day, years earlier, when she had come home from school crying, Mollie sat her down and listened to the litany of insults Daisy had received.

"They're afraid of you, darlin', " Her mother said quietly.

"Why?" Daisy asked, sniffling.

"Because you are brilliant and you don't do things like everyone else," Mollie had replied. "That combination scares the shit out of them."

Daisy had to laugh through her sniffles. Her mantra after that was:
"I'm brilliant.
I don't do things like everyone else.
That scares the shit out of people.
That's their problem."

In stressful situations, she would say this to herself over and over. It worked. Eventually, she began to suspect that someone or something unseen was hearing the whispered prayer. This Accepting Presence was as real to her as the wind and she took great comfort from it. In her fascination with Native American culture, she sometimes fancied the Accepting Presence was actually several entities infusing all of nature. At other times however, she sensed a single Benevolent Friend. At any rate, as she looked about her at the relative grimness with which most people seemed to trudge through their lives, she realized that her reality was much more pleasant than theirs. She saw no reason to change.

In fact it was her perceived difference from other people that had prompted her to embrace her non-existent Native American heritage. She read somewhere that among tribes living on the Great Plains in the old west, people whom the white world might label insane were respected members of the community. The belief was that such people were in touch with the spirits of nature and so their attention was fractured. It was believed that these people were valuable as conduits for communicating with the gods.

It was this accepting spirit that had won Daisy's heart. And so, at the age of nineteen, she faced the rest of her life with complete optimism. In her mind, she now had a mantra to live by and a people to identify with.

But what would her future be? Whereas her mother worried over this question, Daisy did not. She actually enjoyed her job at the market, and she was comfortable in her little apartment. Arthur had told her that her reality was hers alone and no one should judge it. This made sense to her, and although she did not know where the future would lead, she was sure that it would be wonderful.

Her mother still quietly fretted about her strange daughter, however. Mollie was surprised and pleased by Daisy's seemingly smooth transition to adulthood. Whenever she visited Daisy's tiny efficiency apartment, she was continually amazed at how sparsely furnished it was. There was no television set no radio and only one clock. There were, however, books everywhere on a variety of subjects. Whereas most young single women her age might be indulging in romance novels or fashion magazines, Daisy seemed obsessed with books about the natural world and Native American culture.

There were also no signs in Daisy's apartment of any interest in the opposite sex.

Although her daughter was a little heavy, she was naturally pretty and kept her long hair clean and healthy. There was no makeup in the bathroom, not even a hair dryer. When Daisy was a little girl, Mollie worried that her daughter would be incapable of living on her own. Now, she worried that Daisy would live her *entire life* alone. The prospect did not seem to dim Daisy's optimism, however.

"Are you dating anyone?" Mollie had asked her during one visit.

"God, no!" Daisy had responded. "Men are kind of stupid," the girl had explained.

"What about women?" Mollie asked, almost afraid of the answer. Daisy shook her head.

"'I'm not that way, Mom."

"Well, what about girls as just friends?"

"The ones I have met are no better than the men," Daisy smirked. "They're all obsessed with how they look. That crap bores me stiff."

"Well, what do you spend your paychecks on, darlin'?" Mollie asked her. "I know rent, electricity and food don't take up all of it." Daisy shrugged.

"Oh, I just save what I don't need," her daughter responded.

"What are you saving for?" Daisy smiled dreamily.

"I don't know right now, but I will know when it happens. I feel like something wonderful is coming."

## CHAPTER THREE: ANGUS

Angus Merrick loved his job. He couldn't believe his luck when Mr. Bronstien had hired him to paddle about the Indian River Lagoon taking water samples, and checking on the environments of the spoil islands. He thoroughly enjoyed the solitude and being out in the open. He couldn't believe someone actually paid him to do this.

One day, two years earlier, Angus's father had come to Bronstien and asked him if there was any possible employment for his socially awkward, reclusive son. Mr. Merrick was an engineer at one of the large companies in the Sydney area that worked on hush-hush contracts for the Defense Department. Bronstien had known the man since high school and agreed to see what he could do.

"All he wants to do is paddle around the area in his canoe," the man complained. "When he's not doing that, he is working out with weights or reading a book about science or zoology." The man was obviously at his wit's end. "He's twenty one years old, and I don't think he's going to be able to support himself."

Bronstien's ears had perked up when he heard the young man was an experienced canoeist and was apparently in good physical condition. As part of his job, Bronstein was supposed to row out to the spoil islands frequently to check on bird populations, record abuse from human visitors, and to take water samples at various locations on the river. His supervisors emphasized rowing as the preferred method of transportation to avoid disturbing nesting birds with the sound of a motor. Bronstien had gotten fat and out of shape and had come to dread these expeditions.

The next day, Mr. Merrick had brought Angus to meet Bronstien at his office on the shore of the lagoon. The ranger was pleased to see that the young man looked extremely physically fit. When he shook hands with Angus, the younger man refused to meet his gaze, but stared at his shoes instead.

On that first day, Bronstien showed the young man the route he would take, getting to the eight spoil islands for which the ranger was responsible. Angus rowed his canoe and Bronstien sat in the back, occasionally dipping his paddle in to steer. If Angus felt any additional burden by having the large man in the canoe, he didn't show it, but rowed smoothly and mechanically.

At each island, the ranger showed the young man how to look for new birds' nests, and how to make notes on signs of human destruction. He showed Angus how to take water samples, label them, and how to store them to be returned for analysis.

Periodically on the outing, Bronstein would have Angus repeat what he had just learned. Each time, the young man would repeat word for word in a flat almost mechanical voice, everything Bronstien had said. To the older man's consternation, Angus also included times Bronstein had cursed when he was bitten by mosquitoes. To the ranger, it was like talking into tape recorder with muscles.

And so Angus's career as an unofficial park ranger began. Bronstein paid him cash under the table, and felt it was money well spent. The boy was making Bronstien look good to his superiors. Angus's water samples were frequent and informative. The young man also went beyond his duties by picking up litter on the islands and stashing it in garbage bags he brought with him. He also became familiar with those areas of the lagoon where fertilizer runoff from farms and lawns was most likely to cause algae blooms and fish kills. These, he would point out on a map for Bronstien.

Angus was only supposed to do the route a couple of times each week, but he was on the water nearly every day. He felt very protective of what he saw as his little corner of the natural world. To him, the ospreys, dolphins and other creatures he encountered were like family and were under his protection, even the bull sharks. The river and the islands always presented him with something that fascinated him. He could not imagine how much that aspect of his job would suddenly grow.

On this particular day, he reached the farthest island late in the morning. He dragged the canoe onto the wet sand of the eastern shore and picked up an empty garbage bag to bring with him. He walked quietly, studying the trees above him, looking for new nests. He had proceeded about ten yards into the forest when he saw her.

A naked girl with blonde hair and glasses had just spread a blanket under the trees and was opening a picnic basket. The sight of her made him hard and in the past, this would have made him extremely uncomfortable. But this time a feeling he had never experienced before accompanied the lust. He was overwhelmed with the sensation that he was somehow *supposed* to be here with her. The rational part of his mind fought against the feeling sweeping over him. After all, he *did* have a duty to perform.

"You shouldn't be here," He said in his mechanical voice. The girl jumped to her feet at the sound, but when she saw him, she smiled as if she had been expecting him.

"I belong here," She answered, smiling at him. She seemed totally unconcerned that she was naked and meeting a stranger. Unaware of what he was doing, Angus walked up to the edge of the blanket.

"You're naked," He said, unable to take his eyes off of her breasts and her incredible skin.

"You're not," The girl replied, stepping toward him on the blanket. "You should try it. It really feels good."

"I'm not supposed to be naked," Angus protested, still transfixed by her.

"Who says?" The girl asked. Now she was inches away.

"I don't remember," Angus replied. The girl took his hand and placed it on her breast.

"See?" She murmured. "It feels good."

"It feels good," Angus echoed. The girl gently undid his belt buckle. Angus sensed that, like him, the girl was obeying something unseen. Angus found he could not take his hand away from her skin.

"I'm a Seminole princess," the girl whispered, gently sliding her hand under his tee shirt and along the muscles of his abdomen. "My name is Catori."

"Seminoles don't have blonde hair," Angus objected weakly. He was breathing heavily now. "They have black hair like me."

"Are you a Seminole?" She whispered, lifting his tee shirt and kissing his chest. At that moment, Angus wished very much that he *was* a Seminole.

"I'm not sure," he replied cautiously. The girl pressed herself against him and brushed her hands along his face.

"Well, as a Seminole princess," She said softly. "I decree that you are a Seminole prince."

What happened next would seem in both of their memories like a wonderful blur. There was a lot of fumbling and moaning as they locked their mouths together. At one point, Daisy panted, "I've seen pictures. You put it there." Soon the fumbling disappeared and a delicious rhythm swept over both of them, which lead to a shared, sweet agony.

When it was over, they lay panting, looking into each other's eyes. Angus was smiling for the first time since she had met him.

"I don't like people," he explained. "But I like you."

"You are my micco," Daisy crooned, stroking his cheek.

"What is that?" Angus asked, wondering if his newfound love was insulting him.

"It's Seminole for chief," Daisy explained, smiling happily.

"You are my chief and I am your princess. I knew you would come," She grinned.

"How did you know? He asked.

"Something told me that a wonderful thing would happen," she answered. "I don't know how I knew it would happen. I just *knew* it would." She looked at Angus, smiling. "What made *you* come here today?" She asked.

"It's my job," Angus explained.

"What made you make love to me?" She asked teasingly.

"I don't know," The young man answered. "I don't do things like this." He thought for a moment, then blurted: "It just seemed right." The girl swept her fingers across his cheek fondly.

"Exactly my love," she said. "Exactly."


## CHAPTER FOUR: RESCUE

On the map in Bronstien's office the island was simply labeled #78. Daisy began referring to the island as I.O.W.A. (Island Of Wonderful Adventure). Angus's linear mind had a great deal of trouble with this at first. Flights of fancy were not part of his makeup. But the same force that had impelled him to lose his virginity to this strange and beautiful creature reassured him that her eccentricities were more than worth dealing with. When he was with her, everything seemed somehow magical and more vivid than usual.

For her part, Daisy accepted Angus's pedantic addiction to logic. She even took some reassurance from the fact that whatever occurred she could rely on him to point out the most reasonable path to take. She might not choose to follow that path, but it made her feel safe to know that at least one of them was grounded in what the rest of the world thought of as reality. Their relationship quickly settled into a comfortable emotional symbiosis: each supplied the other with something missing.

Whenever their work schedules allowed, Angus would paddle his canoe to the municipal pier in downtown St. Ignacio and pick up Daisy there. She would always be wearing her sun dress and carrying a picnic basket. They would then paddle together out to the Island of Wonderful Adventures. There, they would make love under the pine trees. Over the weeks, the fumbling went away and their bodies responded joyfully to each other. Then they would have lunch, enjoy long conversations and make love some more.

When the mild Florida winter finally set in, she coaxed Angus to come to her tiny apartment instead. He was not comfortable with this change at first, but as was to characterize their relationship for years to come, he followed her lead in faith. Before visiting her apartment the first time, Angus told his parents that he had a girlfriend and that he was going to spend the night with her.

His parents had spent his twenty-one years protecting him from the world as much as possible. Like Mollie, they had realized very quickly that their son was not like other people, and they worried constantly about his safety. So it was not surprising that they greeted this news with a great deal of concern.

"You have a girlfriend?" Mr. Merrick asked, unable to hide the disbelief in his voice.

"Her name is Daisy," Angus replied, smiling fondly. That smile spoke volumes to his parents. In their two decades of raising Angus they had seen him smile no more than a couple dozen times. His usual facial expression was intense concentration, as if he was listening to complicated instructions from within his own mind.

"What does she do for a living?" Mrs. Merrick asked.

"She works at Stoddard's Market," Angus replied. "She's really good with numbers," He added proudly.

"How did you meet her?" The father asked.

"She was having a picnic on island #78," Angus said. Again, a smile crossed his face. "She likes to call it I.O.W.A."

"Iowa?" Mr. Merrick asked. Angus's smile grew broader.

"Island Of Wonderful Adventures," Angus explained.

After their son had left, Mr. and Mrs. Merrick looked at each other in stunned silence for a few moments.

"Should we do anything?" Mrs. Merrick asked, a worried look on her face.

"What should we do?" Mr. Merrick replied. "He's twenty-one." He sighed. "The truth is, we have no real control over him."

Both of them were silent again as they wondered what kind of girl would be attracted to their very strange boy.

The next morning, as Angus and Daisy lay together on her bed, she told him: "I want to buy a goat." Angus looked about the tiny apartment.

"You can't keep a goat here," he said.

"I won't keep it here," She responded. "It's for a friend." Angus felt jealousy for the first time in his life.

"Is your friend a man?" He asked. Daisy smiled at the suspicion in her lover's voice. She felt a little thrill of pleasure that this big, handsome fellow was capable of being possessive of her. She grinned into Angus's eyes.

"No, silly," She teased. "My friend is a goat named Arthur." Angus was quiet for a few moments, apparently trying to wrap his mind around this revelation.

"You are friends with a goat named Arthur." It wasn't a question. Angus seemed to be laying the statement out to make sure he had heard correctly.

"Yes," Daisy answered. "And it's time you met him."

Later that day, Daisy and Angus paddled his canoe to the undeveloped land on the shoreline. Angus had noticed the abandoned building before in his travels, but had never gone ashore there. Daisy directed him to the narrow opening in the debris and they scrambled ashore. They found Arthur lying in the sun on what had been intended as the lawn of the failed condo development. It was clear to Daisy that Arthur had succeeded in cropping much of the grass on which he lay. The goat regarded Angus suspiciously.

"Who is this?" Arthur asked.

"This is Angus," Daisy replied. "He is my lover."

"Goats can't talk," Angus said mechanically.

"Arthur talks to me," Daisy explained.

"I don't hear anything," Angus said. "And his lips didn't move."

"He talks with his mind," Daisy answered, a slight note of impatience in her voice. Arthur watched Angus look at him and then back to Daisy. He saw the young man shrug. Apparently the young man had decided that there is something sacred in Daisy's delusions; something truly beautiful that goes beyond facts.

"I see," Angus said simply. Arthur nodded his horns at Daisy.

"He gets you," The goat said. "Keep him."

"I plan to," Daisy said. "But we're here today to help *you*. I need you to tell me how to get to Winslow's farm."

Three days later, Daisy took money out of her savings. It was Angus's day off, so they rented a van and drove out into the farming country west of town. Following Arthur's directions, Daisy drove them to Winslow's farm near the small town of Oscar. As Arthur had predicted, Winslow was already drunk, even though it was still morning.

"Oh sure," Winslow said when he heard their request. "I got lots of goats for sale." He spat on the ground in disgust. "They're all nannies, though and none of them are producing milk. Someone stole my buck a few weeks back, and none of them is pregnant." Daisy told the man that she simply wanted a goat for a friend to keep as a pet. Winslow scratched his head in puzzlement.

"I've heard of keeping goats to milk or fatten up for slaughter, but I've never heard of anyone keeping them as a pet!" He guffawed loudly and belched. "I mean...they ain't very bright. All they do is eat and shit!" He guffawed and belched again.

"My friend is kind of crazy," Daisy said. "But she would really appreciate this." Winslow shrugged and led them into a pen containing about eight goats. Daisy spotted Clarissa right away. She was the only one with black stockings.

"I want that one," She said, pointing at Clarissa.

"That's one of my best," Winslow said. "I can't ask for less than five hundred dollars for her."

"Three hundred and no more," Daisy said firmly.

"Are you crazy?" Winslow objected. He was about to say more when the quiet young man who accompanied the girl stepped forward.

"Do not call her crazy," Angus said in his mechanical voice, which was so out of place in this situation it seemed even more sinister and threatening. Winslow threw up his hands in resignation. "Okay! Okay! I meant no offense! Three hundred it is!"

While Daisy fished the bills out of her purse, Angus picked the goat up and carried it to the rental van. Clarissa was amazingly docile as he did this. The lovers drove their passenger back into St. Ignacio and proceeded up highway one. They came to the patch of vacant land where the failed condo development was located. Angus pulled the van over to the side of the road and parked.

"We shouldn't let people see us do this," He explained.

"I know," Daisy answered. They must have sat in the van for a half hour until a long enough break in the traffic occurred. They jumped out of the van and Angus threw open the side door and scooped Clarissa into his arms. Seconds later, the two humans and the goat had disappeared into the pines and palmettos beside the road.

The strip of jungle that masked the vacant land from the highway was about thirty yards wide. Daisy led the way, carefully picking her way around the palmetto thickets, her eyes studying the ground in front of her for snakes. Angus followed, carrying the goat. When they finally broke out into the open, he set the goat down. Clarissa raised her snout to the air and then galloped happily off in the direction of the abandoned building. Daisy and Angus followed.

It was the first time they had approached the ruin from the highway side and the full impact of the place hit them. They found themselves walking through what could be described as a "failed paradise." There were paved, cracked driveways with weeds growing out of the cracks. Ornamental trees such as poincianas and mimosas were sprinkled about the landscape. As they drew near the house, they could clearly see how Arthur was keeping the overgrown lawn under control. He and Clarissa were hopping, prancing and dancing around each other in happiness.

"Will this place ever be developed?" Daisy asked Angus as they watched the joyful reunion of the goats.

"Mr. Bronstien says no," Angus replied. "It's being used as a barrier to protect the highway from storm surges." He pointed at the empty, four-story shell of building. "Anything built here will be destroyed like that place." Daisy smiled, knowing that her friend Arthur and his love would be safe for the time being.


## CHAPTER FIVE: MOLLIE MEETS ANGUS


Mollie first became aware of Angus when she visited her daughter's apartment one morning and found him in bed with Daisy. Two things struck her immediately about the young man: How good looking he was, and how very strange he was. When he was introduced, he would not meet her eyes, but stared at the floor, clearly embarrassed. He stayed in the bed, hiding his nakedness beneath the covers. Daisy, however, was not embarrassed at all, and chattered on about how she and Angus had met on the island she called I.O.W.A..

Mollie didn't know whether to laugh or cry. Her fears about her daughter becoming an insane old spinster evaporated that morning. But she also felt some regret that her child was indeed embarking on her own path, her own life. It was at that moment she fully appreciated how much comfort she had taken from the image of she and Daisy facing the world together *alone*. That was apparently over and she was aware of surge of grief at that realization.

Daisy interrupted her thoughts by asking Mollie to face the wall so that Angus could get out of the bed, grab some clothes and escape to the bathroom. Mollie did so, and a few minutes later, could hear the shower going.

"Angus is very shy," Daisy explained. "It takes him a while to get used to new people, and even then, he doesn't say much..." She smiled proudly. "Except to me."

"What does he do for a living?" Mollie asked.

"He's like an assistant ranger. He takes care of some of the spoil islands in the river. That's how we met." Mollie saw her daughter's eyes grow fond at the memory. For a moment, it reminded her of her own infatuation with Mollie's father. The memory of how that turned out prompted her next question.

"So what does the future hold for you and ...Angus?" Daisy could tell her mother was self-conscious about saying her lover's name. The younger woman smiled benignly.

"I don't know," the girl replied, and waved her hand dismissively. "Whatever happens it will be wonderful."

"Do you think he wants to marry you?" Mollie asked. She did not see Angus re-enter the room. He was wearing jeans and no shirt his dark hair was a wet tangle on his head.

"Yes," The young man said in his monotone voice. Daisy laughed in delight and pointed at Angus.

"See? Wonderful!"

As Mollie walked from her daughter's apartment to work that morning, she was experiencing a broth of conflicting emotions.

On the one hand, there was the shock of how quickly Daisy had become a fully functioning adult. Her daughter had never fit into the standard roles our society demands of us. And the young man clearly did not fit in as well. With some envy Mollie realized that neither one of them gave a damn about fitting in. They were their own society and that was all that mattered.

On the other hand there was a quiet sadness at the loss of the constant companion she had loved and protected for so long. Daisy didn't need her as much as she used to, and Mollie greeted that fact with some regret. If she was no longer the much needed mother then who *was* she? As she entered the door of the market to start her work day, she got the impression that she was also entering a new chapter of her own life. It was at once saddening, exciting, and a little scary.

## CHAPTER SIX: CONVERSATION IN THE DARK

A few evenings later, Ron Halsey was in a hurry to get home. The sun was sinking toward the pine trees on the mainland in the west and he wanted to get his speedboat, *Mama Screwdriver*, into her berth in his gated community before dark. His urgency, combined with the many glasses of the boat's namesake he had consumed, caused him to hit the throttle harder than he usually did.

He had gone several miles down the Indian River channel when the nausea hit. The vodka, the orange juice, the fried shrimp he had wolfed down as he talked with his buddies, all came up. Holding onto the steering wheel for support, his 70-year-old body doubled over with cramps. He unwittingly pulled the wheel to starboard, steering the boat out of the channel. He never saw the canoe, nor did he even see the island.

Angus was too preoccupied to notice the sound of the boat at first. He was angry because Mr. Bronstien insisted on tagging along with him on the route today, but kept delaying the start of their journey. It was mid-afternoon when they finally set out in the canoe. Angus put his anger into the rowing and they made good progress going from island to island.

The slowdown came, however, when Bronstien would get out at each island and waddle about on an "inspection tour." The older man took lots of pictures of the landscapes that Angus had cleared of rubbish. Angus didn't mind Bronstien taking credit for his work, but he *did* mind that the older man's tardiness and slow pace was interfering with time he could be spending with Daisy.

The sun was starting to dip below the trees on the shore to the west when they approached the last spoil island on the route--the one Daisy referred to as I.O.W.A. In fact, he was enjoying remembering that first encounter when the speedboat came barreling at them

When Angus finally noticed the boat, he shouted at Bronstien, and tried to make a sharp turn to the left to get out of its path. With powerful strokes, he almost succeeded. But the port side of the prow of the *Mama Screwdriver* struck the end of the canoe right behind Angus. This had the effect of pushing the end of the canoe closest to Angus down and to one side. The curved portion of the prow slammed into Angus's left shoulder and tossed him free of the canoe. He was still under water when the inboard propeller churned by him.

Bronstien was not so lucky. When Angus's end went down, the older man was cantilevered up and slammed very hard into the side of the speedboat as it passed by.

Angus was aware of a searing pain in his left chest as he floundered for a few moments in the water. Then his feet found the sandy bottom four feet below. He stood in the water, the surface in line with his aching chest. He tried to catch his breath, but it hurt to breathe in too deeply so he had to fill his lungs with short, shallow panting. Looking up, he watched the *Mama Screwdriver* slam into the island. It slid up the flat, sandy beach and smashed into the pine trees.

The young man fought to clear his mind of the pain, which seemed to cloud his thinking. Looking around, he spotted Bronstien in his life vest, floating face down, his head almost completely submerged. Angus walked over to him and lifted the man's head. Bronstien's neck seemed to be free of all bone and wobbled grotesquely. He was clearly dead.

Using his right hand, Angus grabbed hold of Bronstien's life preserver and began to wade toward the island, fighting to stay conscious. Blackness seemed to be inviting him to give up and just sleep, to escape the pain. His agony seemed to be aggravated by the strain of towing the large man through the water. It was twilight by the time Angus and his burden made it to the beach. Grunting and moaning in pain, he managed to drag Bronstien's body far enough up on the beach to where only the man's feet were still in the water. Angus collapsed next to him.

Angus was sure he was dying. He reasoned that the collision had somehow damaged his heart. He noticed that since he had lain still on the sand, the pain had subsided somewhat. He was certain that a more powerful attack was coming however, and it would sweep him away. He realized his only fear about dying was separation from Daisy. He tried to focus on Daisy, because it made him feel better.

He knew that Daisy believed in something unseen. She was convinced it had guided them toward each other. As he fought the darkness trying to shut his mind down, he remembered their meeting. He had to admit that his actions at that incredible moment were far from his normal behavior. Something had impelled him toward her. At the time, he sensed that some unseen and unspoken force had sanctioned it. He wished desperately that the same quiet presence could help him now.

He tried to get in touch with it, and quickly found the barrier praying humans have encountered for thousands of years—the clutter of every day existence. Between his mind and the unspoken force Daisy believed in, lay thoughts of her and the dread of his parents' reaction to the destruction of the canoe. He also felt tremendous guilt about being too afraid to move and check on whoever had been in the speedboat. The fragmented thoughts of simply being alive on the earth lay between him and the Silent Presence like that debris barrier over on the mainland in front of the abandoned building. Eventually, he gave into the relief of unconsciousness.

He wasn't sure how long he slept before he became aware of someone sitting in the sand next to him in the darkness. He looked to the left and could make out the form of Bronstien's corpse, still lying where he had left it. He looked up to his right to see a young slim man with dark hair, sitting next to him on the sand. He sensed, rather than saw through the gloom, that this was

Bronstien also—a young, healthy Bronstien from years before.

"You're dead," Angus said.

"You're not," Bronstien said, shrugging.

"You're not real," Angus said in his usual monotone.

"You are," The figure answered.

"Am I dying?" Angus asked.

"No."

"I think my heart is going to quit," The young man insisted.

"It's not your heart."

"It's not?"

"You broke your left collar bone," Young Bronstien said. "Just lie still and you'll be okay." After those words, Angus lost consciousness again.

The next morning at first light, a boat containing two men was heading out to the St. Ignacio Inlet for some ocean fishing when they noticed the smashed wreckage on the island. They slowed down, carefully avoiding what was left of the shattered canoe. Its rounded hull was bobbing up and down a few yards off the island. , They went in for a closer look at the wreckage and spotted the two men lying on the beach. One of the fishermen called 911 on his cell phone.

They tied their boat off to a fallen tree near the shore and waded to the two bodies. They found the older man was dead and the younger man lying next to him was alive and hoarsely muttering something about his collarbone. They wisely didn't move his body, but one of them was able to gently lift his head enough to where he could swallow water from a bottle without gagging.

One of the men walked over to the wreckage of the speedboat and found the body of Ron Halsey tangled in the wreckage.

CHAPTER SEVEN: COMPLICATIONS

Mollie first met the Merricks in the waiting room at Sydney Medical Center. That morning, shortly after she came to work, Daisy had approached her mother who was running one of the cash registers.

"Something has happened to Angus," The girl said.

"What do you mean?" Asked the mother as she handed an older woman her register receipt.

"Angus was supposed to come over last night after work," Daisy answered. Mollie could hear the worry in her voice. " He never showed up and he didn't call. That isn't like him."

"Maybe he worked late and was tired and forgot," Mollie suggested. Daisy shook her head.

"Angus Merrick *never* forgets anything!" Daisy exclaimed. The customer who had just checked out paused in collecting her bags.

"Merrick?" The woman asked.

"Yes?" Daisy and her mom chorused together.

"Well it's all over the news," The lady said, proud to be in the know. "The Merrick boy was found injured after a boating accident last night. Two other men were killed."

Mollie had then given a hasty explanation to old man Stoddard who shrugged in resignation.

"Go ahead," He sighed. "We'll manage."

There had followed the sixteen-mile drive into the city of Sydney to the medical center. It was tense for Mollie, but she noticed that Daisy was amazingly calm. At one point, the daughter caught her mother glancing at her in wonder. Daisy smiled her dreamy smile.

"He's going to be okay, Mom," Daisy said.

"How do you know?" Daisy shrugged.

"I can't explain it. I just *know.*"

In the hospital waiting room, Daisy noticed the Merricks first. Mr. Merrick was tall like Angus and had the same nose. Smiling her brilliant smile, she swept up to them.

"I'm Daisy," she said, offering her hand to Mrs. Merrick. "But my Seminole name is Catori. It means spirit." Mrs. Merrick shook the hand hesitantly.

"You don't look Native American," The older woman said, a quizzical smile on her face.

"No, but in my soul, I feel that I am," Daisy replied calmly.

"This is my mother, Mollie," Daisy said gesturing toward Mollie. Mollie shook hands with the Merricks and the two older women silently communicated that they completely understood the situation: each of them had an unusual child that they loved dearly and were relieved and wary that their child had found a kindred spirit.

"We're very glad to meet you," Mrs. Merrick said, and Mollie could tell that she meant it. Mr. Merrick seemed to be totally caught off guard by the directness of Mollie and Daisy. He smiled, but there was worry and curiosity in the smile. Daisy could feel his questions. She directed her conversation to him.

"I love Angus very much," She told him. "We plan to be married."

"Married?" Mr. Merrick asked. He looked like a deer caught in headlights.

"Yes," Daisy answered, still looking at Mr. Merrick. "I would stay with your son married or not, but it seems to be important to him." She blushed and smiled her dreamy smile again. "Besides, I think I'm pregnant." This announcement was greeted with stunned silence at first. She had not even told Mollie this. Daisy continued, grinning.

"As for myself," She stated. "I don't feel I need to be 'made an honest woman,' but if it's important to Angus, it's important to me."

At that point, the doctor, entered. And beckoned the small group to gather round her. As they walked toward her, Mollie grinned and whispered to Mrs. Merrick, "Sometimes with Daisy, it's best to just smile and nod." Mrs. Merrick nodded, smiling.

"I thought so."

"She really is a good person," Mollie continued. "And she loves your son very much."

"I picked up on that," said the other woman.

"Okay," The doctor began. "Your son is sedated and asleep right now," she said. "The left collarbone had a clean break and the two ends of the bone are in line." She looked down at her clipboard for a moment before resuming. "He did stretch the ends of the bone apart after the injury. I suppose that was caused by towing the dead man's body to the shore." She sighed wearily. "But his chest muscles are so well toned that the bone ends went back into place when the strain was over. They should knit together on their own."

"He towed someone's body?" Mollie asked.

"Yes, it was on the news," Mrs. Merrick answered. "After the collision, Angus waded to a nearby island pulling Mr. Bronstien's body with him." Her voice began to waver. "They are calling him a hero."

"I'm not surprised," Daisy said, smiling proudly. "Once Angus sets his mind on something, he won't give up." Mr. Merrick looked at Daisy as if seeing her for the first time and nodded appreciatively.

"When can he go home?" Mrs. Merrick asked.

"Probably tomorrow," The doctor replied. "He will be wearing a soft cast and a sling for several weeks and he needs to restrict his exercising for a while."

"That will be hard for him," Mr. Merrick said. "He's always on the move." The doctor handed Mr. Merrick a pair of printed pages stapled together.

"Here is a list of what exercises are encouraged to aid in healing. As you see, it is broken down into weeks since the break. To begin with, however, it is very important your son does nothing that will jar the bone ends as they knit together." Mr. Merrick nodded in comprehension.

"Your welcome to see him now, if you wish," The doctor added. "But he is sound asleep,"

All four people went into the room where Angus lay, hooked up to monitors. Even though they knew he would be all right Mrs. Merrick and Daisy still wept softly to see him in the hospital bed. The sight of this strong young man looking so vulnerable affected them deeply. The group did not stay long in the room. Satisfied that the object of their concern was indeed, healing, they left. Mollie and Mrs. Merrick exchanged phone numbers as the two couples split up and headed for their cars.

On the drive home, Daisy turned to her mother with a fond look in her eye.

"Thanks, mom," She said simply. Mollie grinned.

"For what?"

"Meeting Angus's parents made me realize what a great job you did of raising me," Daisy explained.

"How so?"

"You let me be me, and figure stuff out for myself." Daisy looked out the window for a moment before going on. "I think Angus's parents tried to protect him from everything. They're not as comfortable with his being unusual as you are with my being unusual." Mollie had to laugh at her daughter's turn of phrase.

As the Merrick's drove home, both of them felt as if they had walked through a kind of emotional doorway, entering a realm they had never anticipated.

"Should we let him marry her?" Mr. Merrick asked, a worried expression on his face.

"Could we stop him if he really wants to?" Mrs. Merrick asked, smirking. Mr. Merrick glanced at his wife.

"You seem okay with this," He said, a note of disbelief in his voice. The images of Mollie and Daisy flashed in his wife's mind. She sensed, as some women can, that this was the best possible situation for all concerned. She tried to frame her words carefully.

"As dreamy-eyed as that girl is," She began. "I think she understands our son completely and loves him for the person he is."

"Yes, but how will they live?" He asked.

"Well, she has a job and a place of her own. We all know that our son is not afraid to work. He will find some way to earn a living." She turned to her husband.

"Listen, Frank," she said, putting her hand on his arm. "We have spent the past twenty-one years focusing on our special needs son. He is an adult now, and is going to have a life of his own. He is going to be okay." She squeezed her husband's arm. We need to concentrate on how we want this chapter of our lives to be."

He knew she was right. He was a brilliant engineer, but when it came to simply living life, Mr. Merrick had learned long ago that his wife knew volumes more than he did. For the rest of the drive home he wondered what this new life for them would be like. Like Mollie a few days before, he found the prospect saddening, exciting, and a little scary.

# CHAPTER EIGHT: OUT TO PASTURE

Daisy's last conversation with Arthur came a few days after Angus came home from the hospital. She had reluctantly agreed to let Mr. and Mrs. Merrick look after their son for the first few days of his healing. Mrs. Merrick confided to Mollie in one of their phone conversations that he was already grumbling about wanting to be with Daisy.

On this particular morning, Daisy had rented a kayak from Captain Eddie's Fun Port again and had paddled down the river to the abandoned building. Tying the plastic boat up at the usual spot, she walked around the building to find Arthur and Clarissa sitting in the shade of a mimosa tree, chewing their cud.

"I wanted to tell you that I am pregnant and I am going to marry Angus," She told the goat. Arthur nodded.

"Clarissa is pregnant too," He replied.

"Congratulations!" Daisy said to Clarissa, who simply stared at her blankly.

"Clarissa's gift is great beauty," Arthur explained. "Not conversation." Daisy nodded.

"I wanted the wedding to be held on the Island Of Wonderful Adventures," the girl continued. "But there are too many problems with that."

"Problems?" Arthur asked.

"Yes," Daisy responded with regret in her voice. "It would have been a major hassle to get everyone out to the island and then there is the problem of Mr. Halsey's wrecked boat, which is still tangled up in the pine trees." Arthur nodded his horns in comprehension.

"That would have been a grim reminder indeed," He said.

"Anyway, Angus wants to have the wedding in a church, because Mr. Bronstien came back from the dead to reassure him. He feels it would be a way of saying thank you to God."

"How do you feel about that?" Asked Arthur. Daisy shrugged.

"It's okay with me." The girl paused in thought for a few moments before continuing. "You see, as far back as I can remember, I've been aware of someone or something that knew me and wanted what's best for me."

"You mean God?" Arthur asked, a note of incredulity in his voice.

"That's as good a name as any," Daisy responded. "I frankly don't think whatever it is cares about what we call it."

"I can't follow you there, Daisy," Arthur said sadly. "I believe we create our own destinies with no outside help." Those were the last words Arthur ever spoke to Daisy.

She nodded, her eyes welling with tears as she felt the door close between her and her friend. It occurred to her to point out to him the amazing coincidence that brought them together and saved his life. She could have talked about how she knew something wonderful was going to happen the day she met Angus. But she knew his mind was closed. She still loved Arthur, however, and accepted him as he was, just as he had accepted her.

She was to visit Arthur and Clarissa and their kids from time to time at the abandoned condo complex over the years. She would tell the unresponsive goat the latest news in her life. Sometimes Angus would come with her and sometimes she came alone. When her daughter Mollie was old enough, she would bring her to see the herd of wild goats. Arthur and Clarissa had been productive and four kids of various stages of development, now gamboled about in their paradise.

On one of these visits, when little Mollie was five years old, Daisy saw her daughter look at the oldest kid and say, "Why do you say that?"

THE END

## RESURRECTING CLAYTON FENERLY

### CHAPTER ONE: INTERVENTION

One morning in late March, Clayton Fenerly came down the stairs of his condo to find four dead people sitting quietly in his living room. The first light of a Florida spring morning was just filtering into the place when he noticed them.

"Oh shit!" He gasped, clinging onto the wooden bannister for support.

"Clay, watch your language please," said his mother's voice. He descended the remaining four stairs and turned on the light in the dining room. This enabled him to see the figures sitting demurely on his two couches and in his armchair more clearly. It was his mother all right, but it was his mother as a pretty young woman. Her voice was high and pleasant. Her skin was smooth, and her hair was blonde and abundant. This was as she was before years of chain smoking ruined her skin and turned her voice into a gravely basso.

"Am I dead?" Clay asked, breathless. He wasn't surprised to realize that a small part of him hoped it was true.

"No, son," His father answered quietly, and Clayton was surprised by how much affection filled those two words. This man Clayton could never seem to please appeared to be much mellower in death. As he sat on Clayton's couch, Mr. Fenerly was muscular and dark-haired, with no sign of the paunch or the rage that would characterize the last half of his life. His father's hair was slicked straight back in the style of men in the thirties and forties.

"Hey, Clay," Said his brother Jim from the other couch. He was thin and lean—just as he was when he had returned from boot camp at Parris Island. There was no trace of the morbid obesity and the late onset epilepsy that would weaken his heart and take his life at age forty-nine.

"You all look great!" That was all Clayton could think of to say.

"We're not here to show off," His mother said. "We're here to tell you something."

"We know you've been looking at the bannister," Jim said bluntly.

The hairs on the back of Clayton's neck stood on end. For the past couple of weeks, he had been idly considering how to hang himself from the bannister on the landing. It made him feel vulnerable and ashamed that his deceased family members were privy to his innermost thoughts.

"I wasn't serious..." Clayton began defensively, but his mother interrupted.

"Eventually, you will be," She said flatly.

"That's why we're here," His father interjected. "Unless things change, you will be joining us soon."

"It's not your time, Clay," his mother added.

"Moira's not worth that, Clay," Jim said. "She never was." At the mention of his ex-wife's name, Clayton felt a stab of pain in his gut. "See?" His mother pointed out. "You're letting her affect your health. You are well on your way to an ulcer." It was then that Clayton noticed the person sitting in the armchair.

She was a short, slender young woman with a mop of curly brown hair on her head. She looked vaguely familiar, but he couldn't place who she was.

"I'm Nancy," The woman offered "Nancy Williams." Then Clayton remembered her. She was the sister of his best friend, Ron. When he knew her he was a senior in high school. She had been a gawky thing, four years younger than he and Ron. She always wanted to tag along with them.

"Why are you here?" Clayton asked.

"Purely selfish reasons," Nancy replied, grinning. "I was in love with you and you never noticed me." She smiled mischievously. "I just wanted to get a look at you again."

"Are you dead too?" He asked. As soon as the words escaped his lips he regretted how insensitive they might sound. Nancy laughed.

"Yes. Cancer when I was only thirty." Her expression grew serious. "Look, Clay," she explained. "I just wanted to tell you that you are still capable of attracting love."

"It's not too late," His mother said.

"Dig your way out of this hole you're in, son," His father advised.

"Be good to yourself, Clay," Nancy Williams said softly.

"Get off your ass and get outside!" Jim exclaimed. And with those words all four of them were gone. There was no puff of smoke or flash of light. One second the four figures were there and a split second later his living room was empty. Perhaps "empty" is too mild a word. To Clay, the room had never seemed more vacant and desolate.

## CHAPTER TWO: WELCOME TO THE GREAT OUTDOORS

Clayton was scared. He had not been camping since he was a Boy Scout some fifty years earlier. As he drove along the country road that passed through the Central Florida highlands, all he could think of were the animals living in the surrounding woodlands that could eat him. He had actually driven by

a road sign that said, "PANTHER CROSSING."
He knew there were also bears, wild pigs,
and poisonous snakes in the Florida wilds.
Then, of course, there were the Burmese
Pythons that were making an appearance in
South Florida. But these scary thoughts were
immediately shut down by the memory of his
brother's voice: "Get off your ass and get
outside!"

The lady ranger at the state park was a tiny
woman with a grim set to her face. She
confirmed that he had reserved a tent site for
the next three days. He paid the small fee and
she gave him a card to hang on his rear view
mirror. He followed her directions to the
camping area and slowly drove around the
loop where the various campsites were
located. He was glad he made a reservation
many days earlier. All of the campsites were
full.

The campsite numbers were printed on the
pavement next to each driveway. At the apex
of the loop, he found the one he was assigned
to: Space #23. It was also the only vacant site
he could find. He pulled into the driveway
paved with ground up shells and got out.

The first thing he noticed was the smell of
the pines. They towered over his site, along

with a nearby oak tree. It unnerved him somewhat that the site appeared to be rather isolated from its neighbors. At the back end of the cleared area, the jungle began. The trees and brush on either side were so thick that he could not see any of his neighbors. With a funny squirming in his stomach, he realized he was on his own.

The site consisted of a large wooden picnic table and a metal fire ring set into the ground. The fire ring had a grill that could be swung over the fire for cooking. He found a flat spot where he suspected other campers had set up their tents and he unloaded his borrowed tent from the trunk of his car.

His friend Sam had explained that the tent was probably larger than what Clayton would need. It was something Sam had bought years ago when his grandchildren were young and the thought of camping appealed to them. According to Sam, his grandchildren were now sullen teenagers glued to their cell phones and were no longer interested in the outdoors.

Clayton undid the tie on the mouth of the large nylon sack the tent came in and shook the contents out on the ground. He was greeted by a confusing proliferation of wadded up nylon, collapsible fiberglass poles and metal tent stakes. He stared at it blankly for a few minutes, trying to make heads or tails of what he should do next. He was so involved in the project he did not hear the van pull into the driveway behind his car.

"Need some help?" The woman's voice jarred him out of his concentration. He looked up to see a pleasant round face with glasses grinning at him. The face was framed by long, shiny gray hair in a braid that lay across one shoulder. Clayton's knee-jerk macho reaction was to decline any assistance and pretend that he knew what he was doing. But something made him void that alternative.

"I've never done this before," He confessed. The woman got out of the van. She was very short and very buxom. Her movements were quick and sure.

"I'm Sherry," She said, offering a tiny hand.

"Clayton...er...Clay," He responded. Her hand felt warm and smooth. Sherry looked down at the jumble Clayton had been studying.

"Wow!" She exclaimed. "That's a pretty big tent! Are you expecting other people?"

"No," Clay admitted, coloring slightly. "I'm here by myself. I borrowed the tent from a friend." He looked up from the tent to find Sherry studying him intently.

"Tell you what," Sherry began. "I need a place to stay for a couple of nights and I don't have a reservation. If you let me park here behind your car and pretend that we're together, I will help you set up your camp." She saw the look of alarm come into Clay's face.

"No funny business," she said quickly. "I will sleep in the van and you can have your gigantic tent." Clay felt serious misgivings about this, but there was something in the relaxed, almost careless frankness of the woman that appealed to him.

"Look, Clay," Sherry added. "I'm not homeless and I'm not a prostitute. I'm a retired college professor from Oregon and I am traveling around the country in my van, just because I can."

Clay shrugged and to his surprise, found himself saying, "You've got a deal."

CHAPTER THREE: SETTING UP

"My God!" Sherry laughed as she and Clayton stood inside the large tent they had just erected. "You could almost play volley ball in here!" As he thought about what they had just accomplished, Clay realized that he would not have been able to assemble the tent without Sherry's help. They had begun the process with him assembling the collapsible tent poles and Sherry trying to make sense of the jumble of nylon. As he worked, he noticed that she had figured out where the door of the tent was and had spread the nylon out in a recognizable pattern.

When it came time to slide the poles through the nylon sleeves on the outside of the tent, he made the mistake of trying to pull the poles through. This disengaged the segments from each other, and got them tangled in the fabric. Sherry had him retract the poles reassemble them, and then showed him how to gently push the segmented rods through the sleeves. She seemed to understand which poles went through which sleeves. Almost before he realized it, the domed structure had taken shape. As Sherry had pointed out, it was much bigger than he had anticipated.

"So what are you going to sleep on?" Sherry asked. Clay walked over to the trunk of this car and lifted out a limp bit of green plastic.

"This air mattress was in with the tent," Clay said. Sherry took it from him and looked at it. She passed the plastic through her fingers and stopped at a tear.

"This isn't going to work," she said. She looked up at the sky.

"We've got about two hours of daylight left," she said. "There's one of those stores in Lake Wales that sells everything. Let's go there and get you something decent to sleep on." Then another thought struck her. "Do you have a sleeping bag?" Clay lifted a tightly rolled bundle of fabric out of the trunk. Sherry took it from him and unraveled it, letting the foot of the sleeping back lay across the back bumper of his car. It smelled awful. The bottom half of the bag was covered in black mold.

"This thing was packed away wet," Sherry said. "God knows how long it was sitting like this. She tossed it on the ground next to the defunct sleeping bag. "C'mon, Clay," She said. "Let's get you some bedding that won't infect you with something." As they left the campsites in her van, she stopped at the dumpsters located at the entrance and Clay disposed of the ruined sleeping bag and air mattress.

The huge chain store supercenter was not as crowded as Clay had expected it to be. It was a Saturday afternoon and Clay assumed that the place would be packed with people stocking up for the coming week. He disliked crowds and was relieved to find the aisles of the store quite manageable. He and Sherry found the sports equipment area and she picked out a sleeping bag. Then she led him to the bedding department. As they walked she explained what she was doing.

"A lot of people will disagree with me, but I have yet to use an air mattress that didn't leak and end up having me lying on the ground by morning."

"So what are we going to get instead?" He asked.

"I'll show you," Sherry reassured him as she turned the shopping cart down one aisle. She looked along the shelf carefully.

"Ah...here it is!" She said, lifting a box down from the shelf. "It's a four-inch memory foam pad." She looked Clay up and down. He suddenly was reminded of every flaw in his appearance. "You're not that heavy," She said. "A four-inch pad should keep you off the ground."

Sherry also picked out a mattress cover for the pad. Then the two of them went over to the food section. Clay was becoming increasingly aware of his idiocy. He hadn't given a second thought to food for this trip. As she shopped for both of them, Sherry made a point to stack food intended strictly for her self in one corner of the basket.

"You don't have to do that," Clay said. "Your help is worth my paying for everything." Sherry shook her head.

"Nope," She said. "I pay my own way."

On the drive back to the campground in Sherry's van, Clay was watching the orange groves and pasturelands of Central Florida pass by. The land was hilly here, unlike the coastal area where he lived.

"I had forgotten that parts of Florida have hills," He mused.

"This is the Mid-Florida Ridge," Sherry told him. "It's actually a string of prehistoric sand dunes left over from the time the ocean covered much of what is now Florida."

"How do you know that?" Clay asked in wonder.

"I was a geology professor," Sherry explained. "It's why I came through this area on my swing around the country. I wanted to see the ridge for myself." She glanced over at Clay. "What did you do for a living?"

"I was a bookkeeper for a large furniture company." Clay was suddenly very conscious of how boring his career sounded.

"So you're good with numbers," Sherry surmised.

"Yes," Clay responded with a note of regret in his voice.

"Numbers make sense to me," He said absently. "A lot of other things don't."

"Like what?" Sherry asked.

"Like people," Clay answered. "I'm not good with people." He stared out the window at the passing scenery for a moment. "I suppose that's why I chose a career where I stayed in an office and didn't have to relate to them much."

"You sound sad about that," Sherry observed.

"I think it cost me my marriage," Clay stated.

"How long ago were you divorced?"

"Three years."

"So the pain is still fresh?" Sherry asked. Clay didn't answer but simply nodded. He wanted to change the subject.

"So how do you know so much about camping?" He asked.

"My husband and I used to camp all the time," Sherry answered.

"Are you divorced too?" Clay realized he was hoping the answer was yes.

"Widowed," Sherry said flatly. "Joe was killed in a windsurfing accident in the Dalles."

"The Dalles?"

"It's a stretch of the Columbia River where there are frequent steady winds." Sherry frowned at the memory. "Joe apparently hit his head on something and was knocked out. He drowned before any of his friends realized he was down."

"I'm sorry," Clay said and meant it. Sherry glanced at him and saw the sincerity.

"You never get used to losing someone like that," She said as she steered the van into the entrance of the state park. "You just find a way to keep going in spite of the pain." Listening to her, Clay became acutely aware that his pain over the divorce was nothing compared to what Sherry had been through. He was impressed by her strength.

## CHAPTER FOUR: TRUTH TO THE FIRE

The same tiny, taciturn woman who had checked Clay in earlier that day seemed suspicious when he asked that Sherry be added to his campsite as well. Sherry paid the requisite fees, however, and the woman gave her the proper card for the van's rear view mirror.

"There can be no more than two vehicles at a campsite," The woman warned sternly. "Is anyone else going to be joining you?"
Clay assured her that Sherry would be the only addition.

By the time they got back to camp, the sun was almost setting and a pleasant twilight was settling between the pines. Sherry showed Clay how to build a small fire in the metal ring, and closed the iron grill over the flames.

"When the fire burns down to coals, it will be just right for cooking our steaks," She said. She then pulled a camp stove out of her van and set it up on the picnic table. Meanwhile, Clay put his new pad and sleeping bag into the tent and lay down on it. It was very comfortable. As the twilight gathered, the temperature began to cool. The smell of wood smoke and pine trees and the persistent sounds of birds seemed to trigger a primal relaxation in him. He almost nodded off.

Supper was delicious. They each enjoyed a small rib eye steak, some boil-in-the bag broccoli, and some small canned potatoes flavored with butter and parsley. Clay volunteered to do the dishes and he carried the dirty pots and pans to the restroom building fifty yards away. Along the back wall, there was a large sink and drain board that was usually used for cleaning fish. He used this to scrub the pots and utensils from supper. He brought them back to the campsite and Sherry had him lay them face down on the picnic table to air dry. The supper chores having been done, they sat on folding camp chairs Sherry produced from her van, and stared into the campfire. Because it was early April, Florida was still enjoying relatively cool, dry days. As a result, mosquitoes were not yet a problem

For a long time, neither of them said a word, but simply stared hypnotically into the flames. Clay took note of the fact that he felt no pressure to converse and he sensed Sherry was just as comfortable with the silence. After an undetermined amount of time, she finally spoke. There was a sleepy quality to her voice.

"So how did the divorce happen" She asked. Oddly, Clay felt no sense of violation by this question. In fact, he found he *wanted* to talk about it with her.

"Moira fell in love with somebody where she worked," Clay stated. He was immediately aware of what a common, sad little story it was.

"So it was her fault," Sherry said. Clay shook his head.

"Not totally," He said. "It takes two people to ruin a marriage and I did my share."

"What was your share?" Both of them were still staring into the flames. It was as if doing so freed each of them to be more honest. Their truths were being offered to the fire.

"I tend to isolate myself, even from people I care about," Clay began. He was amazed by his own honesty. He had not said this out loud to anybody before. "I like routine and predictability—at least I used to."

"*Used to*?" Sherry asked. "What changed?" Clay sighed apprehensively.

"Here's where you're going to thing I'm nuts," he warned.

"Try me," Sherry said, turning her gaze away from the fire to look at him. So Clay described the meeting with his dead family that had occurred a few days earlier. Sherry was quiet for a long time. Clay felt the need to explain more.

"I guess if I hadn't been so withdrawn and had focused more on her, my wife might not have been drawn to Paul." The image of his rival flashed into his mind: handsome Paul with his graying blonde hair and his limp from a war wound. Oddly, this time the image was *not* met with a feeling of inadequacy on Clay's part. He found that in this moment, he actually felt a little sorry for handsome Paul. Sherry added a small branch to the fire.

"No," Sherry said. "I agree with your brother. It takes two people to make a marriage work, too," She said. "Was this Paul guy good looking?" Clay nodded.

"Yep," He responded. Sherry stirred the fire with a stick, adjusting some of the pieces of wood. There was a wry smile on her face.

"The problem with handsome men," She said. "Is that they eventually open their mouths." She shook her head. "That usually ruins it for me." Clay surprised himself by throwing back his head and laughing. It felt like the first good laugh he had enjoyed in ages.

"So what was your wife like?" Sherry asked. Relaxed now, Clay answered readily

"Too pretty to be with me," He responded.

"How so?"

"She made it a point to be beautiful at all times," Clay said. "She was constantly having her hair and nails done, and only bought the best outfits that complimented her figure." He shook his head in disbelief. "If Moira was to fall off a cliff, I do believe she would find the best way to land that would show off her figure." This time, it was Sherry who laughed.

"So she was a girly girl who fought against aging," Sherry stated flatly. Clay realized for the first time that "girly girl" accurately described Moira.

"Let me guess—she always had makeup on."

Yes." He admitted. "She said she never felt comfortable if she wasn't wearing any." Sherry snorted.

"I don't mean to offend you, but I simply do *not* understand women like that," She stated flatly. Clay shrugged.

"It doesn't offend me," He said. "I guess I just never thought about it."

"But it's so *ridiculous*!" Sherry exclaimed. "Why fight against a natural process?" She gestured at the fire with one hand. "We treat aging as if it were a disease! It's not!" She shook her head in disgust. "Eventually, there comes a tipping point, where the colored hair does not match the aging skin. Then it just looks ridiculous!" Sherry then seemed to catch herself.

"Sorry," She apologized chuckling sheepishly. "I didn't mean to get on my soapbox." Clay glanced at his companion.

"You don't wear makeup do you?" He asked. Sherry shook her head. Clay noticed that Sherry had wrinkles, as might be expected on a woman of her age. But there was a healthy tone to her complexion that seemed to make the wrinkles unimportant.

"Nope and I don't dye and perm my hair," She added. "What you see is what you get." Clay realized that it was her lack of a façade or pretension that had drawn him to Sherry in the first place.

"I'll bet men are comfortable around you," He suggested. Sherry nodded emphatically.

"And I am more comfortable around men than I am around women," She stated. "I frankly don't give a shit what brand of shoes a woman is wearing. And it really burns me when I notice women changing their behavior when men are present." She shook her head again. "I don't have the patience or the time for the games." She looked up at Clay earnestly.

"You're right about preferring the company of men, though. I am especially drawn to less educated men as long as they don't behave like jerks. For many men, a lot of education seems to lead to a lot of pretension." She shrugged. "Good blue collar men have an endearing humility about them." Her eyes became wistful. "Joe didn't even finish high school, but he earned a very good living as a heavy equipment mechanic." She stared into the fire for a moment. "In his own way, Joe was one of the wisest people I ever met."

They talked for a few minutes longer, but both of them were clearly getting sleepy. They bid each other good night and each went to the agreed upon beds. As he drifted off to sleep, to the accompaniment of two owls hooting nearby, Clay realized that he had thoroughly enjoyed the evening without having to rely on television to keep him occupied until sleep came.

## CHAPTER FIVE: NATURE 101

Clay was awakened by something shaking the side of his tent near his head. It was Sherry. Dawn was peeking through the nylon-screened window.

"Clay! Get up!" She whispered excitedly. "You've got to see this!"
Through his sleepiness, Clay was instantly aware of being clad only in his underpants. He grabbed a pair of shorts and threw them on. He slid his feet into his shoes, not bothering to lace them up. Unzipping the door of the tent, he poked his head out. Sherry was fully dressed in jeans and a plaid shirt. Her long gray braid tumbled through the opening in the back of a baseball cap. Clay thought she looked adorable. She was grinning broadly and gesturing at the picnic table. Clay scrambled out of the tent as quietly as he could and stood up.

A doe and her fawn were timidly inspecting the picnic table. The mother seemed particularly interested in trying to figure out what the pots and pans were, while the fawn sniffed around under the bench seats. Clay could tell that the mother was aware of the two humans standing nearby watching them, but apparently she had experienced a lot of non-threatening human behavior. She didn't run away at the sight of Clay and Sherry. Instead, she casually led her baby back toward the woods. They would pause and nibble selected plants along the way.

Clay thought of fumbling in his stuff to find his cell phone and get a picture, but his bladder felt like it was bursting. Grabbing his toiletries kit, he excused himself and shuffled off to the bathroom.

There, after answering nature's call, he washed up as best he could and returned to the campsite. Sherry was already in the process of cooking breakfast on the camp stove. A small pot of coffee was percolating on one burner. He could smell bacon cooking, and realized he was starving. He still had his shirt off, and he thought he noticed Sherry's gaze staying on him as he walked back into the campsite. He went to his tent and self-consciously put on his tee shirt.

"So what have you got planned for today?" Sherry asked him between mouthfuls of bacon and eggs.

"Nothing, actually," Clay responded. He was amazed to realize that this was true. His impulse in going camping was to simply obey his dead brother and get out into nature. He had made no other plans beyond just getting here.

"I'd like to go on a short hike around the area," Sherry began. "Would you come with me?"

"Sure!" Clay said without hesitation.

After breakfast, Clay cleaned the pots, pans and utensils. He set them out on the picnic table as he had done the night before. Even though they had not felt or heard any mosquitoes, Sherry had both of them spray repellant on exposed skin.

"Do you have a canteen?" Sherry asked. Clay shook his head. She handed him a bottle of water. "Carry this." She then had them load any valuables into their vehicles and lock them. Sherry took out the campground map she had picked up in the office and studied it for a moment.

"Okay," she said and they set off on their walk. They circled the paved campsite loop for a while then set off on a marked trailhead. The path was too narrow to walk side by side, so Clay fell back and let Sherry take the lead. He realized he did not care where they were going. He was just glad to be there with her.

The trail arced through a pine and palmetto forest and Clay was fascinated by the birdcalls he was hearing. A single, repeated note seemed to ring through the trees. Sherry stopped and pointed up into a nearby pine. A male cardinal—stately in his scarlet plumage, was singing his heart out.

When they started walking again, Clayton was still looking up at the treetops and promptly stumbled over a root sticking up out of the sand of the trail. He managed to catch himself before falling. Sherry grinned at him.

"Okay—first lesson in hiking is watch your feet first," she chided. "I tend to move my eyes in a repeated pattern," she continued. "I look at where I'm about to step, then glance ahead on the trail a few feet. I then swing my gaze from side to side, checking the brush on either side of the trail. After that, I glance up for a moment, then start the pattern all over again."

"What are you looking for?" Clay asked.

"Snakes, poison ivy, or anything of interest," Sherry replied. As they walked on, Clay tried to practice the pattern of eye movement. It worked. He was able to see much more and he felt more in control. He relaxed.

Sherry got quiet as they walked and he felt the same impulse for silence. There was a kind of reverence he felt at being surrounded by the woods, and he sensed this feeling was Sherry's motivation for venturing on hikes like this. The old Clayton—the man who had seen his dead family a few days earlier— would have imagined terrors on every side. But the new Clayton—the one happily learning from this strange little woman— was beginning to enjoy just being in the cathedral of trees.

The path broke out of the forest and began skirting a large lake. Cattails and reeds lined the shore in most places and the path mounted a low levee, no more than a couple of feet above the tea-colored water. There were more reeds and small scrubby bushes along the top of the levee and the path skirted most of these. Sherry motioned for them to stop and took out her binoculars.

She seemed to be looking along the lakeshore up ahead.

"Yep," She said. "Gator!" As she handed the binoculars to Clay, she pointed at a dark shape lying on the muddy edge of the lake. Putting the binoculars to his eyes, Clayton could clearly see the alligator. It was about five feet long and was sunning itself contentedly.

"I really admire them," Sherry said.

"Why?" Clayton asked.

"Well, think about it," Sherry began. "Their bodies are so perfectly suited to their environment that they haven't had to change in millions of years." Clayton nodded.

"And there's another thing," Sherry added. "Alligators and crocodiles live in a bacteria-laden environment, and they often get injured in territorial battles. But they never seem to get infections." She resumed walking as she talked. "Scientists are studying their blood to see what kind of antibodies it might contain." Clayton had never heard about any of this and he found it fascinating.

As they progressed along the overgrown levee, the lake was on their right. A small pond began to be visible on the left. When they got between the two bodies of water,

Sherry stopped them again. She pointed out reeds that had been matted down on both sides of the levee.

"I think that's a gator slide," She said.

"Gator slide?"

"Yep. It's how they get from the pond to the lake and back again."

Sherry started walking again and Clayton followed her looking back at the gator slide behind him. He didn't see her stop suddenly and collided with her. Instinctively he grabbed her shoulders and held her close to keep her from falling. Oddly, Sherry was smiling as a result of the collision.

"We need to turn back," her voice had a strange breathy quality to it.

"Did I hurt you?" Clayton asked, his face a mask of concern. Sherry's smile broadened.

"No," she said quietly. "Don't you see it?" She gestured ahead of them on the trail. On the other side of some bushes a large gray log seemed to be lying across the trail. As he looked more closely, he noticed that the "log" had bumps on it. The hair stood up on the back of his neck when he realized that the huge tree trunk was actually a *very* large alligator. He noticed that its back looked to be three feet across at the shoulders. Clay stepped aside and let Sherry take the lead, heading back the way they had come. The smile was still on her face.

## CHAPTER SIX: THERE'S NATURE AND THEN THERE'S NATURE

As they walked toward the trees they fell into a self-conscious silence. His mind was clouded with the memory of the feel of her body against him when they had collided. It was as if she had some kind of gravitational pull that surrounded her and even though they were separate now, it was still tugging at him.

The silence held until they nearly made it back to camp. Sherry had them stop at the restroom building ostensibly to wash up for lunch. When he finished, he wasn't sure if he should wait for her, or not. Then it dawned on him that she might have finished first and had gone on back to camp. So he headed down the path to their campsite.

She wasn't there. Not sure what to do, he sat at the picnic table and waited. A few minutes later, Sherry came into their site. She marched up to the picnic table, put down her water bottle, her binoculars and her cap and marched up to Clay. She launched herself at him, her mouth finding his, and her arms flung around his neck. Clay's body took over. He stood up, his mouth still glued to hers and pulled her to him. When they parted, they were both breathing hard.

"The tent," she whispered and took him by the hand, leading him to the oversized structure. He fumbled with the zipper getting the door panel open and then fumbled with it again getting it shut. By the time he turned around from the door, her plaid shirt was off and she was removing her bra. Her large breasts swung free. Clayton's breath caught in his throat. Their eyes locked on each other as they frantically disrobed. What he saw made him nearly dizzy with desire. This very attractive woman was staring at him with undisguised hunger. The sight of that look would reverberate within him for years to come.

The lovemaking was an exquisite combination of tenderness and urgency. When it was over they lay on their backs next to each other, panting. Tiny beads of sweat were on each of them as they stared dreamily up through the nylon mesh at the top of the tent. The sun was illuminating pine needles swaying above them. Sherry rolled over and faced him. In he midst of his reverie, Clay realized it was Easter Sunday.

"Thank you, Clay," she murmured. "It's been a long time for me."

"Me too," Clay said, staring into the brown eyes looking at him.

"Since the divorce?" Sherry asked.

"Long before that," Clay answered. "Moira became disinterested in sex at least a year before we called it quits. I think that's when she started screwing Paul." Sherry shook her head.

"What the hell was her problem?" She asked. "You are wonderful." Clay smiled proudly. In that moment, with those words, it was as if he felt parts of himself that had been fractured, coming together. He sought for reality through the ego rush.

"I think it was a matter of chemistry," He said. "We just didn't have it." He shrugged. "Apparently she and Paul did."

"Was it always that way?" Sherry asked.

"No. It was very passionate in the beginning," Clay answered. "But as the years wore on, things changed."

"Did you have kids?" Sherry asked, stroking his cheek.

"Moira was worried about ruining her looks...so no. What about you and Joe?'

"I have a son. He's works for a computer firm that's based in Portland." Sherry was quiet for a few moments. She propped herself up on one elbow, her breasts swinging free.

"I believe the value of marriage is that it keeps two people together until the next time they fall in love with each other," she stated matter-of-factly. "It sounds like you and your wife never fell back in love at some point." Clay nodded.

"That's a pretty accurate description," He said. "After a while, it just wasn't there any more. We tried, but that's just it—it was an effort."

"Was sex an effort?" Clay nodded sadly.

"Yes. Sex with her was always a big production," he said. "It could only be at night just before falling asleep. I had to bathe and shave first, and she had to have a lot of wine beforehand."

"Oh, that's not good," Sherry said, shaking her head.

"Then there was this long involved pattern of foreplay I had to follow leading up to it."

"It's good that there were no kids to be hurt by the split," Sherry mused. "Apparently the only casualty was you." With that, she rolled against him and kissed him.

## CHAPTER SEVEN: RESURRECTION

Two months later, Clayton Fennerly came down the stairs in his condo one last time. Its new owners would be taking it over in a couple of days. He paused on the stairway where he had stood several weeks earlier when he encountered his dead family and a friend. He knew they would not be present today, because there was no need. He had heeded their warning.

The three nights he had spent with Sherry had rolled back the stone on the tomb of his dark thoughts. The tomb wasn't completely open. He still had bad days of self-recrimination, but these were fewer and no longer had the destructive power they once had. When he stepped through the doorway of his condo for the last time, he was aware of stepping into bright sunlight that felt good on his skin and on his soul.

He locked the door to the condo and walked over to the office of the housing development in which he had lived for three years. He handed in his door key to the chain-smoking lady behind the counter and walked back toward his assigned parking space. There, his new hybrid sedan awaited him. He had gotten a good price for the condo, and because Paul was wealthy, Moira had not wanted any alimony, only the divorce. Her eagerness to be free of him had hurt his feelings three years ago. Now he was grateful to be free of her. His money was his own. He felt light on his feet as he walked through the carefully manicured grounds of the senior development.

Although his new car was not set up for camping, he had done so himself. He knew he wasn't by nature a "handyman," but he didn't care. He had a sheet of plywood specially cut at a home improvement store. With one of the bucket seats in the back folded flat, that became the basis for his bed. He bought a cheap level and some squares of carpet samples. Using the carpet samples as shims, he made the bed level. On top of the plywood, he put the memory foam pad he had purchased with Sherry. On top of that would be his sleeping bag. In bad weather, he could sleep comfortably in his car.

He had returned Sam's gigantic tent to him and bought a small, two-man tent. In good weather, he could pull into a tent site, set up the tent, store his goods in it, and still enjoy the comfort and security of sleeping in the car. In bad weather, he could clear his belongings from the bed by storing them in the front seats. Clayton had already spent a few nights in local campgrounds to make sure his system worked. He was satisfied that it did.

As he drove over the bridge that connected Sydney Beach with the mainland, he grinned with excitement about what was ahead of him. He had made reservations at a campground in North Florida for that night. It bordered the Suwanee River and was reputed to have the only rapids in the state of Florida. After that, he was planning on heading north into the Appalachians. The crushing heat and humidity of a Florida summer would soon be here, and he wanted to get to cooler climes.

He knew that Sherry was somewhere in the west by now. She had stayed in touch with him by email, attaching pictures of the various places she had stopped on her round the country journey. He had purchased a good pocket digital camera with a decent zoom function. His plan was to surprise her with how good a nature photographer he had become.

As he passed through the small city of Sydney, Florida, he did some rough calculating in his mind. He figured Sherry had about a month left before arriving back to her home in Oregon. In a couple of the emails she had mentioned how she wished he were with her to see various things.

As he swung on I-95 north, he visualized his own circuit around the country. He was thinking of following the Appalachians until he got to Pennsylvania perhaps. Then he would swing west and skirt the great lakes. He would cross the Great Plains and head up into the Rockies. He would arrive in Oregon just in time for fall.

THE END

Made in the USA
San Bernardino, CA
22 July 2018